I0847042

BETWEEN *TWO* DOORS

DOORS

In search of Colette

THOMAS *and* MARY MARTZ

Between Two Doors
In Search of Colette

Copyright 2023 by Thomas and Mary Martz

This is a work of fiction. The characters are both actual and fictitious. All incidents, descriptions, dialogue and opinions expressed are the product
of the author's imagination and are used fictitiously.
They are not to be construed to be as real

Cover photograph copyright by the estate of Mary Martz
And by Shutterstock
Cover and interior designs by Nohemy Adrian
Book Edited by Amelia Gilliland with assistance by Kali McNutt

* * *

This book is dedicated to
The greatest French Female Writer
of the 20th Century

SIDONIE-GABRIELLE
COLETTE
1873 – 1954

And to all other strong, brave, women
everywhere

* * *

Mysterious Colette painting,
between two antique stores. Camden, South Carolina, 2004

CHAPTER 1
BOOK 1

It was a dark and stormy night when the ship docked in Honfleur. Early morning that cold mid-May in the northern district of France called Normandy was no better. The morning clouds were giving way to the pinkish cast rays of the first sun. Still, it was cold as the young woman walked swiftly from the waterfront.

She could sense the big man dressed in black was still behind her. He had been since she left the meeting with the small squeaky-voiced man. Although his voice was feminine and his look was frail, it did not hide the meanness that dwelt within his soul. He had given her the package. She had taken it anxiously. She was unsure which scared her most...the frail evil one or whatever was in the package that she now carried under her coat.

After taking the package as she had been instructed to do, she hurried away, getting only several yards. A loud noise. A gunshot! Then a high pitch scream! A splash.... not loud... that of a big man falling. No, this was the sound of a small man hitting the cold dark North Sea harbor's water. She, afraid to look back, increased her steps. Her shoes made ever faster clomping sounds on the cobblestones. She could hear the muted sounds of his shoes not far behind, gaining on her!

As she passed by an Honfleur cottage doorway and approached the door of a second house, a man appeared in that doorway. He was a good-looking man, tall, dark, handsome. He, dressed in a long slender coat covering his broad shoulders, used his eyes to study her momentarily. Dark blue, almost black eyes meeting her eyes. The look was just long enough for her to see a polite but seductive smile form on his lips. He touched the first and second fingers of his right hand to the black, Homburg wool hat, then turned toward the big man in black.

A second shot rang out! She started running. Looking back over her shoulder, she saw the big man fall to the ground. His knees buckled beneath him, his right hand raised to his left chest. Then as if in slow motion, his head hit the cobblestone street with a loud "crack". The other man, the one with the seductive smile and blue-black eyes... was nowhere to be seen.

Down a dark alleyway all had been witnessed by the man wearing a maroon fez. He had been hiding in the shadows, knowing she would come this way. He was waiting.

Across the alley just around the bend, a young boy relieved himself on the side of the church wall. He had not witnessed "Fez" watching her. "Fez" would find the young woman later and...

Colette, now rereading the manuscript written in the hotel room between performances of the play L'Ingenue, was headed back by train to Villa Rozven, a "special" home in Brittany. It had been purchased for her after the divorce from Willy. The purchaser, her long time "intimate friend" Missy. She couldn't wait to get home. This trip had been troubling.

She closed the manuscript. Writing it on the train had been hard. Not because of the rolling motion of the train down the tracks but because it was too different from the others she wrote. Those were stories of her childhood, young womanhood and her adulthood. Stories that told of the oppression women faced from domineering men. The women in her stories suffered from abusive men but usually not physical violence so much as mental control. They, the women and girls of her stories, learned to be self-respecting and independent. Awakening to their desires. Finding what satisfied themselves. Learning how they cared for others.

In those stories, they threw off the chains and escaped the cages men put them in. They learned their own voices. No one would take that from her again! Damn it! Never again! She owned her own story now. She would write it as she lived it...as she felt it...as she wanted it. Looking down at the papers, she was troubled. This manuscript had been different. It told a sadder story. Perhaps a terrible story.

Yet here she was, hiding again. Hiding in her train coach room now. Afraid and trapped! Enough of that! She put the manuscript aside, stood up, and opened the coach door. She stepped out.

A glass of wine and dinner in the dining car. That would settle her nerves. There she would be with others. Surrounded by people not caring for her, keeping her company just the same. Nothing could happen there.

As she walked away from the room, another compartment door quietly slid open. He poked his head from inside. He was unseen at the opposite end of the car. She kept walking. He would follow her shortly. First, he had a more important mission. With agile trained hands, he quickly worked the lock on her door. It clicked. Looking around to ensure no one was watching, he opened her door. There on the small writing table it sat. He picked up the bundle of papers. Quickly, he slid them in the waistband of his pants. His evening jacket covered them. Turning back to the door, he opened it slowly and peaked out. No one was there. He slid it open. Walking back down the narrow hallway, he entered his own room. The documents were a finished novel. A novel by Colette. One that would never be published under her name. When she finally noticed the manuscript was missing, he would be long gone. The secret in the novel was safe for now.

Colette was shown to her table. Her mind reflected on all that had happened over the past few days. She never should have started this book. It was that new genre...a "mystery novel". They were becoming all the rage in England and America. Books that began with that English writer. What was his name? Yes, someone named Arthur Doyle. The American, an older fellow, had written some earlier. God awful if you ask her. Particularly The Murders in the Rue Morgue. A scary story about a fictitious street in Paris. The one by Doyle, something about a dog. A kind of dog of the Baskervilles. Hound!

That's it. The Hound of the Baskervilles. When she had read them as a young girl or woman, she felt the thrill. The scary tingling up her spine. Now she was writing one of them. One in which she was a part of the story. Now, the thrill was real terror. It was a real story.

The young woman, Jadin, had told her the account of what had happened. Both actresses in the play, Jadin was also the singer. Colette and Jadin had shared several nights together. The night she told Colette what had happened...that night... sent chills throughout Colette's body. Why had she decided to write about this tale?

The story began as written in the manuscript. They always began on stormy nights. That night had been a real beauty. Lightning, thunder, heavy rain, and terrible wind. Yes, many mysteries began this way. But this one was different. It was a true recounting of the event that had happened...to Jadin.

After what had happened on the pier and street, Jadin had made it to her room safely. At least she hoped she had. It was a small room in the rundown rooming house. Actresses in this play at this time could not afford more. She studied the package. Sitting on the bed next to it, she touched it. Feeling all around the cloth enclosing. Whatever was inside, she thought, was odd. She knew she shouldn't, yet she did. She opened the package!

The note had warned her not to do that. It, the package and letter, were to be delivered to a man only identified as JS. The envelope on the outside of the package was unsealed. The wax had broken away. Slowly, she pulled out the note inside. It simply said:

> *"JS, the payment. The men are to complete the assignment as decided. When the deaths are confirmed, you will receive the next installment. Great wealth and power ahead. When the first phase is finished, you will need to ensure that VL is eliminated. Then the wealth and power are assured.*
>
> *To our mutual success!*
> *Your American supporters.*
>
> *IOL +1 and GE +1"*

The squeaky man who handed her the package had said, "Another man wearing a maroon Fez is to be the courier. You are to entrust the package to him. Only him. He will know where and how to find you." He then smiled his evil smile. She saw behind him a large man in black approaching and she hurried away, heard the shot, heard the scream, and heard the splash.

Again, she touched the package and picked it up. It was still heavy. It had been earlier too. Having it in her room hadn't lightened it.... nor the burden it carried for her. Whatever it was, it was wrapped in several layers of rough paper inside several turns of oil cloth.... cloth of which a sail is made. The package was to be the object of payment? For what? For assuring deaths? By whom? What reason?

Jadin carefully undid the paper. She knew she would have to cover it back up later. It would have to be done to look as though it had been undisturbed. She shouldn't open it. She knew this. Curiosity and fear were both there.

Her curiosity was too strong. Curiosity won.

With trembling fingers, she began to unveil the object. As each layer was pulled away, what was inside appeared to get smaller. When finally revealed, the object was 18 centimeters long. One end, approximately 15 centimeters wide. The other end, only 8 centimeters wide. As the last of the paper was pulled off the object, her breath fell heavy. It was ugly! A black fist of dense metal. A fist that was disfigured. Numerous bumps of several sizes raised out of the fist surface as though some strange disease had caused the disfigurement. The owner's body, if a real person, would have been horrible. She told herself, "It is not a real fist. Not the real hand of a disfigured man." Still, it was hideous.

She looked closer. There was a small scrape in the black paint. Was it caused by the one piece of jewelry she owned? Her mother's ring? The one given to Jadin on her mother's death bed the night she died of consumption. Her mother's only possession. Had the ring marred the surface? She said a silent prayer that the scratch was there long before she opened the package.

Under the scratch, the metal was yellowish. Gold! Through tearful eyes, she saw the scrape had also cut a small groove across the top of one large bump.

The groove in the surface revealed a bit of red sparkle. A ruby! A very large red ruby! Now she knew her fear was more than justified. This fist was not only extremely valuable, it represented great power and wealth. She was nothing, her life would mean nothing! She was in trouble. And all she knew is trouble wore a maroon fez!

Her hands shook as she tried to rewrap the package. She was unsuccessful! No matter how hard she tried, her trembling hands could not wrap it. In fact, each attempt made it worse. Tears filled her eyes. She ran from the room...from the boarding house. She headed for the only safe place of which she could think.... the theater...and her friend, Colette.

That night after the performance, she asked Colette if she could stay at Colette's room. It was at a nicer boarding house. Colette was the star. The young woman was troubled. Colette could tell. Jadin's voice broke often during her songs and for the first time she had been "booed" by the audience.

Looking at this waif of a child, Colette said, "Of course you can, Jadin. Whatever is troubling you will vanish. We will see to it. You and me. You can tell me your troubles one day when you feel up to it. Until then, you will stay with me."

Though this act was done out of kindness, Colette was intrigued by this situation. After all, Jadin was attractive. In a way, a most appealing little creature.

So, Colette's reason for rooming together was quite different than that of Jadin's...at least at first. But then Colette had no way of knowing what had happened earlier that day with Jadin. She did soon learn a few days later.

The first night brought contentment for Colette and relief for Jadin. Over the next two nights, emotions grew. One night turned into three nights. Jadin's fear gave way to excitement and enjoyment. She told Colette the story and Colette began writing. She would not tell Jadin what she was writing. Only that she must write. It flowed like blood through her veins.

That lasted until the day that Jadin went back to her own rooming house. She only went to pick up her few belongings. Instead, she discovered the object was missing. Perhaps the landlady had taken it.

Colette had warned her not to go back to her room. Jadin didn't listen. During the day, she slipped off between shows.

What an imagination Jadin had. A story of the two men shot. Her feeling of being followed. The description of a black fist, enamel-covered gold, encrusted with jewels, stones of all types. Painted over with black. A black fist!

A fabricated story, Colette thought. A story about two murders. Was this the basis of a new novel? One of the new genres for Colette to try and write? In between performances, she began to do so. She had written fast. After all, Jadin's description told the story. All Colette needed to do was put it down on paper. Would she consider Jadin a collaborator of the story? She would have to think about that. Still, the child did tell an intriguing story. But, what if it were all true?

Had there been reports in the newspaper? It had been a long time since Colette had seen the paper other than the reviews. But, yes, others had talked about two men found dead. One in the water as Jadin had described. The other on the street coming back from the piers. Both men, a small frail looking fellow and a big man dressed in black, had been shot. Just as the young woman had said. Even though Jadin had told her she had felt the presence of someone following her, the story had to be made up. Even as she wrote the story. That changed the night of the last performance.

"Shake a leg! Come on, shake a leg! Jadin hasn't shown up!"

CHAPTER 2
BOOK 1

The dining car was only half full as she had been shown to her table. It was now starting to fill. White linen tablecloth, fine china with the French railroad company's logo hand painted on each plate. Wine and water glasses and silver tableware. The fine dining car was only available for those with compartments. Missy had made sure Colette had a compartment.

Colette sat facing the entrance she had passed through at the end of the car. She ordered a glass of Burgundy. It was from her home region where she was born. Some people looked down on it, Burgundy and its wine. Not as refined as a Cabernet Sauvignon from Bordeaux or a Syrah from Rhone. It was fuller bodied. Since she was having steak rather than fish tonight, she decided the healthy, hearty glass of Burgundy was good. Perhaps a whole bottle! She would decide after the first glass. Tonight she needed it!

As the glass of wine was placed in front of her, behind the shoulder of the Sommelier, she saw movement. A man entered the car. He was younger than her, she being 37. He, perhaps 20...maybe 22 or 23. Tall with broad shoulders. Slim nose on a slim face. Short cut, slightly wavy dark hair. A manly cleft chin. Lips that looked as though they would deliver sublime kisses. But it was the eyes. Even from this distance, at least half a car away, she could see something special, different in them. Deep set and dark.

The Maître D' walked to him. A silent discussion took place. Looking around the room, his eyes spotted hers. Something was said by him to the

Maître D'. The Maître D' turned, looked at her, and turned back to him. A further silent discussion. They now walked toward her table. The Maître D' spoke. "Pardonnez moi, Madame, would you mind if this young gentleman joins you for dinner? The dining car will be full soon and I am trying to assure that all our compartment guests will have places."

Understandable, she thought.

Colette moved her right hand in a motion of acceptance and please be seated to the young man. Then the Maître D' clicked his heels together in a salute, turned, and went back to his station.

In French the young man said, "Actually, madame Colette, what the Maître D' said was not truthful."

She raised her right eyebrow knowingly. A small smile slipped into the corners of her lips. He knew who she was.

He went on. "You see, I was in Honfleur last evening and caught your show. I too am an actor. Though not of your quality." She laughed.

The young man continued, "I thought I would chance that I could ask for your patience in letting me eat with you. It is so much better than eating alone, you see? On this business trip, I have had to eat alone quite often. And definitely not with such a talented and beautiful woman."

"Though your French is very good, Monsieur, I detect a bit of an accent other than true French. Perhaps you are one of our Canadian Cousins?"

"Well Madame Colette, you have the continent correct. Unfortunately, I am not from Canada but the United States. The State of California, in fact. A place there called Hollywood. But then, you should not be expected to know the compartments of the US, which we call States, nor the. cities so far away, any more than I could name all the compartments of France and areas outside of Paris."

He said this with a smile now slipping onto those lips. Again, though, it was the eyes that caught her imagination. Not just deep set, but dark. A dark blue that almost became black. She had seen nothing like them before. A coincidence perhaps? She waited a few moments before speaking.

"You say that you are an actor? Is that what brings you to France? Acting?

"No madame, acting is my hobby. I am here on business. Though the business is related to acting. Have you ever seen something called a motion picture? Pictures that move? Perhaps you have seen a short moving picture by Georges Meliès called "A Trip to the Moon" or perhaps an earlier film called "The Arrival of a Train at La Ciotat Station?"

"Moving pictures? No, monsieur. Of these I do not know anything. Tell me about them."

He did. And throughout the evening, she learned more about what these motion pictures were. It fascinated her as she realized, in some future time, this may transform her own work. Not only the plays she had written and starred in but also the books she wrote.

He was interesting. And very good looking. Perhaps?

The conversation continued for nearly the entire remaining two hours of the trip. Much of the time she was answering his curious questions about Jadin and her disappearance on the last night of the performance.

Finally, they decided that they should end this conversation for a while. They must go back to their compartments to make sure their bags were in order for the departure from the train at the Saint-Malo stop. That was the closest stop to villa Rozven. They agreed to meet again on the platform there.

Mont Saint Michel stop was less than twenty minutes earlier than the Saint-Malo. There a tall, dark, young man with a cleft chin and blue-black eyes hurriedly departed the train. At the depot he hired a carriage to take him north to the town of Cherbourg. From there a ferry took him the next day across the English Channel. The ferry docked at Portsmouth. The home of the largest British Naval base. In Portsmouth Naval Base, he sent a cable to the United States. It was a coded message for the eyes and understanding only of his commanding officer Captain Louis Van Schaick. Captain Van Schaick was the commanding officer at Fort Huachuca, Arizona, home of the Military Intelligence Division.

The cable simply read:

> Information gathered. Payment to JS (Russian). IOL+1 and GE +1 (US) providers. Suspected assassination. Purpose to depose Tsar. Believed large financial benefit for (US) providers. More upon return.
> SM Lt

In two days, June 14, 1911, he departed from Southampton on the maiden voyage of the Olympic, sister ship of the Titanic. The ship made harbor in New York City on June 21, 1911. On board with the young lieutenant was a manuscript. This manuscript would never be revealed to his commanding officer. He decided to keep it himself. One day, he thought, I might be able to make this into a movie...perhaps even star in it. He was young and ambitious.

As he was heading by carriage north to Cherbourg, three days before, Colette disembarked the train with the help of a porter at Saint-Malo. It took a few minutes for her to arrange for his help with her bags. The train to Saint-Malo was full. Though early in the season, the oceanside hotels were beginning to fill.

Now, on the platform, she looked around for the young man. He was not there. She continued to gaze, looking for him. She didn't notice the other "gentleman" coming toward her with a somewhat troubled expression on his face.

A voice called to her, "Cheri, Colette, here I am." It was Missy. As usual, she was wearing her outfit of a dark three-piece suit and tie. It was against French law of the time for women to wear pants. On Missy, often called "Max", it was perfectly proper. Illegal but proper.

That evening, Colette and Missy sat together in the writing study. The place that Colette now felt most at home. Colette had a distant, somewhat troubled look on her face. As Missy spoke to Colette, she had to repeat herself often before receiving a response. This was very much unlike Colette. There was something troubling her.

"Colette, Cheri, what is on your mind? You are not focused on our conversation at all. What are you thinking about?"

"A young man," came the reply.

Now it was Missy's turn to have the troubled look on her face. "Yet another young man? Is this Henry D' Jouvenel not trouble enough for you? When will you learn that men bring nothing but trouble! D' Jouvenel has created problems for us. I wish you had never started writing for La Matin last December. He will play with you, my dear, just as Willy did."

"This is not about Henry, Missy. Leave him out of this. Frankly, I am a bit tired of you bringing up my divergence into affairs with men. You like just the women sex. I like the sex of men and of women. I am an amphibian! Like Lorrain said, 'Just because you blow on the fire does not mean that you don't enjoy using the poker too'. I enjoy the poker! And, I will not have a man or a pretender of a man tell me what and when I can enjoy whoever. But this is not about that. This is a more troubling affair!"

Those words uttered by Colette had a stinging effect on Missy. She would have expected those words from others. Colette was different. She was a woman who had a deeper understanding. Though Colette could be brutally honest. Living with Willy had caused her to have to become so. She was not mean and hurtful. Yet this moment had caused hurt. Something in the relationship was now terribly broken...unfixable. This realization settled on Missy.

With that, Missy's mood calmed for the while. She asked Colette the reasons for her troubles. Though she sensed that the man, Henry D' Jouvenel, was still a deeper concern for them both. It had to be that Colette was forming a deeper bond with De Jouvenel. She must be feeling the loss too.

Colette proceeded to tell Missy the story that had been told to her by Jadin. Missy suspected, yet again, Colette had been unfaithful to her, but at least it was with a woman. The story was indeed intriguing and frightening. When

Colette's telling ended with the fact that the young woman, Jadin, had gone missing, it heightened Missy's concerns for Colette.
"Colette, I am worried for you. And I am worried for me too. Were you followed?"

Colette's answer was to tell of the strange meeting in the dining car with the young man with dark blue-black eyes. The same kind of blue-black eyes described to Colette by Jadin. It was he that Colette was looking for on the platform. They were to meet up and perhaps he would stay the night with Colette and Missy. Of course, only to discuss this idea of motion pictures. Missy hid her anger. She was intrigued and frightened.

The story continued with Collete talking of the unpacking of her bags. There was no manuscript! Had she packed it in the bags before heading to the dining car? She couldn't remember. Had it been in the room when she got back following the dinner conversation with the young man? She couldn't remember. Troubled looks were on both women's faces.

"It was a piece of trash anyway! Not worth my writing. I would have burned it once you had read it. I probably left it in the compartment when I rushed to get back to you." A small smile on Colette's face as she said it. The smile did not fool Missy. Her intuition knew that an end was coming. Would it be the ending of their relationship? Or, would it be the ending of something more permanent. Although she hated either, she hoped it was only the first. The thought of the second frightened her.

CHAPTER 3
BOOK 1

The year 1911 brought changes to Colette and Missy. That year a new book by Colette was published. Not the mystery lost on the train. Instead, a book entitled La Vagabonde was printed. It also dealt with a man who was cruel and controlling of his wife. Following a divorce, the main character in the book becomes a dancer and actress in a music hall. She has a friend, Jadin. Jadin goes missing! The story, of course, was based on the true life of Colette and her short-term paramour, Jadin. The real Jadin was never heard from or found again. No apparent ill fell on Jadin in the book other than frequent frolics in various men's beds.

Colette continued to write for La Matin. Her relationship with Missy further deteriorated. Colette, drawn to the younger Henry more and more, removed her feelings from Missy. That autumn, she moved to 57 rue Cortambert, Paris, with her new love, Henry de Jouvenel. The villa Rozeven Missy purchased for her was given to Colette. The sales documents were in Colette's name when Missy purchased it. The seller would not sell to a woman dressed as a man. Colette's name would have to do. It was only right therefore that Colette kept it and the memories that live there. Missy had no further use of them.

Then it happened! June 28th, 1914, three years and seven days after a young, cleft chin, blue-black eyed lieutenant in military intelligence debarked a ship named the Olympic in New York harbor.

The motor car, an open-topped Graf & Stift touring car, turned the corner. The driver had not realized he made a wrong turn. The hospital was on this route but much farther down the small tight street. Staying on the larger main boulevard would have been safer. That was true even though the earlier event had occurred on that boulevard. The driver made another turn, left this time, parallel with the larger street but still much narrower. The Apple Quai running along the river Miljacka was the street the driver should have taken. Instead, the open-top touring car was traveling down the Frani Josipa.

At that moment, simultaneous coincidences took place. A young thin mustached man came out of the delicatessen, having just finished his sandwich. He stood only four meters from the car and was in awe of this happening. He thought they had failed. The senior officer protecting the people inside the vehicle was riding on the running board of the touring car. He noticed the mistake of route the driver had made. He ordered the car to reverse and go back to the proper route. Some wonder if this was a mistake or part of the plan. The car's gears caught and jammed. The driver worked the gears in frustration. The car didn't move. The officer yelled at him loudly. "You fool! What have you done?" Was the driver's mistake now part of the plan?

At that moment, two shots rang out. One bullet struck the gentleman riding inside the car. It entered one side of his neck and exited the other side. Another, the second bullet, struck his pregnant wife. She crumpled to the floor of the car. The man yelled for his wife not to die. "Sophie, Sophie, don't die! Stay alive for our children!"

Several bystanders grabbed the mustached man, the shooter. They wrestled him to the ground. They took the pistol out of his hand as he tried to use it to kill himself.

By 11:30 the morning of June 28, 1914, in Sarajevo, Bosnia, ArchDuke Franz Ferdinand, heir to the Austrian Hungarian Throne and his pregnant wife, Sophie, were dead. Killed by one of the seven-man assassin team known as the "Black Hand ". "Black Hand", a state sponsored hit team from Belgrade, Serbia, was successful. Only by accident, it seems. Perhaps?

Back in Belgrade, a man wearing his military blue Fez, not the maroon one he wore three years before, sat smiling. His name, Dragutin Dimitrivjeic, also known as "Apis" (Holy Bull). Dimitrijevic was head of military intelligence for Serbia. He sat with a pleased smile on his face. The news was good. It had finally been delivered to him. He was very pleased indeed.

Unknown to others in military intelligence, he was also the head of the secret "Black Hand". His payment for the work of his hit team, a black jewel-encrusted fist of enameled gold. He had put the team together and they had been successful. He was the one who had trained the team. The symbolic payment from JS to his men was really only known to himself and JS. The others had no need to know it all. He only provided them with a few gems. Those, the smaller ones he scraped from the hand. He kept the rest of the gems and the black painted gold fist for himself. No need for the Russian, JS, to know that either. They had more work to do. The fist would fund his work. JS could find his own funding.

As Dragutin sat quietly by himself, he thought about the past. It had been a long journey to this day. This trail had begun for him in Honfleur, France, May 1911. It was an early morning when he had followed the young girl named Jadin three years before. She was a lovely little creature. Small and delicate. But he had no shame for what he did. He knew his assignment. The end hadn't come quickly for her. He had his fun first. In the end, however, it was he who personally had put an end to her story.... At least, he thought so. The small girl said during his interrogation treatment of her something about telling another actor about the fist. An actor? No worries.

Little did he know the actor that the young woman had told was a famous French writer, Colette. Colette had listened carefully to the story the young woman told her. She had written Jadin's story nearly word for word. One day in 2022, it surfaced and sparked a new mystery.

On this same day, June 28, 1914, he, JS, and two others had unexpectedly set in motion the new second phase of the plan. This second phase would eventually kill over twenty million people and seriously wound another twenty million. It was, of course, the unexpected price that must be paid for their eventual financial success.... Greed had its price!

Their plan had triggered what would be called the war to end all wars. World War I began! The true second phase, now became the third phase of the plan. It was the eventual delivery of Russia to the control of JS and the influence of his American friends. The initials JS would later be replaced by the man's name... Joseph Stalin. The initials of the Americans would remain unrevealed. The code of the initials hid their names. A dark eyed military intelligence officer would figure the code out. It would cost him his life.

Joseph Stalin became one of history's cruelest leaders. The last official Tsar of Russia, Nicholas II, abdicated his throne on March 15, 1917. With Nicolas II's abdication, the 304-year rule of the Romanov dynasty ended. On Jully 17, 1918, only four months later, he and his family would be murdered. The leadership of Russia now fell to a man known as Vladimir Llyich Ulyanov...Lenin...VL. The head of the new Communist Party in Russia.

Lenin led the country for a short seven years. His time as head of the country was often marked by him having physically debilitating conditions. During those times, his sometimes friend but increasingly more often his enemy, Joseph Stalin, would step into leadership.

Lenin died mysteriously at a young age due to strokes. The strokes were preceded by seizures...highly unusual in stroke victims.

Perhaps the strokes and seizures were caused by hereditary high cholesterol? Of historical interest to many forensic anthropologists, Lenin had been treated with arsenic. This treatment was a prevailing syphilis remedy of the early 1900s. Curiously, the autopsy at Lenin's death showed he had no signs of syphilis. Why was he then treated with arsenic? Could he have fallen victim to what would become a common method of Russians leaders' handling those who were no longer popular or wanted by other future leaders? A well-known fact might prove this case. Almost any poison causes seizures. Arsenic in the right amounts surely did.

And who was the person with the most to gain by this poisoning? A man with the initials on a package continuing a black enameled gem-encrusted gold fist....JS! Joseph Stalin.

Now, nearly 100 years later in 2022, another man lead Russia.... his initials.... VP! The twenty-first century version of Joseph Stalin.

CHAPTER4
BOOK 1

Following the end of the war to end all wars, November 11, 1918, the not-so-young dark blue-black eyed man returned home. Promoted to captain in the intelligence branch, he had considered staying in the army. Now, 32 years of age, he was ready to get on with his other life. The motion pictures were calling. He was still trying to decide which role he would take. Would he be a star? His looks certainly qualified. At least they had qualified him once. He would have to shave and clean himself up just a bit. His clothes reeked. He couldn't tell it. Others told him and moved away from him.

His confidence in himself, strong. Some might say he had a huge ego. A movie mogul? Perhaps a producer of films? No money. Those took money. He had none. The pittance he had saved during the war was not even enough for him to afford a decent room. A company grade officer's pay had not been much, though he had nothing to spend it on except drinks and women. Small town Arizona during the war had not much to offer. A bar for drinks. A woman for pleasure. All he had needed then. Nothing left now.

He had only one thing. The manuscript he had stolen on the train from the writer Colette. And the story the initials told! They would pay big to keep that secret!

The bar was lonely. He had been sitting in the dark rundown place for some time.

"I'll have another scotch!"

The money he had taken after beating the young man several blocks away was nearly gone. They wouldn't find the body for some time… if ever. His military intelligence training assured him of that. He had become good at that work. When finished with a job, no remorse. It had become easy that morning in Honfleur, France. It became easier with each assignment up to and through the war. On public streets. Behind enemy lines. No matter. Just a job.

The bartender considered him for a moment. Shook his head and filled the glass with another two fingers. At least this fool would not be driving. He would stagger off across the street to the flop house, lay down in the filth there. He did this same routine every night.

"Son, don't you think you have had enough? You would be a good-looking young man if you ever cleaned yourself up and got straight."

"Shut up, you old fool! Lay off! I don't need some alcohol-pushing, old man telling me what to do. I had enough of you guys doing that in the war! I make my own decisions now. Someday you will see this face in the movies and think back to when this guy even bothered to frequent this rundown speakeasy. And, by the way, next year at this time you won't even be here. The Feds are seeing to that! I'll make my own hooch. The army taught me how to do that too! They trained me well, you see. Really well!"

He staggered off the stool and weaved toward the door. Good riddance, thought the bartender. Good riddance.

Back in the flophouse, he sat on the bed. Wrinkled sheets a gray tan color with age and dirt, stained, and still unmade. Hell, he hadn't made a bed since he got out of the army. He wasn't about to begin to do that again. One day his servants would do it for him. One day!

He let out a long sigh. He had to get his head together. That old guy in the bar had something. He had to figure out a plan. He was good at planning. If only his mind was clear.

Glancing to the one piece of broken-down furniture in the room, an old three drawer chest, on top his mind clearing recipe sat. The last of the cheap scotch he had stolen the other night from the secret liquor store. Hell, they won't need the stuff now anyway. The Feds will close them down too. Good thing he had relieved them of it.

He tripped over to the chest, hitting his forearm on the furniture and nearly causing the bottle to crash to the floor. He reached with his right arm and knocked it to the side. It leaned now on its bottom edge. Just as it started to fall, he grabbed it with both hands. He spun around, his back slid down the front of the chest, the wooden knobs hitting each of his vertebrae as he fell. Landing hard, he hit his bum.

Through glassy eyes, he studied the bottle clasped firmly between both hands. He tipped it to his mouth. Leaning back to take a gulp, he smacked the rear of his head hard into the chest. If somewhat more sober, he would have cursed and slammed a fist into the chest. Drunk as he was, he paused for a moment, trying to figure out what had happened. Lifting the bottle to his lips again, he took another gulp, hitting his head once more. This time he rolled to his right, spilled the rest of the bottle around his head, and fell asleep on the floor. His face was in the puddle from the now empty bottle of hooch.

CHAPTER 5
BOOK 1

The drunken stupor ended. He cleaned himself up as best he could. Stole a few items of clothes as he found them. Clothing lines behind small homes provided several items. Things slipped secretly into his bags, coats or pants from stores. Again, his time in military intelligence had served him well. Over time, he had enough to look somewhat presentable. He took on odd jobs, auditioned for a few movie parts, was an extra in some small movies, and hung around the growing picture industry. He met the guy who owned the house. A rich playboy tennis player. Started watching the house while the guy was travelling the world. Life was good again.

Then one day at a small diner, fate happened!

Frank's cafe on Hollywood Blvd had only been open for a year. His odd jobs and living in the wealthy guy's home provided him enough money to have a better style of living. No longer subjected to the flophouse he once stayed in across the street from the now closed bar. He had told the guy the end was coming. Sure enough, it did. January 17, 1920. It and every other legal bar of the time closed. Prohibition passed and ratified by all of the states a year before was now officially the law.

The former military intelligence officer sat at the table sipping a Coca-Cola. The young woman walked into the restaurant. Dark short hair with bangs that reached down almost to the large eyes below. Dark and mysterious eyes. Not unlike his own. She looked like a pixie. Lips perfectly formed. Ones which could deliver either a shy suppressed smile or great inquisitiveness.

Long thin alabaster neck joining a body likewise slim and inviting. Her dress, though proper, clung tight to the shapely curved hips and long legs. The neckline revealed just enough below the bodice of her pert breasts to invite and excite. Small but well-formed waiting to be touched and kissed. Soon, he thought...that would happen.

She, like so many others, was an aspiring young actress interested in getting into the booming film industry. He knew she thought she would one day be a star! Perhaps she might have been.

By 1920, Hollywood was seen as the world's film capital. The film industry was having its effect on society...creating a new morality. It was a place of excitement, fun, and extravagance. Who wouldn't want a piece of that?

He had become more adept at moving through the culture of Hollywood. His looks were still good, though they had not landed him the leading part. His brain was more functional now that prohibition had limited access to booze. However, his friend had stored up quite an extensive stash. His cunning, learned during war, had allowed him to be heartless with his plans. And his increasing desire for wealth and fame pushed him to sobriety and to fulfill that plan. His one weakness was in front of him. A woman!

This young woman would play a part in his plan.

She looked around the dark room. The bright southern California sunlight of the Los Angeles day created a need for adjustment. It took a moment for her eyes to overcome the difference and then she spotted him. The host talked with her. He now nodded his head in the direction of the man sipping his Coca-Cola. He escorted her to the table. Her movements were a glide.

The man raising from the table was just what she expected. Good looking, strong manly cleft chin. Hair that was short, dark, wavey, and graying at the temples. And the darkest deep blue-black eyes she had ever seen. There were age lines around the eyes. But those eyes! Yes, he was just as described.

His eyes surrounded the top of a very sculpted thin nose. A nose very fitting for the face. The lips below? Those could deliver the kisses that would drive the actresses swoony...and the audience watching as well. Yet, through all this...no one could place the face. Couldn't remember it from all the movies they had seen. She knew he was not real. Neither was she. She suspected he did not realize that.

"Miss Chandler, please sit. You are Miss Chandler? Yes?"

She smiled sweetly. Her coaching had been good. Don't ever show the star, director, producer, or executive anything but sweet. Sweet and innocent is what they want. Be sure to let them know how innocent you are.

"Hello," she said as she began to sit. "You are Mr. Miller? Steven Miller?'

"Yes, Miss Chandler. But Steve will be sufficient. All of the stars who sign with me call me Steve." He smiled back at her. The lips forming a perfectly delicious smile.

"Well in that case Mr. Mil...Steve. Perhaps you should just call me Louise." She finished sitting.

Steve signaled for the waiter to come to the table. "Would you care for something to drink, Louise? I'm having a very fine Coca-Cola. Bottled, let's see... ah, yes, 1919. A wonderful year for Coke!"

Louise giggled.

"Of course, I'm sure that Frank's has something a bit stronger somewhere. Am I correct?" he said, looking at the waiter.

"Well, sir..."

"Actually, Steve, a Coca-Cola sounds wonderful. I'll have the same vintage," she said lightly laughing to the waiter. He smiled back and left the table.

"Very good, Louise. That was very quick witted. I bet you will do well with screen auditions. Have you ever auditioned for a movie before? My buddy, Louis, who recommended you to me, has not told me much about you. How about filling me in? Although before you do, don't you find it a big coincidence that your name is so close to my friend's name? Perhaps it is a sign that we should change your name to something more memorable? Hmmm! Got it! What do you think of LuLu?"

She placed her hands on the table. One on top of the other. Nicely formed hands. Just like the rest of her. Sleek and shapely. Athletic perhaps. The hands appeared to be smooth and with no sign of hard work.

"LuLu? It is different. But why?

"It just seemed appropriate based on your name being Louise and my buddy recommending you being Louis. See? Lu and Lu. LuLu! People will remember that name."

She laughed. "Sure, let's go with LuLu. It's kind of appropriate. And fun! LuLu. I like it!"

"So, let's have you tell me about LuLu's background.

"I grew up in Michigan a bit west of Detroit."

"The auto industry capital of the world. Were you ever in Detroit?"

"Only occasionally. Not frequently. My father was friends with one of the founders of an auto company. I can't remember which one now. They had gone to school together back home. But, really I never spent much time in the city. I'm really a country girl. Small town. Small farm. Longing for an adventure." Her sweet smile on her glossy lips. Interesting, he thought to himself. I never would have suspected looking at that beautiful soft white skin and soft hands...

"Adventure? Is that what brought you to California?"

"Oh, yes. Well that, but particularly the movies. I loved watching the movies. I did some acting in school and people thought I would be a natural to become a star." She giggled. "Including my parents. They even paid for my ticket to come out here and try. We always went to the Saturday movies together in our small town. Not much else to do but movies and cows.”

Now Steven laughed. He liked this girl. She had a good sense of humor. Too bad!

“So you want to be in the movies? How did you and Captain Louis Van Schaick meet?”

“Captain?” she said inquisitively.

“Oh, I’m sorry. Yes, Captain Van Schaick. He and I served in the Army together. How did you and Louis meet?”

“The Army? Were you in the war? Oh, that must have been so terrible!” She then whispered in a low voice, “Did you ever have to kill anyone?” A frightened and worried look on her angelic face. “I’m sorry. I should not ask a question like that.” She put her hands to her mouth. “I am so sorry! Please forgive me? It must have been so terrible for all of you men! That is really what I meant to say.”

“Louise…I mean, LuLu, don’t worry about it. We are asked this type of question all the time. Although over 4 million of us served in the war, we are still a small number in comparison to the 100 million population.” He put his hands on the table as she had done earlier.

“Yes, these hands have killed. Yes. Not many, but enough. You never get over it. Was I happy to do so? No. But it was my duty. And I did it as ordered. I wish never to have to do it again,” he said lying. “We do things for honor and country that are not always pleasant. I’m sorry. But, now you know the truth.” His luscious smile back on his face.

“Let’s see. Oh, yes, you were about to tell me how you met Louis.”

A smile now returned to her face, and she began.

“I was on the train from Chicago. It went from Chicago to Arizona. I had to make several stops and changes of trains. I passed through Phoenix,

Arizona. The last real city before we reached the west coast. We had to change trains and stay overnight. The small hotel where I found a room had a restaurant and bar. I met Louis there. He lives in Phoenix. But, I guess you know that. Anyway, he is a nice guy. He was alone at the bar. When I too sat at the bar, he came over to me and began talking. I told him I was going to Los Angeles and hoped to work as an actress. He talked about his friend, Steven. Then he gave me a phone number where he last knew you were. He told me you worked in the movie industry before he met you.

I'm not sure how you learned of my hotel address and phone number here. I just arrived the day before yesterday. I must have left the hotel phone number with whoever answered your phone. Then when I got back to the hotel that evening, your message was waiting for me...and here we are. I really didn't know if you would truly be here."

"And I, dear LuLu, didn't know if you would come here either."

"How is your hotel?"

"Different. I mean the hotels in Detroit and Chicago...the only others I've ever stayed..." She paused for a moment, thinking it seemed..."Well, except for a couple of others like the one in Phoenix, the ones in those two cities are large places. Many, many rooms. Almost too many to count." She appeared to him at that moment to be a very shy and protected girl. "This one is very small. It is kind of dumpy. I think that is the word for it. Clean enough. But, well, you know. There must be other bigger ones? I mean Los Angeles, I guess Hollywood would be included, is a big place. I'm sure that there are large hotels here too. I just didn't find one. It is good enough." She continued the somewhat sweet shy smile at him.

"Let's order some lunch and we can further discuss your acting options. Waiter!"

They ate lunch while he told her of his supposed movie industry connections. She seemed very grateful for his potential help. Finally, he said:

"Here's an idea. I'm staying in a place much too big for me alone. Looking after it while my friend is away. I'm currently looking for my own place. Up in the hills, you know? So, well…what would you say if we picked up all your stuff from that old dumpy hotel and moved you over to this big house. It has 4 bedrooms with bathroom suites, a clay tennis court, and a swimming pool. Heck, other than talking business, you would never even see me. I'm out pounding the streets for my acting clients most of the day. And, of course, if you agreed to sign with me." He made the suggestion very clear. "You would be one of those clients for whom I would pound the streets!" The inviting smile returned to his face. "Living there would provide many benefits!"

"Oh, I don't know! I mean is it proper and all? You really don't know me. Or, I you." She seemed troubled and conflicted to him…but inside she was not at all that way. She knew in the end she would gratefully accept. He would not know that it had been planned.

"Look, LuLu, this makes perfect sense. First, why spend your money needlessly. Second, this happens all the time for new people moving to Los Angeles. It is kind of the expected way for newcomers to be welcome here. Third, I will be working for you. We can practice your audition scripts if need be. It makes perfect sense. Besides, it will only be for a couple of weeks. By then, we will have you in roles that pay. You will be able to afford something in one of the grander hotels that you are used to back home. What do you say?"

She reached across the table and took his hands in hers. Looking up at his eyes from lowered eyes, head just tilted so, "Steve, this is so nice of you. Okay, I'll do it. I am scared, you know. But, all of this life is an adventure. Sometimes scary is a part of that. Okay. Yes!" Her smile and eyes now twinkled at him.

Each one individually thought to themselves, "It worked. The plan is working!" Her plan did. His…ultimately did not.

CHAPTER 6
BOOK 1

"LuLu, I'm home. Where are you, you minx?" No reply. "I know you're home. Where the hell are you? I have good news!"

He walked through the living room, dining room, and sunroom to the back of the house. There she was, lounging by the pool. Her daily routine. He worked. She lounged...naked....by the pool. Alabaster skin coated in glistening oils and sweat. Large dark glasses with 3 inch ovals covered her eyes. They, the only thing she wore. Her long slim legs joined together where her scant dark, trimmed vee pointed toward him. Hiding nothing. Same color as her pixie cut. Was she asleep or pretending? He couldn't tell. She knew he was there. She was tormenting him.

"Hey, you need to protect that skin more! That's our ticket to wealth, you know. Your beauty is what people will buy! You really know how to sell it. That thing is what the producers want!" Double entendre strongly implied.

Her demeanor over the last few weeks had changed significantly. She was not the small town, sweet, protected, innocent she had been. She had transformed before his eyes. She was now quite the "vamp". Innocence had given way to dangerously flirtatious actions. Bright lipstick, tight, little, or no clothes. Whenever and wherever she felt like it. She used her beauty to charm men into doing what she wanted...including him!

That first night together, her control began. That pure, sweet girl gave way to a sexual volcano! She devoured him. She mesmerized him just as she had

Louis back in Phoenix, though Louis wouldn't remember it now. Well, actually, Louis would have a hard time remembering anything now. Her friend ensured that.

Then, she began devouring other men here. Not just him. Some he caught her with after arriving home unexpectedly. Sometimes more than one a day. Was that the case today? Had there been another man or two or more here earlier? Would he find the tell-tale signs on the sheets, floors, in the pool? Or on her?

It was becoming harder and harder to control himself. Yes, he had started drinking again. And yes, his anger would flare. So far, he had enough control to leave the house. Not hurt her. That was becoming more and more difficult. Difficult because now his original plan for her use had given way to a much more financially rewarding possibility. She was magic! She wooed the producers. Her auditions were incredible. And, he had a major offer for her. From one of the big movie companies... Predominant Studios.

"I'm going to fix a drink. Want one?" he asked, holding his temper. Not wanting to look around for the evidence he knew was there. "We have something to celebrate!"

With interest now, she slid the bath robe over her naked body as she rose off the poolside lounge. A slight, but not quite, swipe of a towel between her legs as she did. She hadn't hidden the movement...just made it impossible for him to know for sure. Teasing him.

"Sure! I'll have what you're having. Scotch, I presume? Or are we going for gin today?"

"Let's be exotic today," he said, looking at her body and the gaping robe as she stood not hiding anything from his eyes. "I'll fix each of us a dirty martini. Seems fitting, don't you think? Dirty and exotic!" Letting her know he knew of how she had spent her day.

"Yes, dirty and highly erotic...I mean exotic...Stevie...you know that's what I like!" Sweet smile turned into a sneer.

Later, after he mixed the drinks, they sat by the pool. She, with her robe open to just below her sex, small perfect breasts mostly exposed with occasionally a nipple exposing itself.... finally, she asked.

"Why do we have to go to this place... San Luis Obispo? And what is Hadley Castle? This is a waste of time. By train. God!"

"LuLu, we are going to San Luis Obispo because we will sign the contract there. A guarantee of 10 movie roles over five years. Four of the movies are talkies! You will be the leading lady star in at least two! The studio boss is with Clayton Hadley's nephew right now. Hadley Castle is the name of Mr. Hadley's west coast home."

"So?!"

"Hadley owns over 54 newspapers worldwide! He owns magazines like International Sophisticate. He has large investments in international film studios like Predominant Studio. He can get your name to the world! All you have to do is be there and do what you do so well! Sell yourself with that thing you keep teasing me with! Hell, you do it with just about anyone. Do it now for a good reason!"

"But a train? How long will it take?"

"Overnight. We will have a sleeper. It could be fun."

"Two sleepers and it's a deal! You know how I move around in my sleep!" A sneer planted on her pixie face. "When do we go?"

"Day after tomorrow. 8:00 in the evening. We can eat in the dining car. Then a few drinks, sleep, and we're there. Twelve hours in total. Just two stops. One at 10:00 pm. The second at 5:00 am. We will sleep through it. I have the tickets already. Let's have another erotic...I mean exotic martini and get dressed and go out for dinner. Unless you want to go out like that. I'm sure many would relish it if you did!"

"Tempting, but no. I will wear something provocative but keep them guessing. Martini, yes. Then I can dress. Oh, and I'll keep you guessing too!"

She spun around, letting the robe fly open above her waist. "Have a good look. Want some?"

He did too. He knew she would find a partner somewhere on the train overnight when they left in two days. He was not getting much anymore despite the fact his efforts were producing success. Oh, she gave it to him occasionally, only when she needed it, wanted it. Her sexual desires were unquenchable. It was always her decision when, where, if, and with whom! Usually not him!

Ingrate! At least she could give him some when he wanted it. Not make him feel like a beggar being tossed a morsel here and there. He knew she did it only when she wanted to make sure she had the power to keep him inline...keep him interested. Her control of him made his anger build. One day, she would give it to him on his terms. Like it or not! Then, he would get rid of her for good. By then, she would have served her original purpose! His wealth would be ensured.

How perfect, she thought. An overnight train. She would let HIM know tomorrow.

"By the way...what train will we be on?" she asked with a wink.

CHAPTER 7
BOOK 1

Two days later at 7:00 pm, they boarded the train for the overnight trip. Each had their own separate sleeping compartments as she demanded. Inside each compartment was a large, nearly full-sized bed, a fold down upper bunk, a toilet, sink, and lounge chair. State of the art for the time. The beds were attached to the adjoining wall.

Sure enough, that night he heard it happen. Hands banging against the wall in ecstasy. Loud moans, squeals, shrieks, and pleads, "Make me come! Now, harder, harder, faster! There! There! Yes! Yes! I'm coming! I'm coming! YEEESSSS!!!" All night.

It kept happening over and over again. Although she was having her desires quenched, she knew she was tormenting him...building his frustrations!

He knew it was, though not an act, at least partially an act to show her disdain for him. She was a talented actress! But, he wasn't the co-star in this play. Who was?

Early in the morning, after all the sounds of pleasure-filled moans ended, he heard the compartment door slide open. Tempted to look out, he decided not to do so. Perhaps that was the mistake? That question would never be answered.

An hour and a half before the arrival into the station at San Luis Obispo, he knocked on her door. "LuLu, it's me. It's 7am. We will arrive in an hour and half. Let's get some breakfast."

"Go away! I didn't sleep all night. The damn train kept me bouncing and thrashing around all night. I must have kept you awake too! Didn't I, darling? Poor boy hearing all my movements through these thin walls and all. Every movement must have sounded so loud and disturbing. Sooo sorry. Were you worried for me? Of course you were, sweetheart. I hate myself if that is so. I wanted you to get your boyish rest.! Now be a good little boy and go away! Leave me alone to finally get some sleep. I'm sooo exhausted. What a hard night I had. Sooo hard!

Perhaps the second mistake. He headed to the dining car alone. Frustrated.

Very few people were up. There were two older women, aged 75 or so sitting alone at a table. An even older man at another. A woman with a small boy of perhaps 6 years of age at a third table. Lastly, a very large man about his same age...perhaps a bit older, sitting by himself at the back of the car looking outside.

Steven sat down at a table with his back to the large man. Unfortunately, he was close enough to the two older women to overhear their conversation.

"Yes, they were going at it like rabbits all night long. Surely you heard her moans and screams, Janette? It was God awful!." The woman was talking loudly so her companion could hear and so she could tell everyone in the car too. "Why she probably won't be able to walk for a week!"

Loudly, Jennet replied, "Didn't hear a thing, my dear. You know my ears aren't what they used to be. Perhaps a blessing, don't you know?"

"Well, trust me, they were in some state! She could have satisfied all the troops at Fort MacArthur. That's for sure! Never heard such a thing."

Steven finished his coffee and got up, tired of hearing what he had heard going on next door through the night, retold to him by this old lady. A cigarette on the small platform outside the back of the car was appealing. Then back to the compartments to force the sleeping nymphomaniac off her back.

He got up and walked out. Soon afterward, the large man did too. The man pulled out a cigarette and asked Steven for a light.

Just south of Surf, California, as Steven raised his hands cupping around the flame to protect it from the wind to light the man's cigarette, it happened. The man pulled a knife from inside his shirt sleeve and shoved it into Steven. Stabbing Steven several times in the abdomen as he twisted the knife with each stab, ensuring maximum damage. They struggled. The large man was too big and with the loss of blood, Steven was nearly unconscious. His last thoughts to himself were, "I sure didn't see this coming!"

As he was pushed over the train's railing towards the cliff and the boiling surf below, he made one last grasp for life. His hand caught inside the large man's belt. As the man lifted Steven over the railing, he didn't realize it had happened...until it was too late. Steve's nearly two hundred pounds on a tall 6'2" frame was too much weight, leverage, and pull. Fighting to regain his own balance, the big man lost his own fight with fate. He too was pulled over the rail. Both bodies hit the side of the train car. The large man's arm broke on the rail. They tumbled to the edge of the cliff. With no useful arm free to hang on to safety, slowly, they both slid to the cliff edge and disappeared over it...falling 125 feet to the rocky shore below. High tide was just starting to flow back in. In less than an hour, it would be fully in and then start its slow departing flow out again to the deep blue depths.

Jenette, seeing the struggle and both men falling over the rail, yelled, "My God!"

Her partner, worried about Jenette as the color drained from her face, yelled back, "Are you alright, Jenette? Answer me! Jenette!"

Jenette could only stammer, "thh, thh!" Finally, she got out, "The two men just fell off the back of the train!"

Her friend said, "What? Who?"

The waiter, hearing what she had yelled, realizing that the two men were no longer on the back platform, ran to the emergency cord, pulled it, and alerted the conductor and engineer of the emergency.

The brakes of the train locked. The train continued to slide on the rails, the weight and built-up energy pushing it, almost a quarter of a mile before stopping.

The conductor and several male passengers ran back along the tracks. They covered nearly a mile. No sign of the two men could be found other than the marks in the dirt and stones where they slid to the edge of the cliff and had disappeared below. Neither were ever to be seen again. The outgoing tide saw to that.

After hours of delay, the train finally made it to San Luis Obispo station. LuLu was notified during the stop as the train personnel and male passengers were conducting a search. She broke down in deep sobs and heavy falling tears, giving an award-winning performance. She was terribly distraught that her good friend and lover had been attacked and apparently murdered. Who was this horrible, unknown person who had attacked Steven? She swooned a couple more times while being questioned about him. Did she know of any reason someone would do this horrible thing? Of course, she did not.

"He was such a good man, an honored serviceman who returned from the war to pursue his love of acting and to help young aspiring actors, like me, get into the business. Why, he had even arranged several auditions for me. Now we were on this train headed to San Luis Obispo to sign my five-year contract with the owner of Predominant Films at the Hadley Family home. Then we talked about marriage and our life together. How horrible! We were so deeply in love. I'll never be the same with my Steven gone! How horrible! Oh, my Stevvvviee!"

CHAPTER 8
BOOK 1

A MARVELOUS ACTRESS

Yes, she was a marvelous actress, and she pulled off the sale just as well. After a lengthy interrogation at San Luis Obispo police station, the police captain in charge of the investigation had heard several complaints from both the representative of the Hadley family and the Predominant Studio owner. "Why is this young, distraught woman being subjected to the inquisition?" the police captain very apologetically ended the questioning of LuLu. "Someone as attractive and innocent-looking could not have been involved in this terrible happening," he was told by one of them.

Still, it was very interesting that from the interviews of other passengers, she seemed to have had a late-night visitor. The sounds from her compartment caused quite a lot of stir to the rest of the passengers. Most likely it was this fellow Steven joining her. But what if it wasn't? Would he, the police captain, be letting a suspect go so easily because she was so alluring?

Having seen pictures of the girl, her desirability had intrigued the Hadley family representative, Clayton's nephew. He, a young member of the family, well fit, and used to getting what he wanted, from whom he wanted, when he wanted, decided instantly he wanted some of her.

A couple of days before her arrival, he and the Predominant Studio owner had fully agreed upon a plan for her. The plan would have been presented to Steven had he been alive. His surprising end made that unnecessary. The three men, Hadley, Paramount, and a man in Detroit, discussed the plan over the phone together. Detroit was not upset to hear about Steven. The other two men were unaware of Detroit's arrangement with the girl nor the other fellow who apparently died with Steven. They had suspicions, however.

As the other two men revealed their idea to him, Detroit, seeing that the plan was very intriguing, told them he thought they should go ahead with it. It added a nice twist to what he and his partner in New York had conceived. "Yes," he agreed, "follow through with it. I only wished he could be there to help!"

As the Predominant owner ushered the young woman out to the waiting car, playing that he was saving the police captain's pride, the young Hadley said, "Captain, how about as a subject in the police investigation... a sly smile on the young man's face... 'you require this young woman to stay in the area for a few days? A length of time until you feel comfortable. Then at the appropriate time...' eyebrow raised... 'you notify us the investigation has moved as far forward as possible with her help. What would you think if we have her stay at the castle... for say a week? Would that make it easier on the investigation, captain? You could visit with her often there...privately.'"

The captain suspected this was not a magnanimous suggestion. It instead appeared to be well thought out. He had heard the castle had been the site of other such schemes. This one, the captain realized, would provide interesting possibilities and a variety of enjoyable opportunities for himself. He took a moment before answering. A Machiavellian plan! A plan filled with sly, devious, artfully cunning treachery. The castle was the perfect location. Remote, it stood on its 150,000 isolated acres.

After the pause, he said, "Why, yes! That is an excellent idea. I do have some more questions I would like to ask her. Tell the young lady I have released her into... hmmm... let's just call it your protective custody. She will be under the protection of you and the Predominant movie owner until further notice. If other killers are out there, who knows what harm might come her way? Perhaps as long as a week, maybe more if needed, depending on what she..." his own eyebrow raising..."can provide! Yes, tell her at least a week. She probably has intimate knowledge which will be useful for her to... share with me... hmmm", pausing again as if reconsidering, "Yes, at least a week at your castle. We can start with a week and see if it does the trick. It might just be long enough for the issue to be settled and her safety and well-being preserved. And, for us to uncover all the inside secrets to this case. I'm sure you understand?"

The young man smiled at the captain again with a knowing smile.

"I am sure she will enjoy your full investigation, captain. An investigation that seeks out any inside secrets will be welcomed!" His smile bigger, "She, I think we both can tell, will not want to leave anything unexposed or unexplored."

Following that statement, he lifted his right eyebrow for emphasis and added, "We will make sure she will be open to your full and completely deep investigation of her... on this matter. You will be provided plenty of time to fill her completely with any of your knowledge. That knowledge could be helpful for everyone. Though I'm sure much of what you do might be hard for her to receive! Hard observations in the end will provide her completely satisfied... with the results. This, I'm sure, is what she wants. She seems like a willing young woman. Wouldn't you agree?"

They both glanced out the door at her standing by the car. "Yes, it does appear she will be a willing witness."

The two men shook hands. The young man smiled and left the station. The captain had, at one time, a bit of an unspoken question about her possible involvement in the crime. He no longer did... not now, anyway. He had other things on his mind that had "firmed up"! Below his beltline, it had become quite obvious and even a bit uncomfortable... He had previously had the urge to pee. Now, damn it... he would have to wait!

He sighed and thought, "Sometimes you just overlook some things for the better good!" This "better good" he knew he would soon be enjoying. Looking down, he added to his thoughts, "It may be sooner than my being able to pee." Other things would have to go down... a lot!

As the young man joined the others by the limousine, the captain continued watching her. Without the captain noticing, she caught a glimpse of him through the corner of her eye. She could tell he was focused on her backside and made a special effort of lifting her dress well above mid-thigh height. Then she slipped gracefully, first one cheek, and then the others, into the vehicle. She smiled to herself, knowing what she had done to the captain. He simultaneously said softly out loud, "Yes, that reward will be nice. Nice indeed!"

Later that night, he was appropriately rewarded... more than once... and several more times that week. The first results had been good. Each session was even better. Some of his most trusted and loyal colleagues were called on to add their efforts to the probing investigation. Those results, they would share with each other back at the station over coffee again and again for several days.

After she left the police station, she was taken to the castle and led to the third floor of the stately 75,000-square-foot, five-story La Casa Ingente. On the third floor of this grand structure was a room she would occupy for seven days. A room in a hall of three doors: one door was at one end of the hall; a second door was at the opposite end. Her room, La Condesa Suite, a very opulent room of turquoise color, was between two doors. It was the perfect room, serving well the continuous stimulating reassurance she received at the hands of volunteers.

The large, oversized bed could provide room for several. The stately chairs and couches could be positioned and repositioned again to allow flexibility for participants in the sessions Hadley and Predominant envisioned for her. This was often needed as the sessions required extended time and multiple participants' efforts. All this was explained to her that evening at dinner. Her agreement, she would realize, was necessary to ensure the signed contract.

CHAPTER 9
BOOK 1

After resting and bathing, LuLu dressed for dinner, which was scheduled for 7:00 p.m. There was champagne to toast her and her planned success, of course, after the consoling statements by Hadley and Predominant. There were also a few other guests, including close friends of the movie mogul and Hadley, the police captain and his lieutenant, and four curiously big male movie actors who fascinated LuLu. They would continue to fascinate her for the rest of the week.

Once the toast and consoling statements were made, and the champagne was drunk, the group left the outer room and entered the grand dining room. Nearly three stories high, made of dark mahogany wood, the table in the center of the space was long enough to seat more than twenty people. That night, only fifteen people were gathered for dinner, but later in the week, more people would fill the space and an extra table would be brought in for them.

Mr. Predominant explained that dinner would be served, and then he would tell the guests about the arrangements for the week to honor what he knew would be his newest rising star, the beautiful Miss LuLu. Loud applause filled the room, and dinner began.

Throughout the meal, LuLu found it hard to eat due to nerves and questions being asked of her. She felt all eyes on her, especially the constant stares of the four big actors who seemed to have knowing smiles on their faces, indicating a secret they shared.

Another person was also closely watching her, a woman whose face had a sweet smile but also showed a hint of concern. LuLu wondered if the concern was for herself or the woman. The smile was below two big brown eyes of the most beautiful light brown-skinned black girl LuLu had ever seen. She was one of only three other women in the room: the other two were a young, nice-looking girl, and a middle-aged frumpy woman who looked stern and did not smile.

Dinner ended, and Predominant stood. "Gentlemen," he paused, looking at each one, "and ladies," he paused again, scanning the room. "It is truly an honor for us to be hosted at the Hadley Castle this week, following the untimely death of Miss LuLu's betrothed. I'm sorry, my dear! Our sincere condolences," he said, looking at her as she acted with appropriate made-up sobs and tears.

"But we are also here to celebrate the ascension of this young woman to the stars!" Loud applause filled the room. "It will not be an easy ascension," he looked at her and continued, "no ascension is, now is it, my dear? Why, all one has to do is ask our savior about that! Right?" This time laughter filled the hall.

"In the end, the rewards will be great! Of that, we can all be assured. We who fill this room are all your new friends. We want to aid you in overcoming your great grief. We also want to provide you with support. We will do this by coaching, counseling, and acting. That is why each of us is gathered here to be with you this week."

"Tomorrow morning we will begin in earnest. Tonight, we will let you get some much-needed rest…" a smile forming on his face…"though some of us may come to your room to provide you with special preparation for tomorrow. Oh, and I believe the captain and lieutenant may need to probe some troubling issues regarding the investigation. Other than that, the work will begin after breakfast with the first of your screen tests."

A shocked look appeared on LuLu's face.

"Yes, my dear, a film crew arrives tomorrow for filming before a live audience of these friends here gathered. Several other friends, soon to be your close friends, will be arriving tomorrow to assist us."

Turning from her to the others, he said, "Sleep well, everyone." Then turning back to her, "You too, my dear. I will come to give you some private instructions on your role for tomorrow, in just a few minutes. That will give you time to prepare."

The dinner broke up. The four big actors and the Hadley young man escorted the beautiful woman away. The frumpy woman took the other young women with her. The rest of the men adjourned to the billiard room for cards, billiards, and discussion of the fun in store for the next several days.

A little while after she returned to the room, there was a knock on the door. Before she could respond, the door opened, and in walked Predominant. Shocked, she was about to say something when he began to speak first.

"Good, you are only in your undergarments. This will make it easier for our practice."

"Tomorrow's screen test will involve role-play, my dear. I want to see your performance with a variety of different players. You will be asked to take on the appropriate role with each. As an example, one player will be a Catholic Bishop. We can practice the role you will have with him now."

"Let me set the stage for you. You have run into the church naked. Let's see, yes, you must take those undies off to put you in the proper mood. Go ahead now. Be a sweet girl. That's right. A sweet young, most innocent thing."

She did as she was directed.

"Very good. You are much more beautiful than I even imagined. And, as a movie company owner, I have quite an imagination and significant experience of other women's bodies to judge against. Yours is right up there with the best, my dear. The very best."

Having her continue to stand naked in front of him, and not in any hurry to speed up his close look at her, he finally went on.
"Each performance will have two aspects of your role which will need to carry throughout. First, you will have a bad case of 'female hysterics'. Caused, of course, by the loss of your lover. The hysterics nearly drive you crazy with need. They must be cured as each participant will try to do for you."

He paused, looking at her nakedness in front of him. "Spin around slowly and let me have a good look at all of you from all sides. Very nice, my dear! Very nice, indeed! Your body will serve you and others...in our business...well. Extremely well!" He continued to look at her closely, for some time. Again, with no hurry to relieve her awkward situation. After a few moments, he walked over to her, put his hands on her, and touched her in her most delicate areas. Then he spoke, again.

"You will also need to display in each role the fact you are grieving." He paused for a moment as though he was considering what she would be grieving.

"It is obvious she thought, you old fat fool, I'm grieving Steven's death," LuLu thought to herself.

Then he spoke again.

"Yes, you are grieving...but not for the loss of Steven."

"But what then? He was my fiancé!"

"Yes, sweet girl, of course." A sly smile turned up in the corner of his mouth. "That will give you great natural emotion to draw upon in the roles. Experience in real life can help us use it in our roles." Continuing, "But, in this case, you have come to the Bishop to seek pardon and redemption for your sins!"

Becoming more uncomfortable and not just from being naked in front of him or still being touched, she was uncomfortable about what she thought he would say next...and he did! He said it!

"You are seeking forgiveness for leading Steven to his death!" His eyebrows both raised knowingly. "His murder!"
A shocked LuLu stood there dizzy, nearly fainting.

"Now, my sweet girl, kneel before the Bishop and earn your redemption. Kneel, girl, now!" And with that, his pants fell down, and the first practice began.

CHAPTER 10
BOOK 1

The next day, a film crew arrived from Hollywood. They filmed a week full of episodes. The resident of the estate and the head of the studio had advised the willing helpers that the girl was not to be harmed in any way. She was, after all, recovering from the loss of her fiancé's murder. They were there to provide compassion, consolation, and assist her in the screen tests. She was the studio's valuable commodity.

But still, they insisted, there could be no long-lasting blemish, discoloration, swelling, contusions, or injury. The visitors were there to fulfill her needs, help her learn her craft. Did they clearly understand these rules? They all did! Over the week, they all provided a large variety of help for her as she was appearing in constantly changing and difficult roles. Their efforts were exhausting, but they persevered with great personal sacrifice. And all week, their hard work was filmed. They truly were special men...and yes...women too.

The four big male actors had two responsibilities. They provided their special talents to help her with extremely difficult roles. During those enactments, the other guests would be gathered to watch their unique talents as they were applied with her.

And so, all of the willing participants made her a star of seven complete days and nights of filming. It was a special collection of films. This was also filmed for medical posterity. The attending family physician was there to supervise. He mandated LuLu be inspected from time to time. He personally did the inspections. He wanted to ensure no long-term damage had been done to her. It was always...after the fact.

His studies that week made him a leading doctor in the field of women's health. His film library became extensive. Those medical films, as with many of the others, would be preserved in his private medical collections. He studied them often, used the techniques again on other patients. Some patients would remember their actual use. Most under medication, of course, would not. He liked his patients that way. Sedated patients always gave him greater access.

And so, after first setting rules, the action and filming commenced. The films were not really talkies as few words were said. Mostly the sounds were of her in emotional release. Her howling animalistic sounds were all recorded on the film.

Each and every one of her releases was captured as they occurred. Usually, they were multiple. Some were continuous. One day there were more than twenty continuous releases. The applause and cheers that day grew with each release. When finished and near collapse, she received her first standing ovation! Encouragement for encores rang out from the audience. Best of all, every release, every one, had been preserved for eternity...on celluloid!

The viewers all agreed to be filmed. They each wore masks for the filming project to protect their identities. Many were prominent businessmen and politicians. The congressmen from the local district, a senator home from Washington, a gubernatorial candidate among them. Of course, the chief of police, the captain and lieutenant were there. Clergymen from several faiths, owners of large San Francisco and Los Angeles department stores, other actors and actresses, radio and newspaper owners, oil tycoons, and others. All gathered to assist this young woman in her time of need...and help her become a star. Families and the public had no need to know of their wonderful philanthropic efforts to aid LuLu. They were all anonymous "donors" in the efforts. That was all they cared about.

Men visited her at night, occasionally accompanied by women, though it was not common. When they did visit, they provided the poor girl with muchneeded consolation, given her fragile condition. The women, in particular, understood better than the men what was required by this lovely creature. They had several unique methods at their disposal, and they employed all of them to comfort her.

The women always had a special touch, smiling with pleased faces that understood well where her strong tensions lay. They knew where and how to relieve those tensions. Perhaps she would need to find female friends once she left the castle. Men and their attachments were nice, but the women had special knowledge! Yes, their comfort was indeed needed by the grieving girl. They gave, and she received, and it happened repeatedly, with a grand release! She loved them.

The one who provided the best relief was a beautiful, chocolate-skinne girl named Cheryl.

Finally, to mark the title of each reel of film once filming was completed, a card bearing the type of role she played was made and filmed. Each card mentioned hysteria, and each recorded her "fictitious" responsibility in Steven's murder.

She was indeed a mega-star! She had portrayed the agony of female hysteria and the sin of Steven's murder.

Thus, those seven days of marvelous acting provided the first professionally produced and filmed pornography movies by a major producer and studio.

CHAPTER 11
BOOK 1

Her response to all the consoling efforts was so good that Predominant, at the end of the week, decided her contract should be extended to a full ten years, not five, with perhaps many more future options, depending on her continued willingness, of course. If she was unwilling, he had copies of the films made that week that could probably ensure her willingness.

As a bonus, her new contract gave her six leading roles, four of which would be in the new "talkies". Those would be "talkies" with words, not guttural shrieks, squeals, and howls. She had sold herself hard that week. She had been exhausted, somewhat sore, but very well satisfied. God, being an actress was hard! Very hard indeed! But oh, the satisfaction it brought!

Likewise, the magnanimous Hadley newspaper chain determined she was such a remarkable talent that they decided to run constant updates on her successes. Those updates ran each week for the entire ten years. They reminded the public continuously of her effort to overcome the tragic loss of her true love, Steven. And, of course, the unwavering gratitude she showed all of the caring men and occasional women who helped her prove how special she was. They truly enjoyed her natural talent. So gifted. All of her...so gifted! They would remember how special it was to aid her fully in her time of great need.

Predominant decided that a script should be written and a movie should be made. Only one problem: why did the murder happen? No motive could ever be determined. Greed seemed to be the answer. If the movie was made, she would have to be the leading lady. That was only appropriate. Yes, a movie should be made...one day. A movie about greed!

CHAPTER 12
BOOK 1

At the end of the week, she was escorted back to Los Angeles by the Predominant Executive. He wanted to personally ensure she was secure and safe. He felt it was important that he stay with her a few days longer, given her hysterics had been so strong that week. She might fall into an uncontrollable relapse. What would she do by herself if this were to happen? This would also allow him to get to know her even better, something he felt was important with each of his aspiring starlets. She, of course, showed him her appreciation many times. Following the first episode of ensuring her safety and needs, that evening they sat by the pool with martinis in hand.

"So you're staying in this home? Owned by 'Big Bill'? Isn't that kind of odd? I can't see him providing a girl like you what she needs."

"Steven was a friend of his. They met through some other actors or something. Steven never really told me how they met. Anyway, this 'Big Bill,' whom I only met once, seemed a bit limp-wristed or light in the moccasins, as we would say back in Michigan. He is out of the country on some world tennis trip or something."

"Why do you suppose he has the nickname 'Big Bill'?" she said with eyebrows lifted.

"Anyway, so he, 'Big Bill,' asked Steven to look after the place until we found our own home. Now that will never happen, and I'll just have to find a place of my own."

"Yes, LuLu, I know you are all broken up over the loss of Steven," his eyebrow now raised too. "But you are a young, beautiful woman, becoming a star. It's best if you were single for your career. It allows you to be more interesting, especially alluring to the male filmgoers, you know? Causes a bit of heat with the women, however. The catfight syndrome, you might say...but the sexual allure of a young free-spirited actress? That's worth your weight in gold! To you and to me!"

"There is a place not far from my own you should look at, by God! I forgot about it until just now." He said as he looked at the light swim coverup hanging off her shoulders, barely covering the nipples of her naked body. His eyes followed the gapped open garment down to the dark brown shaded area between her legs. "Yes, by God! It will be a grand place for you! I think I will help you buy it so that you...my newfound star...have a most appropriate place to be displayed."

"And you and I can share..." his eyebrows raise again as he lifts his martini. "...drinks together with each other and, of course, continue our fully deep discussion! Ones just like we have had today. A rather wonderful way to ensure your star rises...don't you know?!"

Three days and nights later, he decided it was time to leave. He had pushed it with his wife. She knew of his adventures with starlets. Divorces were always messy and costly. It was time to end his enjoyment for the moment. LuLu would be close by for his continued consoling. He assured her she would have a new place in two months. Until then, the consoling sessions could continue here.

While he was staying with her at "Big Bill's" house, LuLu had found a way to make a private phone call to a number in Detroit. This had been hard to do with his eagerness to enjoy her abounding recovery.

The recipient of the call was an unknown person. She explained the situation of the deaths arranged for Steven and Louis, and did her best to also explain the unexpected death of the associate he provided.

It was not a problem, she was assured. "He was a good man and will be missed." The voice on the Detroit end went on, "It is exciting news about your acting career. A ten-year contract was reported in Hadley's New York paper. How wonderful for you! My associates and I will be watching your career develop and blossom. We also learned of your extended stay at the castle and why you are just now reporting in. I know the consoling sessions aided you greatly." She could sense his snicker over the phone. She feared learning that he knew all of this. How? From who?

"We learned that you were very deeply appreciated, my dear. Deeply appreciated by all who were there! Our friends were helpful in filling us in about you." With a laugh, he added, "Just a little bit different than how they filled you in, huh?! If you get my drift?!" He chuckled, letting his whole meaning be understood. "Stay well, my dear. Stay well. Enjoy your new life! Use your God-given gifts, especially that one between your legs. That I'm sure others will be enjoying with you! They sure did last week. I saw some of the films earlier today. Very impressive. Not acting at all. Truly responding to all efforts. I could tell!"

The call ended abruptly.

Her message was passed from Detroit onto another person in New York. He too had received copies of the films. That person was equally pleased at having the opportunity to watch her being used. With the films, now all the arrangements for their first plans were almost complete. Only one more to handle. JS would see to it.

The best part was that no one alive now knew the coded names of the suppliers of payment to JS. Their story was gone with three men's deaths. The girl? She knew nothing. Besides, she was just a paid twat. They had copies of intimate films of her. Their supplier of the films would watch over her to ensure she stayed in line. Both men would have a future time with her. Enjoy her. But she would never know who they were and their past involvement in her life. She was just like so many others in Hollywood. They could just imagine, from the descriptions and films they received, how she fell backward into this contract which they had arranged. She was a knockout! Of that, they agreed. It would now be easy to track this rising star. Off of her back and into the stars! An arrangement they had made for her. Maybe they both should buy a bigger piece of her. Was the rest of

Predominant Studios for sale? They knew they already owned most of her. Owning it all might be fun! When out in California next, he decided he would call on her. He guessed his wealthy Detroit friend would too.

One missing issue remained...they didn't know of the stolen novel.

CHAPTER 13
BOOK 1

LuLu's career blossomed as the contract agreement proved successful. She was an inspirational actress admired by all and lusted after by men. Her impact on Hollywood and the nation was felt for two decades and more. Her pixie haircut was all the rage, as were her short dresses that swirled up her thighs - dresses with long, top-of-the-thigh cuts, fringed and slinky, tight-fitting, low necklines that revealed some breasts. Could a hopeful eye catch a glimpse of a nipple? Well, men could hope! There were other intriguing characteristics of that look too: dark silk stockings with a hint of garter belt clasp showing - a small detail that drew male eyes, enticing them where she wanted them and keeping those eyes wanting more. She challenged them to dare to release the clasps and free all that could eventually be revealed. Oh, yes, she could tease, and tease she did.

She knew well her effect on men! Her looks and actions challenged other women to follow her style. Follow her or lose their men to women who did. LuLu became the flapper's iconic look throughout the '20s, '30s, and even into the '40s. Sexual inhibitions and restraint disappeared; fun and frolic were where it was at. This change was all led and created by a young, shy farm girl from Michigan - a naive girl who became a movie actress named LuLu. She was all the rage!

With the purchase - mostly a gift by an eager male friend - it was time she cleaned out her things from the international tennis player's home. His alternate sexuality was of no use to her. She was sure that was true for him too. He was good-looking, however, and it might be fun to try to entice him.

No, there were others who would serve her needs better and with less work for her. Though he personally loved movie stars and the crowd of characters they attracted, he was not lover material for her. It might be fun watching him and his boyfriends, perhaps? Amusing maybe? Maybe someday if she was drunk enough? Besides, she was a star now. She had her own mansion. She didn't need his or anyone's charity.

Tempted to just throw Steven's sparse belongings away, instead, she gave them to a charity shop for the downtrodden. Those people needed it, right? It was the least the star could do to show others she cared.

Clothing and personal belongings were useful to the "Virgin Mother's Hands" charity. LuLu loved the idea of a virgin's hands and what the virgin used them for. It was an inside joke to herself. Bet the Nuns wouldn't approve! Or would they? What did their hands do at night?

The charity accepted everything but had no use for a manuscript written in French. The order that took care of the charity only had one Nun who spoke and read French. She was in the hospital seriously ill, not likely to survive. The other Nuns decided it would be of interest to a small used book dealer who specializes in odd items. It was written in pen and ink and looked interesting, with words scratched out and lines rewritten. It was not saleable in Los Angeles, but San Francisco, perhaps?

So, one day the manuscript made its way north in the satchel of a bookseller and was transferred from dealer to dealer three times before it finally found a home. It arrived in San Francisco, coinciding with a young writer who was beginning to flourish. Fortunately, he spoke and read French. It is unknown if he could tell who the original writer was - probably not. Though Colette, by this time, had an international following, it is unknown if she signed the manuscript.

The story intrigued him, however, and he purchased it. He kept it as the background, the hidden "why" to the answer behind his future novel about human greed.

Yes, human greed had indeed followed this novel's story and it had flourished. Would that ever change?

CHAPTER 1
BOOK 2

Sitting in the sun, moving paint from palette to canvas, were four people: Albert Marquet, his close friend and lifelong protector, a larger man named Henri Matisse, a strange Spaniard named Pablo Picasso, and the owner of the property, a woman writer and amateur artist named Colette. With them was a fourth man, somewhat younger, also a writer. His name was Jean Cocteau.

In 1926, Colette had moved to her new home, La Treille Muscate, in Saint Tropez. She and the man she had loved for a while, until his infidelity became too much, Henry de Jouvenel, separated in 1923. Of course, her own affair with her stepson, Henry's 16-year-old boy, had perhaps been a contributing factor to the separation. She divorced Henry in 1924 after meeting her next and last husband, Maurice Goudeket. With Henry early in their life together, she had a girl child who would never marry. Colette had a step-granddaughter by her past lover, her stepson, and this granddaughter would figure later into the story.

Right now, as the small group of friends was enjoying the bright light of southern France, Picasso and Matisse were using bright colors on the somewhat abstract-looking subjects filling their canvases.

It was Albert Marquet's paintings which had his more muted coloring and less defining lines than the other two men. His paintings were also truly representational landscapes, each displaying his well-developed, graphically correct skills, nearly draftsman-like. In his paintings, he never made up a scene. Instead, his canvases were filled with images that were true to nature and reality. His were not the momentary glimpse of the light, here one moment and gone the next, of the Impressionist painters, those were fellow artists slightly before him, such as Monet, Renoir, and Degas. Nor were his paintings similar to those of his two friends painting alongside him, Matisse and Picasso. His was his own style. Some critics later would say his work did not break through the barriers of time but stayed in the past.

Albert was a small man. Born in Bordeaux in 1875, he was now 54 years old. He was two years younger than his close friend, the woman painting nearby. She had invited them to her house for the week to enjoy the sun and to paint. He admired her greatly and had many fascinations with how she had lived her life. She certainly could have fit in nicely with the many erotic real women he had sketched and painted in his 20s and 30s. Unfortunately, she was not. Still, he had his fantasies, thinking what might have been. A man of his stature often relied on fantasies and goodwill.

In his younger years at school in Paris, the 16-year-old was befriended by an older, much larger man. That man had become his champion. Matisse protected the younger and more frail Marquet physically from other students as well as on the streets of Paris. He also argued on Albert's behalf against the harsh criticism from their teacher Gustave Moreau. Matisse felt that perhaps Gustave was a bit envious and threatened by the artistic skills of the young Marquet. Though he himself was not, still with even Matisse, there was envy for the pure talent of this young man.

Fifty-five years after the four artists painted together, a beautiful movie about a fictional artist, Monsieur Ladmira, was released. Each movie scene was a magically impressionist painting. Perhaps the artist Albert Marquet was the basis for the story. That movie, "A Sunday In The Country," was by Bertrand Tavernier.

However, on this day in the country of Southern France, it was the fourth artist painting that captured all their attention. Colette, the amateur, why was her painting so dark and mysterious?

Albert Marquet was the first to question her. "Colette, my dear, why is that painting so sad and foreboding? I feel as though it is telling us something.

Here we are in the sun of the south, and you are painting the sadness of Dickens's London last century."

Picasso joined in, "Yes, Madame Colette. You need to liven your strokes. Be less worried about the form. Free the spirit. You have wonderful cube-like structures to work with; let them form together and move. This is a painting of old...and sad. Make it new and bold!"

Matisse held his tongue until he had heard enough of the young Spaniard. "Colette, don't listen to the foolish Spaniard. He hasn't painted a good painting with form since he was so poor he could only buy blue paints. Someday someone will give those paintings a shameful name, something like 'Picasso's blue period.' They will not realize he was just a poor fool. They will instead attest to his talent. His boldness! Their silliness! Still, he used color to fill his images...though only blue. You must do the same, Colette! Fill the objects with color...more than Albert here. His paintings are pretty. The future is bold, not pretty! Let the color speak for you."

Picasso, not left for words when his rival interrupted him, jumped in again. "The problem, mademoiselle, is you have never been my muse. Our relationship would give you great freedom and inspiration. I freed Fernande, Olga, Marie-Therese, and others. You must be captured by me. Subject to my animal sexuality, let me tame you! Be bewitched by me! Let me ingest you and crush you onto my canvas!"

"You arrogant fool! Leave dear Colette alone! She is not one of your unthinking followers. She doesn't desire this foolishness. She is a brilliant writer. She also shows much talent. Correct, Albert?"

Marquet, quiet and on the sidelines, just shook his head that Matisse was correct. He walked quietly over to Colette while the other two friends, sometimes enemies, and full-time rivals argued on. Jean Cocteau joined Albert and Colette.

It was at this moment that Colette began to tell Marquet and Cocteau a story that inspired what she was painting. A story that had haunted her for years...19 to be exact. This painting was a scene from the story in a novel she had written. A true story. The manuscript of this novel had disappeared or been forgotten on a train from Honfleur to Saint Malo. She began...

"When I was in Honfleur performing my play, there was this young actress, Jandin. She came to me distraught one night. The poor girl was shaking, crying, and her eyes were filled with terror. She asked if she could stay with me that night in my boarding house room. I thought she was just reacting to the terrible room she had been staying in or perhaps that she had run into an abusive man. Of course, I said to her, you can stay with me. So she did for several nights.

Both men listened intently to Colette as she continued.

"Then one night, I think it was the third, she began telling me the story of why she was so afraid. She said, one night during the performance she had noticed a man at the back of the theater, his eyes watching her closely. It was not unusual for men's eyes to be drawn to her. You see she was quite lovely, though in a very unsophisticated way. She was a petite country flower, you see. Though she knew her way with men. She was not unsophisticated in that way," this said looking directly at Albert. "I'm sure you understand Albert? Oui?"

Albert knew exactly what she was referring to...in either direction...he guessed. He knew Colette too well to suppose otherwise. It didn't take Jean Cocteau long to also figure it out either. Though his own interest lay in one way only.

"This night following the performance, she was walking home when the same strange man, this time with a maroon fez affixed atop his head, cornered her on a side street not far from her rooming house. She was scared and about to scream when he held out a fistful of French Francs. She thought he was suggesting she might be a willing demi-mondaine. She could be interested."

"Is that what was requested?" Jean asked.

"Non, the man wanted to pay her to go to the dock the next morning and retrieve a package for him. It was to be off-loaded from a freighter coming in from an area of North Africa. The man she was to receive it from was described as a frail fellow. One not hard to recognize because of his high-pitched voice and dark complexion. For such easy work, she would receive 5 Francs then and another 5 Francs when he, the man wearing the fez, picked it up from her at her rooming house. What worried her was that he seemed to know where she was staying. He must have followed her earlier."

"His eyes told her that she had no choice but to accept the offer. So she did. Early the next morning following a terrible storm the night before, she went to the docks. She saw nothing. She waited a few moments and then decided to leave. She would return the 5 Francs to the fez fellow. Just as she turned to leave...there in front of her was a small dark frail fellow. He handed her the package and told her to leave now! She didn't hesitate. He was a frightening-looking fellow. She could see the same meanness in his eyes that she saw in the fez man's eyes too."

"So she started walking away. Just then she heard a gunshot. She heard a high-pitched scream and a splash of someone falling into the harbor. She looked over her shoulder at a large man dressed in black coming toward her. She hurried off. As she passed a doorway, in the doorway ahead of her, a man stepped out. He smiled at her, tipped his hat, and walked past her in the other direction. Then a second shot. She turned and saw the large man fall to the ground. She ran home to the boarding house."

"It was there that she saw the note on the outside of the package warning her not to open the package. She said she knew she shouldn't. Ultimately she gave into her curiosity, and she opened it, however. It held an ugly black disfigured fist. Bumps all over it. A scratch revealed that it was black enamel over pure gold. The bumps were large jewels. A jewel-encrusted black-enameled gold fist!"

Jean's eyes grew larger and larger as he listened to the story, until he let out a shriek. Colette and Albert turned to look at him, and even Matisse and Picasso stopped their argument to stare at him.

"All I can say is, 'Oh, my God! Oh, my God!'" Jean exclaimed.

The others asked him what he was talking about, and Jean explained.

"I was in Paris last week, visiting an American friend of mine who is also a writer. He had a magazine with him called 'Black Mask,' which features serialized stories. In this magazine, he showed me a story about a black enameled gold and jeweled bird. I think it must be related, Colette, to the story you're telling us. It's a story of greed, with no other purpose but for greed."

"Perhaps," Colette said, "but I haven't finished Jadin's story yet. She opened the note, and it was from two Americans whose names were in code. The note said that the first was to be delivered to a man identified only as JS. It was payment for two assassinations that occurred in 1910. In 1914, the assassination of Archduke Ferdinand took place. Do you suppose..."

"Was the victim of the assassination identified in the note?" Jean asked.

"No, Jadin didn't know that," Colette replied. "There was something about a second payment following the second assassination. That victim was identified only by the initials VL."

"Oh, my God! Oh, my God!" Jean exclaimed again.

They all looked at him.

"Am I the only one who sees this? Am I the only one who understands?" Jean asked.

They continued to stare at him.

"The first assassination was of Archduke Ferdinand of Austria! The second one was Vladimir Lenin!" Jean said breathlessly. "The JS has to be Joseph Stalin. Don't you all see?! This was payment for the assassination that led to the First World War! For all that misery! All those deaths! It was also payment for the future assassination of Vladimir Lenin! Look who's in power in Russia now! JS... Joseph Stalin!"

"But who were the Americans mentioned by initials in the note?" Albert asked. "And where did Colette's manuscript go? How did it disappear? And who is the American writer who ended up with it, or at least heard its story?"

Colette thought for a minute and then replied, "Jadin told me the man who stepped out between the two doors was a tall, good-looking man. The hair she could see at the side of his hat appeared well-trimmed but dark in color. She said when he looked into her eyes for just a moment, they were the darkest, deepest blue eyes she had ever seen... almost black."

"The one who she thinks shot the large man dressed in black?" Albert asked.

Now both Matisse and Picasso listened intently, having missed the story of the two shots and apparent murders while they were having their argument.

"Wait a minute?" said Matisse, "You mean someone was killed? Shot?"

"No, not just one. Jadin told me of two men shot. A small, frail man. He was shot by the big man. That man chased after her. Then the man came out of the second doorway and smiled at her... Oh, yes, she said his smile was extremely seductive. I remember that because how could she have even considered a seductive smile after hearing a man shot? Anyway, she ran. Then, as I told the other two a few moments ago while you boys were fighting, she stayed with me for a few days. The day of the last performance, she went back to her room to gather her things. That night... she went missing! She didn't make the performance. I tried to check on her over the next few weeks any way I could through other acting troupes. No one had heard anything more about her. A few knew of her. But no, nothing was learned. No one knew where she had gone. She just disappeared."

"You think she was killed too?" Picasso asked.

"You Spanish fool! Of course, she was murdered. What else could have happened to her?" Matisse said angrily.

Colette, Albert, and Jean all looked at the two of them. Finally, Marquet, known for his kind, soft-spoken way, said, "Why don't you children behave, keep quiet, and listen to Colette!"
Shocked by this statement from the gentlest of men, they both stood quietly and waited for her to continue.

"To answer your question about where the manuscript is, Albert, I think I must have left it on the train. The last I saw of it was in my compartment. Just before I met the man in the dining car."

All eyes were fixed on her, and Jean said, "The man? What man?"

"It's probably nothing, but a young man asked to be seated with me. He too was dark, good-looking. I remember thinking that his kisses from his lips could cause a woman to swoon. And..." she said with a pause...

"And what?!" they all exclaimed.

"And... he had the deepest blue-black eyes I have ever seen. One could get lost in them."

"What happened?" Jean asked.

"We had dinner. But as I think back on it now, he said he had been in our performance the night that Jadin went missing. That last night. He was an actor from Hollywood, California in the United States. Though he said he was on a business trip associated with the film industry that was just getting underway. At that time, I knew nothing about movies. We had a wonderful talk. But as I was going to say, now that I think about it, he asked a lot of questions about Jadin. Lots!"

Jean Cocteau, known for drama, let out a large gush of air. "I bet he stole the manuscript. Where did he go after dinner?

"We were supposed to meet up again at Saint Malo. He was going to come to my house and talk more about the movies. He never got off the train there. Of course, Missy was upset, as she usually was, with me when I met good-looking younger men." Said with an attempted smile.

"Was there a stop before that stop?"

"Yes, it was at Mont Saint Michel. Why? Do you think he got off there?"

"Yes, my dear," Jean replied. "I think he got off there. He probably hired a carriage and went north to Cherbourg. I bet he took a ferry across the channel to England. Let's see, yes, as I recall, there is a large British Navy base in Portsmouth. I bet he somehow got word back to America from there."
"I would bet anything, my dear Colette, that this young man was an American spy. He was either working for the two Americans mentioned in the note on that mysterious package, or he was an American government spy trying to learn about what the two Americans were up to! If he did get to the navy base, I would bet he was an American military spy!"

"Do you remember anything about the Americans' initials? You said there were two sets of initials in code?"

"Jean, you are asking me to remember back 19 years. I don't know if I can do that. Let me see. Ok, I do remember that the initials of one were three letters and a plus sign and a number 1. The other initials were just two letters but again had the addition sign and again a number 1."

"Well, let's play a game and figure out who the Americans are. Surely with all of the intellectual talent within us, this cannot be that difficult. Let's assemble our facts just as we would if we were writing a play. First, we know they are two Americans. We know that they have provided a rather odd method of payment for not one, but eventually two assassinations. We have presumed the first assassination was of the Archduke of Austria, Ferdinand. We further assume that VL, who died of a stroke in 1924, was also a target. It also appears that the initials JS certainly stand for the name Joseph Stalin. Colette's manuscript went missing on a train between Honfleur and Saint Malo. She had met a man on the train that now appears to match the description of the man that Jadin suspected had shot the large man in black."

As Cocteau was explaining all this, he was pointing at the figures that Colette had painted on the canvas in question. He continued, "Colette stated that a man in a fez was responsible, perhaps, for the disappearance of the young Jadin. He is pictured here spying on her. As she told Colette, he seemed to have followed her before. He certainly is displayed sinisterly here, Colette. Nicely done!"

Pausing for just a moment, he drew attention to one of two other figures on the painting. "But my dear Colette, why did you paint this image of a boy peeing on the side of this building here in the foreground?" They all looked at her.

"I just thought the painting needed more figures. Perhaps a little light comic relief from the horrible story that was told. What could be more amusing than a young boy relieving himself on the side of the church while horror was happening around him? I also felt that someone should be delivering the wine of the day, and that is why I added this fellow too," she said, pointing to a man with a wine carrier over his shoulder and back.

"Well done, Colette. The sign of a true playwright. Make the audience question the scene!" Matisse injected.

"Back to our facts as we know them at this point," Jean continued. "The dark-eyed man, who we think was enticing to both the young ladies, Jadin and our own Colette," he said with a smile and continued. "He disappears at the same time the manuscript disappears. We suspect he is a spy for the American government or for the two people with the coded initials. We have no idea where he is or what he is doing. We do know that the missing manuscript of Colette's appears to have ended up in the United States. It became the background, perhaps, for the new serialized book I have mentioned that appears in the magazine The Black Mask. How appropriate, don't you think? A magazine called the "Black Mask" has a story about a black bird that resembles Colette's novel about a black fist!"

Then Cocteau shrieks, "I just remembered. Wasn't the organization responsible for the assassination of the Archduke called 'The Black Hand'?! I'm sure it was. We have to check later to be sure. If so, this must mean we are onto something!"

"Jean, when was the last time you did opium? Isn't the reason our dear Colette invited you down here to her home to help you in your efforts to overcome the addiction? I think she has failed. I think you are smoking opium again!" Matissa, the oldest of those in attendance and with less acceptance of human folly, continued.

"All this is just connecting unrelated assumptions. We have nothing of pure fact to guide us to this story of yours as being reality. All that you have mentioned could be explained as purely circumstantial or coincidental."

Colette now joined Cocteau's side, saying, "But Henri, yes, this could all be coincidental, but you have to say that these coincidences are interesting...fascinating. Suppose Jean has something here?"

"And by the way, Henri, I have been weaned off my opium habit now for nearly a year. My mind is clear...and if I might add, a bit quicker than some aging artists I know. I resent you implying that my mind is impaired. You want facts to back up these assumptions. Let's find the facts. How? you ask! I say the old-fashioned way. The way that all evil tends to be tied. Let's follow the money! Who has the most to gain by what transpired with the assassinations and the resulting war? Who had the largest financial gains in America for all of these occurrences? Then we match the initials and see where the names fall out."

Now it was Picasso's turn to enter the conversation. "I think you have hit on brilliance, my friend! I think you have come up with a way to solve the mystery!" Picasso also liked the idea that it was not his rival Matissa who had been so creative. "Well done!"

"How do you propose to do this, dear Jean? Uh? How?" Matissa, not wanting to let go of an upper hand he did not hold but hoped no one would notice, asked.

"It may take me some time, but I will solve this question. I will reveal to us who it is. Then we will celebrate once again. Here at Colette's fine home."

With that, they each went back to their paintings. Matissa muttered to himself of the foolishness. In his heart, however, he admitted to himself that perhaps there might be some truth to what Jean had concocted. Laughing quietly to himself. "Jean had concocted a Cocteau...a surreal idea of reality!" Albert pulled a chair up beside Colette. "Here, Colette, let me guide you a little." He took her hand in his and helped her move paint to the canvas in a compassionate, unobtrusive way. Making slight changes to the image that only another artist might be able to see. A painting now with two different brushstrokes from two artist hands. One was a gifted student. The other was a kind and caring, likewise gifted instructor and friend.

Jean Cocteau slid off quietly to his room to write what he had heard down in his journal and make notes of the questions he must follow for the answers.

Across the country, a phone call was made from New York to Detroit. The person in New York had just learned of the serialized book in the magazine Black Mask. When the phone in Detroit was answered, his message was quick to the point. "We have to meet! It appears we have a problem! I'll be there the day after tomorrow!" and he hung up.

CHAPTER 2
BOOK 2

LuLu, a success, was worried. Well worried, perhaps not. Concerned? A little. Well, maybe a lot. If nothing else, she certainly was perplexed. She was entering into the last year of her ten year contract. Not just six movies and four talkies. She had starred in more than twelve. And all but two had been talkies. She was the largest box office draw for those entire nine years. People loved her. Loved her look. Loved her sexiness. Loved the way she lived a free and exciting life. Loved her! What was happening? Why no talk of extending her contract.

Cheryl looked up from between Lulu's legs. "Hey, girl, what's going on? Here I am ministering to your sweet parts and nothing is happening! Where is your mind, LuLu? It certainly isn't happening down here!"

"Sorry, Cheryl. My mind is somewhere else. You were doing great. Really. I'm just not into it today."

"You sure aren't, baby! Why, I'm just wasting my time and my pucker too! Usually by now ol' tongue's swimm'n in da swamp!" The actress's southern accent was deep.

Cheryl, originally from a small North Carolina town near Beaufort on the Atlantic, was one of the few black actresses who had steady work in Hollywood. Mostly thanks to her friend LuLu's efforts. She had been kidnapped as a 16-year-old girl. Drugged and taken clear across the country, she was forced by a middle aged white guy into prostitution to pay their way.

Hell, no one cared on that day that some black child went missing! No effort was ever made to find her except by her momma. She ended up two years later with him in east Los Angeles. Then the squarely mean guy just damn well keeled over one day dead from drink...but mostly from a heart attack.

Not knowing another trade and without skills, she continued plying her trade by herself. She eventually became a favorite "piece of play" for a young rich guy from the mid northern part of the state. The creep loved to "slum it" as he put it, and mess with the "easy girls". He could afford high-priced dames. No, this guy was a man who liked to show girls how much power he had over them. "Contempt", he called it. An easy thing to accomplish with a girl without power. His treatment of her and the other girls was always rough. The way he liked it.

Cheryl became his favorite toy. He used her in all kinds of situations, usually with multiple male playmates of his. She had a very exotic look. Perhaps that look came from the white slave owner of her grandma. She wasn't dark but a sought-after chocolate coloring. She was sure that was why she had been stolen as a girl. Tall, slender, with long willowy limbs, she became quite striking despite her forced life. "Puss" he liked to call her, didn't know why but her joints could almost disconnect. That flexibility is what he really liked. The positions her body could obtain were not to be believed. Not really normal. He used them all.

He was one mean, conniving son-of-a-bitch! His friends, four huge men, equally abusive, often joined him with her. During those times, he got his kicks watching them ravish his "Puss".

Those four men had been the "protective guards" of LuLu at the castle.

He brought Cheryl to that strange castle house for that week. That's where she and LuLu first met. They became close friends. Shared the same interests. Had the same thoughts about men. She would never let her friend be with those men again!

Cheryl raised her dark naked body up from between LuLu's legs and sat down hard next to LuLu on the couch. "Come on, girl! Spill it to me. What's got y'all upset? Perhaps ol' Cheryl can help. Hell, nothing else is working!" Or, I got a good idea!" With that, Cheryl spread her long black legs and took LuLu's hand and placed it on her own thatch of short curly hair. "Perhaps you can take your mind off your worries by working on me? Whatcha say, girl? I'd like that!"

"Cheryl! NO!" Even though she said "no", her fingers absentmindedly, fondly, started caressing the softness of the girl's female lips. LuLu was completely disconnected from her fingers' actions. Cheryl was not. She began enjoying the soft up and down sliding finger. After several moments, the finger's actions took effect. The oily film formed, and the ease of finger glide improved. So much so that Cheryl's hips picked up a rhythm. They started their own slow circular movement. Moving in time to the fingers' widening spread of her small female gash at the joint of her thighs.

LuLu said, "Okay, this is the problem. This is my ninth year of my ten year contract. The studio should be talking with me about a renewal. But nothing! I haven't heard anything! No message of "we need to talk". No message about holding me to a continuation of the binding non-compete contracts with another studio. What the hell is happening? I'm their money bag. I'm the cunt that delivers the dough. And they are doing nothing! I don't get it!

"Honey, they need you as much as I'm needing you now!" Hips starting to move faster. "Look, baby, you're the one who owns the juices that cause their spunk to flow. They know that! If they don't have you, their damn well dries up. Worse than yours is doing today!" Looking at her good friend, she asked, "What about that movie studio owner who splits your legs from time to time? Isn't he the guy you should be talking to?"

"His wife got on to us. I haven't, as you said, 'split my legs' for him in a couple of months. She told the guy if he continued, she would take every cent he had. He would never see his kids again. Hell, his youngest is two years older than me! I think what really freaked him out was when she said she would cut it off in the middle of the night and flush it down the toilet. That probably was what did it!"

Now Cheryl's attention focused solely on the action between her legs and lost any and all concentration on the conversation. Instead, her center of attention was on the heat flowing from the south.

"That's it, girl! Yes, keep that going. Right there! A bit harder and a little deeper. Yes, now faster. Faster! Damn it! I said faster! Yes, that's it! Yes!!!" And with that, a scream and her first crash of ecstasy hit with shudders and shakes.

LuLu, now aware of what she had caused, pulled her finger off the spot that had triggered the urgent explosion between Cheryl's legs. The spot itself, still wet and swollen, begged for more. Although it wanted more attention, but not receiving continued motion from the finger, still had enough left over sensation to start the next bodily response. The fingertip left its target's tip just as the second explosion hit. Cheryl's legs quivered like jelly. Another third fierce quake quickly ran up through the full length of the girl.

CHAPTER 3
BOOK 2

Several days later, a phone call came through to LuLu. It was from a strange voice that identified as being a member of the studio management. She had never heard the voice before. In the late 1920s, changes were taking place within management, so perhaps this was not so strange.

What seemed strange was she was told a new ten-year contract was ready for her to sign. Great! However, again she would have to make the trip to San Luis Obispo. Not by train this time but by a limo from the owner of the castle. The car was already dispatched to pick her up. It would arrive at her house by noon tomorrow.

The voice told her that he knew she was filming at this time. The filming would be on hold for a few days for her to make the trip. After all, they owned the studio. She was told not to tell anyone where or why she was gone. Don't worry about it. Be ready to leave tomorrow!

"Many have enjoyed watching your movies over the last ten years...especially the early ones that started your career. Not great acting so much on your part as your willing responsiveness. You gave your audience what they wanted. Those films have gone through several re-releases, you know! They still are appreciated for your incredible and unique talent."

With a chuckle, the phone call abruptly ended.

Now she did worry about it because she was headed to where that long week had taken place ten years before.

Over time she came to realize all of them tried and were successful in humiliating her. Allowing the humiliation to be stored and finally its reality to be revealed to the victim...her...by a phone conversation ten years ago to Detroit and now ten years later! Totally used by all of them.

At first, LuLu thought she had proven herself and had won. The contract had been doubled when they found out for sure what her looks and sex could do, because even the best of them ending up seemingly to have worshipped her cunt! The big guys too!

That was all a façade. They were waiting in secret to further humiliate her now, ten years later, with the truth. Evil. Pure evil! But why?

All but Cheryl. She treated LuLu with nothing but kindness and respect..

LuLu accepted what she had gone through to end up with what she wanted: to be a movie star, the queen of the celluloids. Still, it had happened ten years ago with a body that was ten years younger. Her body could take long hours and multiple strains then, but she doubted it could now.

Just then, the door to the house opened, and Cheryl came in. She had been on the set of a movie to be released the next year starring a former Olympic swimmer, a man of the jungle called Apeman. Although Cheryl was not in a leading role, they needed an athletic, beautiful black woman to play several of the female "tribal women" parts. There were not too many black women, especially as beautiful as her, in American cinema to choose from. Therefore, she was asked to play multiple roles. Good makeup artists and camera angles made it possible. She was tired as she stepped through the door.

Seeing LuLu on the couch looking worried, Cheryl walked across the room and sat down beside her. "You ain't looking good again, girl. Looks like your cat is sick. You menstruating, girl? Your little kitty sick?" She touched the V between LuLu's legs. "Tell old Cheryl what's it this time? Here kitty, kitty!"

LuLu laughed for a moment and said her pussy was just fine, not the problem. Then she told Cheryl about the phone call. While she was being told, Cheryl kept saying softly over and over, "Don't like it, girl. Don't like it one bit! Not one bit!"

Then she looked LuLu straight in the eye and said, "You can't do that! You can't! Something just ain't right, not right, about it. You can't go, love! I won't let you go!"

"Cheryl, it isn't that easy. I have to go. That is where they want to sign the damn contract...for some reason. But..." She paused, trying to figure out if she wanted to go any farther. Tell Cheryl almost all that was there. Or most of it. "Oh, God! This is so hard!" she said.

Cheryl could tell there was something more. Much more. Then she said, "Look, sweetie. You are my best friend. You got me out of a really bad situation and into the movies. I owe you a lot. Don't you go holdin' back on ol' Cheryl now. Tell me what is really botherin' you. All of it!"

And LuLu began the story from the very beginning, starting in outstate Michigan where her father was an itinerant preacher of "whatever they wanted to hear". Her mother had passed a few years before from her husband's beating LuLu supposed. Who would want to prosecute the preacher? No one in that community. He used to laugh and say of his congregations, "They prayed in the parlor and practiced incest in the barn." So much for her learning about the "Good Book". She had been gilded since birth that human nature was pretty evil, especially evil to good looking girls like her...and Cheryl.

Her father had drunkenly tried to practice what he had preached on her one night. He had tried before but she managed to get away. That night he almost accomplished the act having pushed her drunkenly onto his bed and ripping her pants off her. She grabbed for and found the bottle and hit him with it . It knocked him out cold, though it could have been the drink that really had done it. That night the 15 year old Louise lit out on her own. Hitchhiking and using her body as she had to do to finally make it to Detroit.

"My God, girl, that sounds like ma' story ya be telling!"
LuLu continued. After making it to Detroit, which was hard to do because several men had forcibly tried to keep her for just their own use, she escaped each of their clutches by her instincts, wit, and cunning. Overall, it had taken nearly two years and the use of her by several men to travel only 147 miles. She was now just 17 years old.

She learned a lot about what her body could take and do during that trip. She learned a lot about men too. She found she had a way she could control and use them when it was for her safety and good.

"I could be real cold-blooded too. Several men would never be the same again physically down below!" Her quick use of knives made sure of that.

"A couple even, when the cut had gone deep enough into the leg after slicing through its target, had to be "gotten rid of."

"You mean you hada bury them?"

LuLu looked in Cheryl's sweet brown eyes and said, "Well, one made it to the bottom of an old well on the deserted property we were on. Can't say it was truly buried."

Cheryl, with big eyes, giggled. "Golly, girl! You are one wild ass white girl! Man, I couldn't come up with stuff that fast. Hell, no wonder ya's a star!"

"Then in Detroit I met up with a guy in a bar. "Yep," she said, smiling at Cheryl, "a guy in a bar. Well, this guy as it turned out ran a string of what were called "High Class Escorts" or call girls. He paid me some upfront cash after trying me on for size. And that's when I learned my real value. I was wanted a lot by his clients cause he said they all wanted that young, wholesome, naive, pure girl. I was just the type. That's when I learned I could act!"

"Well, this went on for about a year. Then one day, the guy came to me and told me he was sending me to California to become a movie star! Imagine that? He tells me I am going to be a star. Seems some powerful guy had used me a few times and thought I would be perfect for the movies."

"My manager," LuLu laughed, "said the 'client' of mine and another man owned a big piece of a movie studio in Hollywood. I only had to do two things."

Cheryl, on the edge of her seat with this story, said, "What? Tell me! Come on, girl, Cheryl wants to know. What two things?"

"I was to meet up with a guy in a bar in Phoenix, Arizona, when my train stoped there for the night. The guy would know in advance that I was headed for Hollywood and that he was to tell me about his friend out there who was an agent. Now I'm thinking, right, an agent just like you!"

"Nope," she said. "The guy would connect me with someone who is 'trying to be an agent.'"

"Steven?" Cheryl asked.

"Yep, one and the same! Not a successful agent. In fact, the contract I was offered was the first one he had delivered to any of his...clients...all female actresses, of course."

"Damn, girl. But what do you gotta do? That can't be all? Meet a guy in Phoenix who will set you up with a guy tryin' to be an agent."

LuLu, with eyes downcast, now paused before saying, "No, Cheryl. That was not all. I was to lure each of them into a place or situation where an associate of the rich guy, a big man, could appropriately take care of them."

"Give them a reward? Why, you haven't been made a star yet. Why they getting a reward? Makes no sense to me!"

"Not a reward...I was supposed to lead them into a place where the big guy could have his associate dispatch them!"

Cheryl, with a confused look, said, "I ain't understanding. He was sending them somewhere?"

"Cheryl, no!" Shaking her head and chuckling, LuLu said, "Kill them! Both of them were lured into a trap that killed them!"

"Damn, girl! That's four! Any others out there I should know about?" She smiled at LuLu as she said that and held her hand.

"Wait, so this Steven dude was not your love? All that stuff at that castle was not to make you better, which by the way, I never bought into 'cause no gal gets better being used the way they all used you. Still, girl, you can act!"

"Actually, I feel kind of bad for the way I tormented Steven the last couple of weeks before he was murdered. Poor guy was dying...guess that's a poor choice of words...to have a piece of me. All I wanted to do was torment the guy. I did a good job of it too!" A big smile of remembrance on her face.

"I bet you did, girl. Hell you could torment the spunk ta spurt out of any man. And without him getting some of that thing," patting LuLu's pussy. "Why I bet the man was near crazy with blue balls! Didn't ya give him noth'n?"

"A couple of times...but I made him really work and beg for it. Men are so easy!" Both girls laughed at the thought.

"Wait a minute! If'n they's agonna kill them fellows...why did the need you in all this? Makes no sense ta me. None so ever!"

"I'm not sure either. I was supposed to ask the two fellows about their pre-war years. Find out if they either mentioned a strange object and a fellow with the initials J.S. Neither had. I told a man on the phone that. I had to call a number in Detroit to do so. Thought he believed my story, cause it's true. I have no idea what it all means."

"Honey child, there is no way Cheryl gonna let her lovely sweet white ass girl go into this alone! You can bet my pussy on that girl, cause I'm a sure bet'n yours on it and I ain't aganna lose this sweet kitty of yours, girl! It's too sweet!" With that she patted LuLu's vee again. "No, sir! Ain't agonna lose that sweet thing!"

CHAPTER 4
BOOK 2

Exhausted later that evening, they fell asleep in each other's arms. The next morning when LuLu woke...Cheryl was gone. There was no message in the bedroom or kitchen. When did she leave? Must have had an early morning at the movie lot. That was the only answer.

LuLu was right in one sense, it was an early unscheduled meeting Cheryl had hurried off to. She was going to an unscheduled meeting with a man in women's leopard briefs.

LuLu packed up a couple of days' outfits. Sexy ones as usual! Dresses with her trademark low necks, with up the side slits to hip and fringed. Of course the dresses fell a bit short of mid-thigh...quite a bit. Hell, if she was going into a lion's den she might as well be a tasty meal. Her looks and sex were her best weapons! Both she had learned how to use well.

Cheryl, after taking two trolleys, finally arrived at the movie lot. She knew just where she would find him.

MBM studios were next in size to the Predominant Studios that owned LuLu. They didn't own him, however. Neither did MBM, who was starring him as Apeman in their movie. The studio sure wanted to. An exclusive contract with the man who owned sixty-five world swimming titles and five Olympic gold medals was a wanted property. His male body was the equivalent of a male LuLu. Men and women were both highly attracted to his athletic looks.

Cheryl ran up to the small star bungalow on the rear of the set and started pounding on the door. After a few more bangs and quiet moments, the door opened. There he was, not in women's leopard undies. Nope, the dude was naked with the smallest white towel wrapped around his waist just barely hanging over his cute and naked butt. It also barely reached below, what she could tell by how the cloth hung out and off it, his very large male attraction . She stood there breathless and mesmerized for a moment.

Then she screamed, "Apeman! I need yo help!!"

CHAPTER 5
BOOK 2

"Aren't you the mulatto girl on my movie set? You have multiple roles. You look different, all dressed up. You know, you can really act. Come on in. I'll go get some clothes on. Then you can tell me why the racket so early in the morning."

"Sweetie, you don't have to put any clothes on. You're just fine the way you are! I can tell them things because of what my profession used to be before I became a movie actress. I can tell you've got some mighty fine apparatus there hiding under that towel! You just stay the way you are and just listen to this girl because my friend needs you badly!"

"Have a seat and tell me about this friend. What's going on?"

And so Cheryl proceeded to tell Apeman all about the who, the what, and the why of what was happening to LuLu. Her story began with the beginning of the movie offer and the need to take the train to San Luis Obispo...

For an hour, she talked. Apeman asked a few questions, but mostly he listened. Apeman was known for many real-life heroic acts. He had saved a number of people's lives, including eleven people one day from drowning after their boat crashed into rocks. Yes, if there was a hero who could help LuLu, Cheryl knew Apeman was the one.

Finally, the story was finished. Apeman told her to stay where she was. He was going to make a phone call and put some clothes on. Then they would go see "The Man!"

"The Man" turned out to be the owner and president of MBM Studios. He not only was a competitor of the slightly bigger Predominant Studios, but he and the owner of that studio were archenemies. With no hesitation upon seeing that it was Apeman with a young black female in tow, the secretary immediately let the couple into the president's office conference room. There, already assembled, were the other key members of the management team.

"Apeman, this is good news. I have an idea! We have to work quickly, but I think we can pull it off."

With that, he instructed the executives to load all of the filming equipment, actors, especially the largest men, and the Pygmy tribesmen onto the company buses and cars. Next, he directed that all of the elephants, tigers, lions, chimps, and the great ape be loaded into the company trucks. They were going to shoot "on location!"

"I want everyone loaded and ready to roll by noon tomorrow! If we don't have enough trucks, find some. If we don't have enough cars, find some! This will be great! So great!" With that, he took Cheryl by the hand and said to Apeman, "You two are coming with me. We have some planning to do. Let's go." Then he turned to the others and said, "By noon tomorrow! That's an order! Anyone not ready by then can look for a new position at another studio! Understood?" Heads nodded up and down, indicating that all was clearly understood.

He took Cheryl and Apeman into his office. Turning to Cheryl, he said, "So you are LuLu's close friend. The one who informed Apeman of what was in store for her at the castle? How do you know? And don't leave anything out."

Cheryl once again told of what had gone on at the castle ten years before. She told about the abuses that LuLu had endured in order to secure the contract. ..which, by the way, would lapse in a few weeks. There was no current renewal of the non-compete clause since no contract had been signed yet.

"Excellent, yes excellent! And do you believe if she were offered another contract from a different studio that was better than the current contract she was to sign that she might jump to another studio?"

"Ya, sir, I sure would advise such an idea!"

He yelled out to his secretary, "Miss Ryan, get my brother Lieutenant General Morgan at Fort MacArthur on the phone! Tell him I need to talk with him right away!" Then he turned again to Apeman and Cheryl.

"Then here's the plan..."

At the same time, the plan was being explained to Apeman and Cheryl, a large car pulled up outside Lulu's house in Beverly Hills. The chauffeur got out of the front left and opened the rear door. The man she often had "split her legs for" stepped out of the car. She hadn't seen him in weeks, hadn't heard a thing from him about her contract, and now here he is. She thought a well-placed kick between his legs was in order. Well, a girl could dream!

"Lulu, dear! How good of you to agree to join me on this adventure. Back to the place where all dreams came true...right, sweetie?"

The kick idea was getting stronger and more satisfying!

"George here will get the door for you. Get in, dear. We will have a wonderful visit and enjoy this ride together. It will be fun!"

Lulu started to get into the vehicle and suddenly saw the four other occupants. One in the front passenger seat, the other three on the seat somewhat hidden from her view by a side post of the car. They were the four big actor guards from the castle.

Lulu tried to step back, but a hand clasped over her face to block any scream, and she was lifted off the ground and forcibly placed on the floor of the vehicle in a most unflattering way. The other three men now securely tied her hands and feet behind her with her knees bent. Another piece of rope was slipped between her arms by the men. Then the same thing was done with the other end between her bent legs at her feet. The rope was tightly tied. Legs bent at the knees and arms and legs tied together, finally, she was rolled on her side. Her dress nowhere near covering any part of her below the hips would remain that way for the first couple of hours of the trip...as would she. More ropes were tied onto the first ropes and were attached to special eyebolts on the floor. Then those too were pulled tight, leaving the girl unable to straighten her legs, move her arms, or get in any other position. A gag was placed in her mouth, and a bag pulled over her head. Although she wanted to scream, she couldn't. Nor could she figure out why the bag was placed over her head. Hell, she already had seen the men. Oh, that could be bad news. She had seen her abductors!

"Well, my dear, our trip has begun. I know you recognize your co-stars from the past. They have been asked to join us to reenact the times we enjoyed nearly ten years ago. It will be a reenactment for two very special guests to witness in person and perhaps participate with us. They also have a few questions to ask you. Oh, yes, a few other of your old friends have agreed to join us too. You know, for old times' sake!

Following the two special guests' questions, we will sign what I believe will be a very agreeable contract for you. Understand, my dear?"

"Mumph muggish agruph!"

"What's that, my dear? I cannot understand a word you are saying. You just rest yourself for a bit, and perhaps later we can find a more enjoyable position for you. Sounds good?"

"Mugah keish gugadama balugs!"

"There, there, sweet one. I'm sure you don't really mean it. Do you? Why, you would have one hard time in the position you are in, legs and arms tied so sweetly comfortably behind your back, to as you say, 'kick my God damn balls in!" The five men laughed. "You just stay curled up there sweetly and relax. Though the countryside outside is quite nice to look at, we gentlemen have a very pleasant view here inside the car too. Quite pleasant. Agreed boys?" They all agreed.

Back at the MBM Studio the phone call came through from four-star general Wade Morgan. He began.

"BB, what is so goddamn important that you need me to call? Hell, I was just about to mount up for polo practice." He always referred to his older brother as BB for Big Brother.

"LB (Little Brother), I need your help. And quickly too."

A short pause before the general replied he said, "BB, is this going to cost me again? The last time I helped fund one of your productions it really didn't pay off. Not interested in doing that again."

"LB, this is a very different request. You will be doing a great service to a special person. Why I only think it will take a couple of your battalions of soldiers and say a couple of dozen tanks."

"What the hell?! Are you crazy?"

"Now, LB, calm down. You army guys always get so worked up. Let me explain the mission. You remember the talk of rehabbing our favorite golf course at Pebble Rock? The one that I own considerable interest in?"

"Yes. So?"

"Well, I would like for you to take your troops up there as my favor to you to have them run maneuvers there. And I think it can be especially helpful for the tanks to do so. While they are maneuvering it will just happen to be on the layout of the revised fairways."

"You want our tanks to lay out your fairways?"

"Yes, and I will assure you that some of the fairways will be laid out for a lefty like you, LB. Will you do it?"

"Well, it is an interesting idea. It allows us to see how quickly we can organize and maneuver on unfamiliar territory. I suppose so. When are you thinking of doing this?"

"Is tomorrow too soon?"

"What!!! Tomorrow. How the hell…"

"LB, now don't go getting your panties in a wad. I bet you boys know how to organize this type of thing to be pulled off even quicker. Let's call this emergency war practice. How about it? Can you get them up there by late tomorrow evening? Be a sport, LB. Don't let your BB down."

"Okay, I'll get the battalions together and two dozen tanks for the maneuvers. I'll have my G3 (operations/training) and G4 (Logistics) to issue the orders now. We should be prepared to move out at 0700 hours tomorrow morning. That should put them at a site to bivouac by tomorrow evening at 2100 hours. I think they will be in position to begin maneuvers the following morning at 0500. Sound good?"

"That's great. Ah, just one more slight addition."

"That's?"

"I need a company of tanks to make the wrong turn and go up the road to La Casa Ingente."

"You what?!"

"Make a wrong turn and go up the road to La Casa Ingente. Oh, and then to have the tanks not see the gate at the top of the road…and…well…accidentally crash into and through the gate. Think you could arrange that?"

After some continued heated discussion, it was finally agreed. In agreement to a full lifetime membership at Pebble Rocks Club for the LB and his General's staff, a large plaque at the entrance of the golf course commemorating the Fort MacArthur effort to create the new golf course design, tanks would crash the gate the next evening at La Casa Ingente. The gate would fall at exactly 21:00.

What the LB, General Wade Morgan didn't know was that following the departure of the tank company, the house would be invaded the next day.

Not by soldiers, but by elephants, lions, tigers, chimpanzees, a great ape, African warriors, pygmies, and a hero named Apeman. That information BB had kept to himself.

CHAPTER 6
BOOK 2

The car drove along Highway 101 out of Los Angeles. The new road had finally been commissioned in 1926, just three years earlier. Though the trip would normally take approximately six hours, today it would take a bit longer. There was a scenic side tour planned for Lulu.

The interior of the Pierce Arrow was roughly eight feet wide. As the car passed Santa Barbara, three hours into the trip, it was time to rearrange the girl. The trip would become rough soon.

Predominant told two of the men to hold her tightly as the third man riding in the cab with them untied Lulu's legs from her arms. Finally, the girl could extend her cramped legs straight out, though her ankles were still tied together. The movement of the legs was painful. After a few moments, the cramping began to subside enough that her groans through the gag became less continuous.

The men were now ordered to pick the girl up and place her sitting on the seat facing the rear seat where the four men, including Predominant, would be facing her. She still had the sack over her head, mouth gagged, and her arms tied tightly behind her back. She was placed down roughly. The men did not hesitate to let roaming hands touch areas of her. She was completely under their control.

"Untie her feet and attach one of the ropes to each of the door handles. Good, now spread those beautiful legs!" There she sat, spread nearly four feet between two doors. Her short dress's skirt raised high on her thighs, allowing all four men a most delectable view. Her bottom barely sat on the edge of the seat, and with her arms behind her back, she had no way to maintain her balance when the car hit bumps in the road.

"Well, my dear, I am sure you are much more comfortable now. We can have that hood removed from your head so you can see us and so you can fully understand what I will say about your future. The gag will remain in place until we are sure that you are in a fully agreeable mood." With that, he signaled one of the men to pull the hood off her head. He did it as roughly as he could, making her feel like her nose and ears would be pulled off too.

"Good! Always so much better to see that pretty face of yours, LuLu. Such beautiful eyes. That mouth. Oh, yes, that mouth. What it can do! From pout to pucker! And, of course, the screams of excitement! It's one of your most marvelous attributes. You drive men wild with it... and I assume some women too. Women like that negress... what's her name... oh, yes, Cheryl. That's it, isn't it? Cheryl."

Turning to the men, "You boys remember Cheryl, don't you? Damn, we should have invited her to join us. Why, I bet we could figure out some impressive new ways to use the girls. Well, there is always next time, I'm sure."

LuLu's anger and contempt for this loathsome man continued building inside her. Thinking to herself, "okay, you repulsive piece of garbage. It's one thing to make me go through this crap, but don't you go bringing Cheryl into this. Damn, I wish I had a knife. I'd ruin your day for sure. That thing between your legs and its attachments would be fed to a dog only after I stomped them flat! All four of you guys! Oh, hell, all five. The chauffeur isn't getting away either! He's the guy who put his hand over my mouth and forced me into the car!!"

"In just a few minutes, we will leave this modern road 101. We will enter a stop by the road called Las Cruces. This road, 101, will turn northeast. We won't. We'll take a slight sightseeing tour on a new road that used to be called San Julian Road, right driver?"

"Correct you are, sir."

Predominant continued, "Now, my dear, it is called California State Road 1. Not much of it is yet paved... just gravel and ruts, you know. Hard on the car. Much harder on a girl curled up on the floor. So, aren't you thankful I am so good to you? Letting you sit up so pretty and comfortable and all? Why, I bet every bounce will have a wonderful effect on you. Make you feel pretty and all for your five gentlemen here. You just have fun?"

Through her gagged mouth she made noises. "What's that you say, dear? We really should get you diction training before we sign the new contract. I'm afraid your speaking sounds...well...are a bit unclear and strained!" The men all laughed.

Driving now on the rutted road all the travelers were being tossed around like being on a bucking bronco, especially LuLu. Twice she slid completely off the seat and was held hanging inches off the floor by her tightly tied legs, arms useless and head bouncing off the car seat. The men laughed at her awkward and unpleasant position. They debated leaving her like this. Finally they were told by Predominant there would be enough uncomfortable positions for her over the next few days. "We can give her a break now!"

That position and unhurried relief from the position would occur several more times on the trip as the next phase of the trip got worse. The car made a turn off California state road one at a small town of Lompoc. Turning left, they were on an even smaller and bumpier dirt trail. Dust flew into the car steadily from the hard packed rutted dirt road. Although the temperature outside the car was in the 90s, the riders were thinking it might be better with the windows closed. LuLu, caked in dirt covered sweat from the strain of trying to keep her bottom on the seat, was increasingly miserable.

"Look at her boys! Why she looks like some cheap prostitute we found on the side of the road and not some famous actress. Perhaps this is a premonition of where she will be in a few years. A cheap slut selling it for what she can get. And not much at that!"

Another thirty minutes of dusty, bumpy, misery they made it to a river called Santa Ynez River. As the car cleared a slight rise there before them was the Pacific Ocean. LuLu, facing the rear, did not see it at first. She did see a small sign at the "Y" split in the road telling her they were on a small road called Lasalle Canyon road. It made a 90 degree turn to the south and as it did she saw a sign that said, "Surf California, population 15". She also saw the thundering tide of the Pacific Ocean.

A short distance later the car pulled off the road onto a small flat area of dirt.

"Untie her, Frank. We'll take her for a little walk like we would a bitch dog."

As the man named Frank freed one of her legs, he made the mistake of squat-standing right in front of LuLu. Swiftly her leg flew up and the full force of her shin caught him completely between the legs. The sound was a loud thump. Frank grabbed his groin, keeled over in an agonized fetal position, and moaned loudly.

The other two men grabbed her by the legs and pulled hard each way spreading the girl even more than she had been spread previously. Frank, in increasing agony as the aching nauseating feeling spread through him, wretched, threw up, and passed out cold inside the Pierce Arrow.

"Put the hood back over the bitch and drag her out of the damn car! Tie a rope around her neck and as you untie the other leg, watch out! We don't need another situation like what happened with Frank!

"Damn you, girl! You're one pain in the balls!"

The hood now secured over her head and a rope tied around her neck neither man was daring to let loose of the leg they clutched. As much as she struggled, it was no use. They pulled her off the seat by her legs, making sure to avoid the still curled up Frank. Also, making sure not to drag her into the vomit, pulled her out of the car on her bouncing butt. Then they dumped her unceremoniously on the dirt.

Frank, beginning to regain consciousness, holding himself and groaning in his continued nauseating agony just lay there.

"Frank, when you recover, I want you to clean your mess up! You hear me!"

"You three hold onto the bitch by the arms. Watch out for those potent legs. Poor Frank will probably never conceive any more kids. Now pick her up. Follow me!"

Fighting as best she could but being lifted by her arms, which were still tied behind her back, she was dragged, falling and stumbling up a small rise. At the top of the rise, Predominant gave an order to remove the hood.

With the hood removed, LuLu found herself standing at a spot she remembered. Less than fifty feet in front of her were the railroad tracks of the Southern Pacific railroad...and the cliff just beyond. The last place two men were seen before they had slid silently together over the edge to the rocks and into the swirling surf 125 feet below.

"Drag her over here, boys. I'm not sure she can remember this clearly enough. Can you, LuLu?"

The men continue to drag the fighting desperate girl. Finally right at the edge, Predominant said, "Fellows, show this cunt what it looks like when she is leaning out over the edge as far as she can. What it must feel like to be flying! Let her sense what her lover Steven must have felt ten years ago when she...lost him so tragically."

"We sure wouldn't want to lose our LuLu that way...just as she is about to sign a wonderful new ten year contract. So, you boys make sure you have a good grip on her arms as you lean her out. You hear? Just to make sure, George and I will hold onto the rope around her neck. Hate to have anything bad happen to this pretty useful piece of...beautiful woman...now would we?"

With that, LuLu was suspended out over the edge of the cliff nearly horizontally held only by her two strained arms and her slipping tippy toes. Suddenly the sand and pebbles beneath her toes gave way. Her legs swung out from under her and flew out over the ledge. The two large men holding her arms fought for their own balance and fell backwards...thankfully pulling her on top of them.

As the men pushed her off and stood dusting themselves off, Predominant said, "Well that was exciting, wasn't it!? Guess you owe these good men a big thanks....and Frank too. I'm sure you will take care of them appropriately this week. Won't you, sweetie? Gosh, you probably owe them your life!" He started laughing. "Yes, LuLu, these fine men are your heroes. You plan something really special for them. Really special. You hear? Oh, yes, I'm sure your friend Frank can think of something equally exciting and memorable as that which you provided him a bit ago. I bet he will have great joy in giving it to you. We'll enjoy watching you receive your gift too. Won't we, boys?" They all agreed it would be a great pleasure to see Frank deliver his gift.

"Okay, boys, drag her back to the car. I doubt she can walk. Look how she is shaking. You boys are shaking too. Anyone mess themself? No, okay, let's see if Frank is finished with his work. Then we will be on the road again."

Once back at the car, the stench was manageable with the windows down. They were on their way again after retying the girl in the same uncomfortable position she had been in earlier.

"Here is how it works, dear. You will be a wonderful participant this week. Right? Just like you were ten years ago. Remember you are still a female...with hysterics...don't you know? Why, I bet those hysterics are even stronger now and would even cause a loving woman like yourself to want to visit the site where you lost your sweetheart. We can arrange that, you see. And, God forbid! Well you know we would do all we could to try to stop you...but honey, I bet your hysterics might cause you to want to join your love. Yes, what a movie scene! I can see it! The tragically sad young woman wants to join her love! And...well...she throws herself off the cliff ten years later to join him!"

"Wouldn't that make a wonderful movie? So, emotionally intense! I bet it would win all kinds of awards! Perhaps we will make it. Of course, you couldn't be the star. We would need a real live star, don't you know. Understand, my dear? Why I'm sure your friends, the police captain, the lieutenant, and even the chief of police would see all this clearly happening this way. Such a tragic story...but oh, so true and believable!"

"You just sit back and think about it...real hard, girl. I think you need to think about life as it is and how precious it is to you and how precious your life is to us."

They arrived later that evening at about 8:00 pm. LuLu was too exhausted to eat. The studio owner and the boys were ravished. Predominant told her to get a good rest this night as work for her would begin again in earnest the next day about 6 pm. It was that time when the two special visitors would arrive for dinner. Questions would be asked of her. Then the fun for the week would begin. Until then, there may just be a practice session or two. Something to get her into the proper mood. But not until at least noon tomorrow. Everyone needed their rest.

"See how sympathetic and kind I am, sweetheart? Good night! Sleep tight!"

CHAPTER 7
BOOK 2

At 07: 00 the next day, two battalions of eight hundred infantry troops were on board trucks and heading out. Ahead of them were flatbed trucks carrying a light tank battalion of twelve French Renault Six Ton M1917 tanks. A second battalion of twelve British heavy design tanks, the Tank Mark VIII, "Liberty" with each weighing over 30 tons were on a train of specially equipped flat cars. It left Los Angeles at the same time. The train tracks had been cleared due to the special arrangements agreed upon by the US War Department and the Railroads in the National Defense Act of 1920. General Morgan assured its use. These tanks could easily take down any roadblock or iron gate anyone put up, even the one at La Casa Ingente.

Joining the convoy with the two battalions of infantry were two companies of engineers. They all headed north together. The addition of the engineers was a special surprise of LB for his BB. Engineers would be needed to make sure that the fairways were laid out appropriately, especially the left-handed holes. An easy tracing of the original new holes' layout allowed for the tracing paper to be turned over and glued down. Now the plans had a reverse image of the original fairways. Perfect for the left hander. Better yet, no need to employ another architect.

At noon that day, another convoy of trucks and cars headed north from MBM Studios. On board these vehicles were the film crews and cast of a movie called "The Apeman of Africa," and other special guests.

The day at the castle turned out to be uneventful for LuLu. Predominant had second thoughts about shared activities with her by the men prior to the important and influential guests arriving. She should be kept fresh for them. LuLu pretty much stayed in her room - the same one between the two other doors that she had occupied for ten years before. It was filled with memories for her, none of which were agreeable to her now.

When she came down for breakfast and lunch, she felt the five men's lust-filled eyes on her, especially Frank's. They followed her every move, with a slight smirk on his face giving her a sense of what he might have in store for her.

The two guests were running late and did not arrive at the castle until nearly 7 PM. Each of their private planes sat down within moments of each other on the mansion's landing strip, a smooth piece of land about a mile from the home. Dinner was delayed by an hour until 8 PM to give them time to settle in and freshen up. At 7:30 PM, LuLu, the five men, and Predominant were gathered in the formal living room with cocktails. She was very uncomfortable. Her gut told her that she would most likely be served up for the men's dessert. Still, the gifted actress would not let on to the fact that she was scared to death, especially about Frank and his plan to get even. She could do nothing but endure.

At 8 o'clock promptly, the men entered the room, both like the five other men were wearing masks. Though she could not see their faces, the size and structure of one of the men reminded her of a "client" in Detroit whom she entertained on a few occasions nearly twelve years ago. Could it be him? She knew the man was from Detroit. The other was from New York City. Yes, this must be Detroit that she recognized. Could he also be the mysterious person on the other end of the phone calls...the calls about Louis and Steven? He was in the automobile industry, wasn't he? That seemed to her to be right. He had to be the one who sent her to Hollywood to become a star and who set up Steven's death. Suddenly she was glad he kept his identity hidden with the mask. The less she knew about his true identity was probably in her best interest.

Formal greetings consisted of introducing LuLu to Mr. X and Mr. Y. Those were the only names used. Unlike the other diners, LuLu was not allowed a mask. Her ravishing face was totally revealed to the guests. As soon as dinner was finished, they would be treated to the revealing of the rest of her. Of that, they were assured.

A mile short of reaching the San Luis Obispo station, the special train apparently broke down. Then the heavy tanks and their brand-new recently developed 30-ton Semi-Trailer Recovery Tank Transporters were quickly offloaded. The weight of all of these would have significant effects on the local roads of San Luis Obispo.

The police captain and his lieutenant, hearing of this situation at their homes, raced to the police station, gathered a few men, and headed out to confront the military units. Uncoupling each of the 24 cars from the train with enough room in between the cars to allow the tanks and trucks to back off the rail cars took an hour. It was now 7 PM as the captain, lieutenant, and other officers arrived at the site.

Less than half an hour behind the train's arrival, a second truck convoy carrying twelve lightweight tanks, 800 infantry soldiers, and 100 men each from two engineer companies arrived at the scene. As the discussions with the police captain and his men were going on between the commanding officer, a full colonel of the first Tank battalion, a four-star general, Wade Morgan exited his 1918 Cadillac Type 57 touring car.

"What's going on here?" the general boomed.

The army colonel turned in the direction of the voice, came to attention, and saluted. Then he replied, "General, this police officer and his men are telling us that we cannot use the city streets to transport these tanks from this location to our rendezvous location. The train has broken down. They are saying the vehicles and tanks weigh too much for the roads, sir!"

The general now turned his attention to the police captain and said, "Is that a fact? You intend to interfere with a military operation because of your damn roads, officer? Really? I don't think so. As you can see, you are now facing these twelve heavy tanks, twelve more light tanks, and over 1,000 armed military men!"
"How many men do you have, son?"

The police captain stammered, trying to come up with an answer that would not sound entirely stupid.

"Tell you what we do, boy! We'll figure out a compromise for you!" Asking his driver to go to the car and bring the army topographical map to him, he continued.

"It appears there is a lot of open land east of your town now, isn't there, sunny boy?" The captain shook his head yes, with his eyes still focused on the over 1,000 soldiers now congregating behind the general. The driver brought the map and handed it to the general, who laid it open on the hood of a truck.

"How about this, son? We unload the tanks here and we maneuver to this open land until we get north of your town. Then we use this tiny little road here to cut back west and regroup with our men in this area of San Semien? Does that work for you?"

The captain, shaking his head no, said, "But sir, that is private land owned by the newspaper chain owner. I don't think you can cut across his land like that without his permission, General."

"Boy, I don't think you quite understand. I really don't need no permission, son. I have two things working on my behalf, son. I have the National Defense Act of 1920 and..." Looking behind him..."I got these 1,000 plus armed men to ensure that we get where we are going...one way or the other. Now, boy, which way will it be? The road or the open land? Make a command decision now, son. You hear me!"

"Yes, sir!" the captain said, coming to full attention. "I think it is best to use the open land, General, sir!"

"Good decision, young man. You definitely have military officer potential. You come to see me one day if you ever decide to give up that uniform for a better one like this one. Hear me, boy?"
"Yes, sir!"

With that, the colonel told his men to unload the tanks. An apparent quick decision was made on the direction they were to head, though it had actually been made the day before at the general's office. Unloaded, they headed out... in the direction of the castle!

Inside the castle, just as dinner was finishing at 9:00 pm or 21:00 hours military time, there was a steady, heavy rumbling sound outside. The noise became louder and louder: multiple loud motor sounds and rumbling. They could sense the earth moving. It had to be an earthquake! Then they heard a loud boom as the huge iron gate and granite support columns were destroyed by the "misdirected" heavy tanks, one after another crashing through the mangled gate. Much of the stone wall a quarter of a mile away was destroyed too. The sound was so loud it seemed as though it was right outside the door and soon coming into the house!

Everyone, including LuLu, ran to the front door and stepped out to see what was happening. At the base of the hill leading up to the castle, they could see huge war machines doing circles around the front lands.

The young Hadley, who had arrived with the special guest for a week of fun, threw up his hands as though praying to a god and said, "What the hell is happening?!"

They all continued to watch in disbelief as the circus of circles continued. Then one tank broke away from the others and motored toward the castle's front door. Stopping just short of the open front door, it remained there for a few moments. Finally, the small hatch on the top of the tank slowly opened, and a military officer peeked out: a full-bird colonel.

"Beg your pardon, folks, for the interruption. It appeared we took a wrong turn down the road a piece. Yes, I believe we did. Well, you see, our transport train broke down at San Luis Obispo, and we needed to unload and head overland to meet up with our operations tomorrow at Big Sur. Made a wrong turn and, well.... here we are. Sure, sorry about that gate down there!" He pointed in that direction. "The Army will happily pay for a new one. Probably even better than the one you have. More costly, I'm sure. You know how the federal government is with the cost and all. Sorry!"

Hadley continued to stammer, no full words coming out.

"Now since we already made a mess of your property, I don't suspect you will mind if our 1000 plus people and twenty-four tanks, trucks, and other equipment just bivouac here for the night. Would you? Good! Thank you kindly! We should be out of your hair tomorrow morning at 0500; that's 5:00 am in civilian talk. Have a good time with the rest of your evening... don't give us another thought! Good night, y'all!"

With that, the colonel closed the hatch, and the tank circled around through the flower and shrub plantings and headed down the hill.

Less than two miles south from there, another encampment was being set in place. This one could have been mistaken for a circus, except for all of the actors there. It was the film crew and cast from MBM studios.

CHAPTER 8
BOOK 2

At 4:00 a.m., everyone in the castle heard the bugles blurt out "Reveille!" Shouts and screams followed as noncommissioned officers yelled out orders. Forty-five minutes later, one by one, the huge tank's motors roared to life. Fifteen minutes later on the dot, 24 tanks of two different sizes once again did their circling dance, tearing up more front land of the estate as well as the wall. Then, sluggishly but powerfully, they motored off in a large cloud of dust.

At 5:30, the young Hadley stood there shaking his head and lost in horrible thoughts. What would his uncle, the owner, say? How would the nephew who was supposed to look after the estate explain this? Looking out at the incredible amount of destruction, he felt like crying. Hell, all he wanted to do was have another one of his fun times with a woman...that woman! Instead, he knew he was facing being fired from his cozy job with all of its fringe benefits like the ones he had planned for this week with her.

Worse, he knew he faced being disinherited by his uncle. He was a nephew by the wife's side of the family, not truly a Hadley but actually a Barton! His grandmother Barton had run a successful brothel which she passed on to the mother and sister! The sister had married a Hadley brother. His mother had only left the business when one of her clients, also a Hadley relative, had decided he wanted to marry the girl for who knew why.

His uncle Hadley enjoyed times like those planned for this week. He too had enjoyed LuLu ten years before. He was going to be here this week, arriving in a couple of days. The young man thought, "Oh, God! What am I going to do?"

Then he heard the voice. Turning to find the two men, the special guests, one of them said, "Jerrold, it is time we leave. The newspaper and radio people will be swarming this place soon. Much as we would love to stay for the week's activities, we will not. It would not be good for our business interests!"

"But, gentlemen, I'm sure we can control this. My uncle will be arriving in the next day or two. I am sure he would like to see his two good friends. Please stay!" His hope was having them here would be a distraction to his uncle about...he looked at the disfigured land...that!

"No, boy. Our minds are made up. But before we go, we would like to ask the young woman some questions. Can you have your men find her and prepare her for our 'rough' questions? We need to be on the plane in one hour. Thank you!" They turned and walked away.

The young man found the five others in the dining room having breakfast. He ordered them to find LuLu and bring her to the specially prepared room that Predominant and he had set up for the week.

Inside the large ballroom, all furniture had been removed except for two leather club chairs and five other dining room chairs sitting against one wall. The leather chairs were facing the same direction; however, they were separated from each other about eight feet. Between them was a coffee table with fresh coffee and croissants. Hanging from the ceiling were two ropes. Each rope ended about seven feet off the ground as they hung down from the enormous center rafter beam. Separated from each other by five feet or more, attached to each one was a padded wrist cuff. Trailing out from one of the legs of each chair, the ones nearest to each other, were similar ropes and wrist cuffs.

The two guests sat down and sipped coffee. Suddenly, at the far end of the room, a door opened and four men carried a struggling nude LuLu into the room, with a gag fitted tightly in her mouth. Each man had an arm or a leg in the grip of his arm, held tightly against his own body. She was suspended horizontally between the four men, squirming and bucking. Frank, the fifth man, carried two things: a step ladder and a paddle measuring 18 inches in total length. It spread from a two-inch handle width to the working paddle head of five inches. The whole paddle was a half-inch-thick, solid red cherry wood. Frank had a big smile.

Frank opened the ladder under one of the ropes. Instead of being handed an arm to attach to the ceiling rope, one of LuLu's long legs was lifted to him. He slipped the cuff strap tightly around her ankle and stepped down. Now he did the same with the other leg and the other cuff strap. There she dangled, naked, upside down and legs pulled apart, her head appropriately at Frank's waist height, two and a half feet from the floor. The juncture of soft feminine split and its small sentinel barely peeking out, all fully exposed, four feet above the ground. She was now positioned for a forceful arm swing from the 6-foot-5-inch-tall, powerfully built Frank. Looking at her in this position, his smile widened.

Frank now did the same procedure to the girl's wrist with the ropes from the chair legs. Spread eagle, she hung there twisting and turning.

Just then, Predominant entered the room through the same door with showman flair. He too had a large smile on his face.

"Gentlemen! Hello and welcome to breakfast! I hear that you will only be here for the first act of the show. We are most sorry that you will need to depart shortly. We certainly understand that business and last night's experience here have caused you to reconsider the enjoyment that has been planned for you. Needless to say, we hope that this morning's performance will give you a taste of what you will be missing. Perhaps one day we can arrange a restaging for you both? Until then, we also understand there are some pressing answers to questions which you need our lovely performer to provide. Answers to, and which I am sure a most agreeable LuLu will be pleased to answer..." Looking at LuLu now, "...for you after she is fully prepared. My Noble Assistant Frank will be most happy to perform the task of preparation now!"

"Frank, would you please warm the sweet girl up? Frank, take it away!"

With that, Frank's arm raised the paddle high above her splayed legs...paused for a moment, looked directly down and into LuLu's eyes to allow LuLu to see and fully anticipate what would happen next...

...as Frank prepared his downward swift swing towards the open target, everyone heard the girl scream through the gag,

"Wait!!! I think I know the answer!!!"

Frank raised his arm again. At the pause, he looked into her eyes once more for emphasis and began his forcible downward swing.

Predominant yelled out, "Frank, hold off!!

The paddle stopped less than a centimeter from its target. LuLu felt the swift air on her tender spots. She cried in anxious relief, tears flowing from her eyes.

"Let's see if she is receptive to the men's questions now. If not, I think a hard swing at that lovely thing will truly be in order. Especially since you have all your "man's strengths" back."

The tears of relief continued to pour out of the girl's eyes and fell to the granite floor beneath her.

"Frank, please remove the gag from LuLu's mouth. With that thing in it, nothing more can fit in or come out. Let us view that pretty thing unobstructed so we all can fully imagine what her beautiful mouth can do. Look how well she is acting, gentlemen. Her lips are shaking, quivering. What a feeling that would provide. Such a wonderful actress! Let's see if she is also a good witness. Gentlemen... She is all yours!"

Through sobs and tears, she tried to answer the questions as best she could, though much of the answers were just what she had provided Detroit by phone some time ago. And so, with frustration building on Predominant's part that the first act of his play had not been fully acted out...something he so wanted to see...he told Frank to prepare again. Unhesitatingly, Frank gleefully raised the paddle high.

"Wait! Please! I remember now! When I gave all of Steven's goods to the Sisters of the "Virgin Mother's Hands," there was a manuscript!"
"A manuscript? What did it say?"

"I don't know! It was in French or some other language. It was handwritten. Appeared to be a couple of hundred pages. Scratched out words and letters. A real mess. I have no idea what was on it, I swear!"

"A manuscript, you say?" Detroit paused with hand to his mouth and thought out loud. "Hmmm, that could in fact be the answer! You gave it to the nuns? What did they do with it?"

"I have no idea!" The sobs became sniffles. Still, she was tensely shaking. "I was just glad to get rid of the stuff. Can you make them put me down now? Please?!"

Predominant walked over to the girl...then spoke. "But dear, you look so alluring that way! A real crowd pleaser. Isn't that right, men? Why I bet all eight of us would like to help you the way Frank was about to do. Bringing back your memory so well. Continue to warm you up, don't you know, for all the fun we have in store for you this week!"

"By the way, good job answering the questions at last." Patting her female parts, he continued, "I'm sure each of the guests would like to thank you similarly the way you thanked Frank the day before yesterday. Helping him feel his manhood so well!"

Turning to the guest he continued. "What say, gentlemen? Would you like a swing at this?" Pointing now to her split labia and its little guard.

"Let's all help her feel her womanhood before parting?" Patting her again there, "I'm sure she would be grateful to us all! One swing? Just one each? Or perhaps two! I'm sure she would be"...pausing before adding... "open to that."

"Surely you could spare that amount of time to help this needy girl! Couldn't you!" A cruel smile, and sadistic eyes on his face.

Eagerly both men shook their heads in agreement and stood.

Just then noises from outside. A booming roar! Several roars and the pounding of thunder. Continuing loud overlapping noise. Not the same roar of tanks. No these were...real roars...several continuous in fact. And then a most notable and unique yell. It rang out for ten seconds perhaps longer, sending chills to the participants!

"Aawooahwoahaaawwwwoooohhhaaaa!"

CHAPTER 9
BOOK 2

Crashing through the fifteen-foot two front doors of the castle's main entrance came a twelve foot tall seven ton Asian male elephant. Riding on its back was a muscular wavy haired handsome nearly naked man. Again the yell rang out from his mouth!

"Aawooahwoahaaawwwwooooohhhaaaa!"

Following his elephant was a slightly smaller female Asian elephant. It stood only ten feet tall and weighed five tons. Riding on its back was the beautiful chocolate colored friend of LuLu's, none other than Cheryl. Cheryl was appropriately dressed in a scant native costume that revealed much of her exciting beauty.

Then through the doors in fast succession were two huge male lions and their female mates. An even larger white tiger, three chimpanzees, a great gorilla, and more than two dozen pigmy actors, and several very large black actors. All were dressed in appropriate costumes. With them, filming every minute, were three film crews. One behind the action and the other two filming from each side of the action.

Overhead two airplanes swooped down from different directions over the castle. Each was fitted out with a movie photographer and an Eyemo and Akeley 35 mm motion picture film camera manufactured by Bell & Howell. They captured the whole experience of the invasion from a panoramic view. Shortly after the first two passes, they filmed two men racing out the back of the castle to a car which sped away. One of the planes followed the car swooping low and recording the escape.

When those men jumped out of the car and ran as quickly as old men's feet could carry them, they climbed aboard one of the planes. Moments later it thundered down the grass airstrip and rose to the sky...followed behind by the filming aircraft.

As that was happening Apeman and Cheryl dismounted the elephants which each had kindly kneeled to allow them to easily slide off. Apeman, with a 10-inch knife in hand, raced to LuLu and cut first the wrist straps and then one by one those that held her ankles. While doing so, he firmly held her upside down body safely to his.

The chimpanzees, great ape, and lions had the five other men cornered in the back of the room. All of them, afraid to make a move. Predominant and young Hadley were off to the side by themselves, guarded by the Pygmys, black actors, and the head of MBM Studios. The 9 foot long, 400 pound, white female tiger was by MBM's side, growling and showing its dagger sharp teeth to both men.

Cheryl grabbed the tablecloth from the adjoining dining room and quickly covered LuLu with it. Then they both walked over to stand with MBM facing Predominant and Hadley.

MBM was explaining to both of the men what was about to take place.

"You two will be most apologetic to this young woman for her abduction, sexual attack, and attempted rape. You will also agree to the use of the film that we have produced today so it may be used in an upcoming film "The Apeman of Africa and the Castle Rescue". The film will star both of these young women and this handsome fellow."

"Further, Predominant Studios will release this young woman from her contract and from her non-compete clause! That will allow her to accept the offer that I am prepared to make for her today. You, further, will not attempt any legal actions on the damage that was done to the property, either what we have done today or what the US Army did yesterday. That you will take care of between yourselves."

"Lastly, gentlemen, you will provide to this young woman any originals and copies of the films that were made of her this week and all of those made of her ten years ago when she was here on these premises. You will further assure her that never again will these films be distributed or viewed!"

"This is what these documents in my hands agree to along with the signed confession statement of the crimes you have committed this week against her as well as the crimes you committed on her ten years ago!"

"Should you fail to sign this agreement and confessions, all the information we have gathered today and in all of the recorded past will be turned over to the FBI and the justice department for prosecution.'

"I believe that they might also be interested in the fact that two former military intelligence officers came to harm due to yours and your friend's actions. Therefore, the US Army may additionally investigate you both.... perhaps for treason. A firing squad offense, I believe!"

"With the signing of this agreement, I am sure that this beautiful woman will be willing to let bygones be bygones. Is that agreeable to you, LuLu?"

LuLu with the dining room tablecloth wrapped loosely around her naked body walked forward. Standing right in front of Predominant, she looked at him then turned her head toward MBM and said, "With just one more clause added if I may?"

MBM replied, "Why, of course, LuLu. What can we add?"

Looking now at Predominant she said, "Only this...". With that her right leg flew up quickly and caught Predominant solidly between his legs with a resounding thud! It landed with full impact right on his three male parts. The force significantly and appropriately squashing them all, making them useless.

Predominant, with a surprised look on his face, staggered back momentarily until full understanding of the impact hit him. His eyes fell back in his head. His hands grasped what was left of his manhood. His knees instantly turned to jelly. His body quickly sagged and he fell into the most pleasing fetal position before the young woman. Unhesitatingly, she aimed her leg again and caught Predominant squarely on the chin with her foot's kick. The foot's fast movement, though solid, slid off his chin and into his nose, breaking it. Still in agony from the first kick, his hands instinctively shot up to his now painful chin and bleeding broken nose... leaving him fully exposed.

With an even harder swing, LuLu's foot shot out again and caught him solidly with her full instep on his now most vulnerable and already pain filled squashed parts. Castration would have been less painful, all male observers thought. Every man in the room grabbed their own groin. Hadley fainted.

"The clause I ask to be added...is this...". Watching one man waggle around on the ground in agony and not knowing what part of himself to hold, she added..." both of these men may never attempt this with another woman!"

Pausing and looking at the unconscious Hadley, she said to herself out loud, "Oh, what the hell!" She then placed a well-aimed kick on the unconscious Hadley. It too caught him full in his groin. The excruciating pain caused him to wake up to an agony he wished he did not find. With that final kick completed, she closed her statement with a premonition of her own.

"Should they attempt something like this ever again, they will certainly wake up with their boy parts cut off, stomped flat and fed to a dog!" Looking at the tiger beside her, showing its large dagger teeth as it twisted its head growling at the two men, she added, "Or a pussy like this one!"

Looking over at the other five men, she added, "And that goes for you "boys" too!"

Loud cheers and applause rang out from all the cast and crew as LuLu, with full grandeur of the movie queen, turned. The tablecloth was now draped around her like a royal gown. She stood tall...and walked with a stately stride...exiting the room walking between the two broken down doors. Her beautiful friends and heroes, Cheryl and Apeman holding the tablecloth gown's train, proudly escorted her majesty from the room.

CHAPTER 10
BOOK 2

The man's body, which was wracked with tuberculosis, walked back slowly to his apartment. Each step caused anguish in his lungs. He made it up the first two flights but had to sit on the stairs before continuing the third and last flight, to the top floor. The building was too old and too small for an elevator. It was the best he could afford, though his books were starting to sell. Only 34 years old but he felt 90. Thin and frail, he could easily be a character in one of his novels. His suits all appeared several sizes too big on him. Most of them had been purchased at second hand and thrift shops. As he would walk by people in the street, he would often hear one whisper to the other, "Who is that pathetic looking thin man?"

Finally making it to the top of the stairs, he walked down the hallway to his apartment number 416. Fourth floor room 16 at the rear of the building looking over the rooftops and the alleyway behind the building. Not hard to figure out. He inserted the key. As he pushed the door open he right away felt there was something terribly wrong.

The window curtain at the end of his entrance hall blew in the San Francisco bay breeze. Although he was twenty-three blocks from the San Francisco Bay each way, and farther from the Golden Gate Park beach, the late evening breeze blew steady at times, cooling his apartment when he was there to open the window. He had not been. And, he knew he did as he always did. He had made sure the windows were closed and locked.

As the thin man walked down the short apartment hallway, he detected more problems. On the floor barely visible he could tell someone had thrown his papers all around. Entering the living room he saw...it was a wrack! Furniture drawers pulled open and dumped on the floor. Pillows on his only two pieces of furniture, an old second hand couch and chair had been sliced open and the stuffing pulled out. Then he realized...his stack of manuscripts, and finished and unfinished books were thrown in a heap in the corner by the kitchen. "Why?"

He pulled out a chair from the kitchen table and sat down in a slump. "What could the person have wanted? Surely they could see this was a place of a person with no wealth? Why?"

Several minutes passed. He suspected he should call the police from the downstairs community phone. Thinking about climbing down the stairs and then back up caused him to pause. He could do that in a little while. "Think! What would one of my detective characters do in a case like this? How would they handle it?" He sat there eyes unfocused and focused, trying to make sense of it.

Finally, his body rose slowly from the chair. The oversize pant legs seem to follow the slow lead of the legs within them. Both legs and pant legs were finally standing straight up. He turned slowly, surveying the kitchen, dining area, and small living room. With aching steps, he walked to the other side of the living room and into the bedroom. It too had been torn apart. Clothes pulled off the closet hanger rod and off the shelf. The one chest of four drawers had been dumped on the floor next to the overturned mattress. Fortunately for him, they had not sliced the mattress. At least he had something he could sleep on tonight. The bathroom that led off the hall and from a door in his only bedroom was much the same as the rest of the place. A mess! He was as close to crying as a 35-year-old man could be. "Why?"

Suddenly, it dawned on him! The only significant thing in his life that had happened in recent months. It was the serial publication of his new book. Perhaps some deranged fan of the newly published writer had broken in and done this. That didn't make sense. Why would his new book be important enough for this to happen? It was a fictitious creation based on notes from a French manuscript. Again, he was shaken by a thought, "The manuscript!

Where is the manuscript?"

As fast as his weary legs could move, he walked back to the living room and the thrown pile of manuscripts laying on the floor by the kitchen. He sorted through them. Not just once, or twice, but three times. It wasn't there! The old mysterious French manuscript was gone! "Why?"

He sat back down in the chair to think. A glass of bourbon sounded good. It would help his thinking. Only problem. He had to get up again. After some time, he did just that. Slowly he rose, his pant legs once again following him. Taking a half used glass, all his glasses were half used as were all the other dishes in the apartment, he poured himself two fingers of cheap bourbon and sat back down, bottle on the table beside him, and tried to think.

After a time and two more drinks, it became less serious for him to figure out the "why". The old hack job of a French manuscript had inspired him to write a good published book about greed. The French fictional manuscript had tried to describe greed too. It obviously had been a failed book. It was unfinished. It had no real plot. He had just used it to fashion a successful book of his own. Why bother with it? Hell, his French wasn't that good anyway. He had a hard time understanding most of it. "It's gone. Forget it. It served its purpose. You need to clean up this mess!" He sat there. "Sometime soon I'll do just that! I'll clean up this mess!" He poured himself a fourth two fingers and proceeded to do just that...forget about it.

A week Later in an Upper East Side Apartment in New York City

The old industrialist automobile giant sat with aged Courvoisier Cognac in hand, looked at the other old man, the son of his first partner, and said, "Well, with this manuscript the story will end."

"What about the woman, the actress, the one we were invited to have fun with. What about her? Isn't she a loose end?"

"No. She got what she wanted in the beginning. A successful movie career, a star, someone idolized by millions. Besides, though she didn't know the reasons, she was complicit in the murders of the two army intelligence officers. She, MBM, and the others are all part of the coverup now. No, all of them know they have far more to lose than to gain. None of them know the whole story either. They, like us both, are greedy, treacherous, and loyal only to themselves. No, nothing to worry about."

"What else is left for us to do then?"

"See that fire over there in the fireplace? We are going to each tear this manuscript up and feed the pieces into the fire. A celebration of success."

Thinking for a moment, downing the rest of the brandy in his glass, he walked over to the man from Detroit and took half of the pages of the manuscript. "I guess you are right. A celebration of the success that brought both of our families great wealth. Too bad my father isn't here to celebrate with us. He would be pleased to know what his loan to you to start your company had created." With that said, he tore some of his pages in half and fed them into the fire.

As the first pages curled in the fire, turned brown and then to ash, the man from Detroit stood, walked over to the large ornate old marble fireplace, and began to do the same. After a short time all the pages were ashes. The fire began to decrease in size back to the original wood logs. They continue to burn down as the New York apartment owner poured another glass each of the fine brandy. They both sat looking at the fire, a smile forming on Detroit's face.

"What's the smile for? Something funny?"

"Perhaps. Not funny so much as interesting."

"And that is? What is interesting?"

"I think you and I just invented 'Time Travel'."

Curious, he said, "How so?"

"We just traveled to the past...and closed that door. Now we are traveling to the future and opening that door. We have traveled through time and are now BETWEEN THE TWO DOORS!"

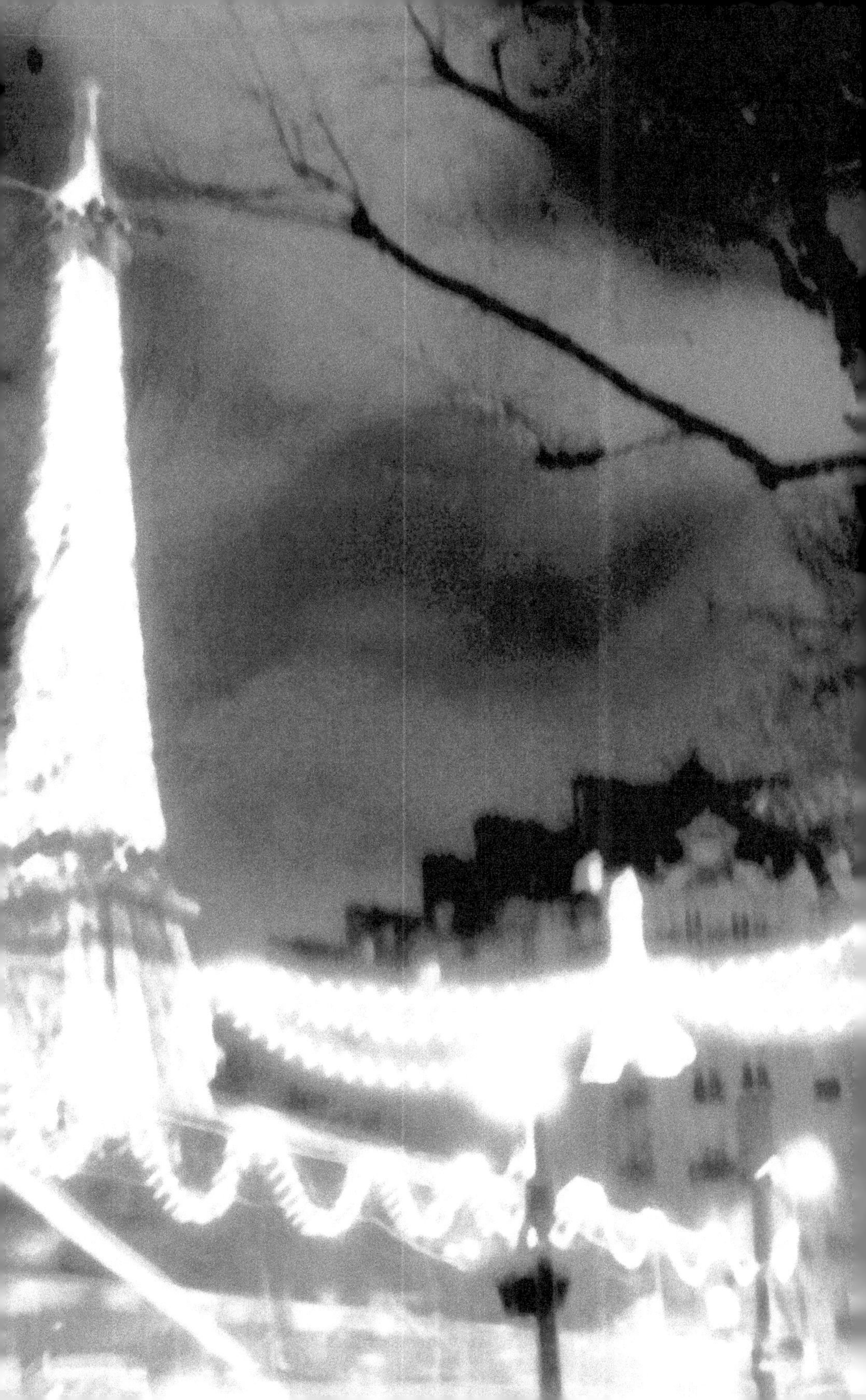

Eiffel Tour at night. Chirstmas 2003.
Candid photo taken on slow shutter sped while walking. Photo by Mary Martz

CHAPTER 1
BOOK 3

They parked the car on the gravel lot and walked toward the arched entry gate through the stucco garden's wall. Entering inside, they were standing between two doors...one door was on the larger of the two antique stores to the right. The other door was on the smaller store to the left.

The courtyard itself was a typical southern scene. Spanning a distance of close to two hundred feet from door to door, it was merely twenty-five feet wide of lush green garden, short-cut weedy grass, and a tall canopy of large willow oak and chestnut trees giving ample shade on a warm Carolina summer or fall day. Today, fall 2004 was a warm one. It hadn't rained the night before as predicted, but the humidity was high even at 10:30 in the morning. The tree canopy gave relief from what would be a burning hot day.

Ten feet ahead in the cross of the sidewalk spanning the four sides of the rectangular garden was a five-foot-wide circle of old reclaimed stacked red bricks. Pansies and weeds shared the planting space inside, surrounding a large old moss-covered two-foot-tall cement pineapple structure. The pineapple was one of several other garden art structures in the whole garden. It and other garden art caught Mary's attention. That was the art she was looking for on this day: unique items to put in their Rock Hill, South Carolina yard.

Curiously, the entire space of the garden was strewn with all kinds of other antiques. These items had been set out for a joint garden sale the previous day by the two antique stores' owners, left out all night. Luckily it had not rained as predicted.

Tom's eye was instantly attracted to a whole different type of art. A canvas oil painting too had been left out. It was a French painting, he could tell, an old village scene. Kind of dark but interesting. It was tilted, lying slightly on the old brick circle. The painting was of a Charles Dickens-like scene of Tudor house structures in a nearly monochromatic style of grays and soft pinks. Perhaps an early morning following a stormy night as the sun was just creeping through a leftover storm cloud cover.

"Interesting," he thought and picked it up. Only sixty-five dollars. "Hey babe! Look at this painting. What do you think? It's French. Signed on the front and back. Honfleur, France. What do you think?"

"I don't like it much," Mary replied. "It's dark and foreboding. Kinda sad-looking."

Tom continued looking at it, set it down, picked it up again, sat it back down, started to walk away, picked it up once more and said, "You know what, I kind of like it. Only sixty-five dollars. How about I offer them sixty since it doesn't have a frame?"

"Really? You like it? Really?"

"Yeah, I do. It says it is Honfleur, Normandy, France. Done by an artist in 1929 – 31 named just Colette."

Mary now put down an item she had previously picked up and walked thirty feet over to Tom, who was holding the painting still examining it. "I think it tells a story of some kind. Interesting characters in the painting. See?"

"Do you suppose that is The Colette?"

"The Colette? What do you mean, doll?"

"The Colette. The famous writer and dancer of France in the late 1800s and early twentieth century. You know, Colette! Surely you have heard of her. She was one of the first women to dance topless at the Moulin Rouge!" Now that got Tom's attention.

"Nope, but I kind of like the painting so I think I'll see if they will take sixty dollars for it. Really, she danced topless at the Moulin Rouge? Wow! What a find!"

"Wait! You're going to buy a painting simply because the artist may have danced nude? Really? That's your criterion for buying a painting?"

"Of course not. Didn't you say she was a famous writer or something? Well, being a nude dancer just adds icing to the cake! Get it? Nude dancer? Cake?"

All Mary could do was roll her eyes as Tom gave one of his "Hoosier shoulder shrugs," and off he went to the store, painting in hand. Mary followed him, shaking her head.

Inside the store, Tom went up to the store clerk, who happened to be the store owner, and began to negotiate his purchase.

"I found this painting sitting outside on that round brick planter. Looks like it had been there all night. Still has a bit of dew on it. You have a price of sixty-five dollars, but there is no frame. Would you take...hmmm...sixty for it?"

The owner called to the back of the store, "Hey Gwen, there is a man here who is interested in that painting that was outside. Says he will offer sixty dollars for it. It's the one of that old village in France somewhere. Will you accept that?"

From the back of the store in another room came a voice, "Sure. But cash only."

"Well, there's your answer. Cash only. Is that acceptable to you?"

Tom pulled out his wallet, paid the price, and asked, "I don't suppose you have the frame that was on this, do you?"

"Not sure. You will have to talk with Gwen about that."

Tom shrugged his shoulders again, smiled, and said, "Ok, but I'm going to take this painting out to the car and look around the store some more. Who knows what else I might find." Off he went out the door.

Mary, hearing and watching his negotiations while looking elsewhere in the store, wandered back to where she had heard Gwen's voice coming from. Upon finding Gwen in a room down a few stair steps, Mary realized this store was much larger than it appeared from the courtyard between the two doors. This particular store had a frontage to the Main Street of Camden. There was no usable door into the store, however, only large windows all along the store which let the light into a room filled with fine antique furniture.

"Gwen?"

"Yes?"

"I'm Mary. My husband, Tom, is the person who just bought that painting of the French Village. Would you mind if I ask you a few questions about it?"

"Sure. But I'm not sure I can tell you a whole lot."

"Did you find it in France?"

"Oh no. It came out of an estate sale in New York State. It was part of a group of paintings owned by an art collector. The guy collected art from American and European artists of the same vintage as that painting. Early twentieth-century art."

"Was it framed when you purchased it?"

"Yes, it was framed by a really plain white frame." This intrigued Mary as she, an art student in college and an artist herself, knew that the artists of that era, including the impressionists, framed their art in plain white frames. The frame was merely the way the art was protected when moved from place to place while being painted.

"Do you still have the white frame somewhere?"

"No, dear, I sold that separately to someone. I never saw that person before. Most likely I did the same with him or her as I did with your husband. Asked for cash only. By the way, does he always negotiate for a deal? I mean sixty dollars instead of sixty-five?" She laughed.

"Oh, yes, that is Tom. Mister 'negotiate the deal'." Mary laughed too.

"Don't tell him..." looking side to side to see if he was back yet, "I probably would have taken fifty dollars for the painting. I don't like it much. Too...oh, what would I say...sad or foreboding in some way. Don't you think?"

"Yes, I agree. But, he likes it so that's what matters. I won't tell him about the fifty dollars, though. We will keep that between ourselves. Male ego, you know." Said with a wink and reply wink. Mary left the store with Gwen's phone number and other contact information, just in case she thought of other questions to ask later. Mary would think of some. Unfortunately, not much else would be learned from Gwen. But, Gwen's information proved only to be the beginning.

CHAPTER 2
BOOK 3

Upon returning to their home in Rockhill, South Carolina, Tom stood with his butt resting on the back of the white couch, staring at his new purchase. He was between two doors: one leading into the living room where he now stood, and the one leading on into the study from the living room. He continued closely studying his new purchase, a painting of Honfleur, Normandy, France, painted by Colette from 1929-1931, as Mary peered at him from the kitchen.

Mary came out of the 1929 kitchen decorated with the hand-stenciled fleur-de-lys. She and Tom had stenciled the fleur-de-lys as a border around the top of the wall shortly after moving into the house in 2001. Mary had created the handmade stencil herself while he was away at work at UNC Charlotte. He came home that evening, and as he drove into their long circular gravel driveway, he could see her through the kitchen window. She was perched high on the step ladder doing something. He soon found out what. Dinner was delayed until they both finished the project. A truly beautiful old French-looking kitchen!

The hand-painted blue and white small square tiles on the walls reminded Mary of Monet's kitchen in Giverny. They had redone the tile of the kitchen purposely that way. Mary had purchased the hand-painted tiles while she was still living in Kansas City, Missouri. The pattern she had chosen was so complex that the tile mason had her lay them out on the floor to ensure that he would not screw the pattern up.

This evening in 2004, she walked through the soft yellow-walled dining room, again reminiscent of Giverny, and entered through the living room door off the home's entryway and stairway to the upstairs. She paused, observing him again, and said, "Admiring your new find?"

"Yeah, I guess. It is an interesting painting. Looks like it is telling a story." He handed it to her.

Mary studied it closely, reaffirming what she had noticed earlier in the day. She had only had a quick look at it before Tom raced off to purchase it. She had been right. It really was as she had seen. She handed it back to Tom, and he looked at it closely again.

"So?" she said, "what's it telling you?"

"Well, having wanted to be a cartoonist as a kid, I think it is a frame from a storyline. You know, several of these scenes could form a book."

"Interesting. I think I agree. Do you suppose...," Mary said, "It could be a scene from one of her novels? I bet it is! Perhaps she was designing a book cover for the novel."

"Also," Mary added, "I noticed at the store something interesting. Let me look at it again."

Mary took the painting that Tom handed her and examined it from top to bottom, side to side, and bottom to top. She repeated this action several times and even turned it upside down to do it a couple of times that way. Tom watched in wonderment of what the heck she was doing.

Finally, she said, "I thought so! There were two artists who were painting on this canvas. Both are very good, but one is an accomplished artist and appears to be instructing the other, also very good, on how to do some things."

"Seriously? You can see that?"

"Yep. Here, take a look." She handed the painting back to Tom and proceeded to point out minute changes in the brushstrokes which were used. Only an accomplished trained eye could see them. As she pointed them out to Tom, he could now begin to see them. Or, believed he could...perhaps.

"I'll be darned. You're right. There does appear to be a very slight difference. Not sure how to describe it. Something like the brush strokes used on small areas of the painting are more assured. Brush strokes look lighter and quicker.

"Yes, exactly. A bit more length to the pull of the brush of the paint. No hesitation. Still, they are both very close. Whoever is the teacher has an excellent student. We should assume the student is Colette. Wonder who the teacher is?"

She then added, "and you can tell that both are right-handed?"

"Really?"

"Yep, by the slight angle of the strokes. See here and here?" She said pointing out small areas on the painting. Tom couldn't see it but said, "Oh, yes. For sure. Both are right-handed. Sure enough!"

"You can't see it, can you?"

"Nope. But I trust you can. That's good enough for me!"

Mary walked around the couch and sat the painting on the arms of a chair. The painting was now across a four-foot square coffee table from the couch where she and Tom sat down.

"You really like this painting?"

Sheepishly he replied, "Well, yeah. And not because it was painted by a nude dancer, though that is intriguing".

He placed his hand on Mary's thigh. She glanced down at it and then at his face. She smiled and laughingly said, "You didn't get enough 'excitement' as a young man, did you?"

"Why, whatever do you mean?"

"I mean your love for nudes."

"Well, you do have to admit they have some allure. But this one has no nudes in it...though I suppose one or two would have helped brighten the scene."

Smile.

"I'm surprised you bought this painting and not one of the nudes she had hanging in the store instead. Heck, when we go into a gallery that is what draws your attention every time."

"There is only one nude that really interests me."

"And which one, dear sir, is that?"

"The watercolor I did of you, of course. Don't you like it? Didn't you enjoy posing for it? Didn't you like what it developed into? Hmmmm?"

Shaking her head and laughing, her hand now fell on his thigh too, as they smiled together remembering that time. Lost in memory, they sat looking at the painting.

Suddenly, her hand flew from his leg with a shout of "I've got it!!! I've got an idea!!"

"What? The bedroom or here?"

Looking at him and laughing hard, she said, "No, foolish boy. Perhaps later. Right now here is the idea. Neither of us really love this painting. Right?" Without pausing she continued. "And we don't really know if Colette painted it. But let's assume she did. Let's investigate it. Let's investigate Colette. Let's go IN SEARCH OF COLETTE!"

Intrigued now, though fighting giving up his hopes on what a discussion of nudes might have delivered, Tom replied, "How do you propose we do this?"

"First, we need to find out as much as we can about Colette. Let's read anything and everything we can on her. Let's see if we can find information as to whether she was indeed an artist, painter, in addition to being a writer...and of course a nude dancer!" Said smiling at him.

"Then, let's figure out what this painting is really about. Let's find out how it ended up in a New York State estate. How did it get there? Once we do all that we can figure out what we want to do with it. It may be worth a lot of money. Perhaps we will sell it. It could be a national treasure of France if it really was done by Colette. Perhaps we give it back to the nation of France. This could be great fun! Another adventure. And, it may lead us back to a trip or two to Paris. What do you think?!"

"Hmmm, next to a trip to the bedroom, a trip or two to Paris sounds exciting. Okay, I'm in! Let's do it. Let's go IN SEARCH OF COLETTE!"

CHAPTER 3
BOOK 4

At 5:50 Tom's 2004 Honda CRV turned into the circular drive off of Walnut Ridge Road. He could see Mary and their yellow lab dog, Duke, sitting together on the covered front porch of the 1929 "colonial saltbox" home. The white siding house had for many years served as the Rockhill Methodist Church's rectory. Eighteen years before Tom and Mary bought the home in January 2001, it had been purchased and moved 5 miles from the downtown location.

The Methodist Church had determined a new youth center was more important than a rectory. They decided to demolish the then fifty-four-year-old, three bedroom, 2,000 square foot house. At the last moment, the church council came up with a different idea. Why destroy a perfectly good home? Instead, they held a silent auction to the parishioners. The best offer would win the house and then they would have to move it to a new location within the year.

The auction was held on a Sunday with the silent bids placed in a secured box. Only one problem. There was only one bid made. It was a bid from a young newlywed couple named Hugh and Daphne. Their bid: fifty dollars!

The young couple didn't have a lot of money so Hugh and a couple buddies worked all year taking the roof off the home, labeling accurately each board and beam. Hugh had learned from the moving company he hired that there were two ways to move the home through the city streets. Leave the second floor in place and take down all the utility lines along the five mile trip. Or, fold the top floor walls onto the first floor ceiling and move it without too much trouble other than blocking roads for a considerable amount of time. In effect, the home became the same as moving a double wide mobile home...and much less costly to move.

Less than a year later, the home sat on its new spot 5 miles from the church and on two acres of beautiful wooded property. Eighteen years later, as their family grew in size and a swimming pool was desired, Hugh and Daphne decided to sell the home. The lucky buyers...Mary and Tom Martz.

Duke as always came bounding his big lumbering way up to plant wet licks all over Tom's arms and attempted to do so on the face. Arms were okay, but face was reserved for only one thing. The evening kiss that sweet Mary always gave him. That evening was no different other than the bigger than usual smile on her face. And, she always had a big smile. That evening he suspected something.

"I see a really big smile on that beautiful face of yours. I suspect you have a surprise or something. What's up?"

"Come on in and let me show you!" She took him by the arm and led him up the front steps and into the house. To his left, he saw on the dining room table several of their books on France. Of particular note was a large coffee table book open with a post-it note attached to a page numbered 72.

"Take a look at this!" she said as she began reading a marked passage.

"The Opal Coast, which stretches from Belgium to Normandy, derives its name from the milky-white seas that wash and sometimes lash it ....Seaside resorts continue southwards...This coastline has constantly produced idiosyncratic maritime villages. Le Crotoy...The village passed successively from the English to the Burgundians and from the Burgundians to the French...Jules Verne, COLETTE, and Toulouse-Lautrec were all entranced by the spot."

"So?"

"This whole section of the book is Normandy...and particularly Honfleur! Don't you see! This specifically states this was a frequent place that COLETTE visited! Proof that she was there...and with other artists and writers too! I think we are really on to something!"

Now noticing his arms full of books, she said, "What you got there, buddy boy?"

"More homework for us. I picked up these books from the UNC Charlotte library. They had quite a collection on Colette. I was surprised. And the librarians helped me request some other volumes they didn't have sent over to us at Charlotte from Chapel Hill and State. We have these for two weeks but I bet we can renew them beyond that. Looks like no TV for a while with all the reading we will be doing!"

Mary thought that would be no problem since they had lost the cable hookup anyway. They did get the PBS and three broadcast channels out of Charlotte but no other TV to entertain them after the visit by the phone company following the landline issue.

Mary had been home and Tom was at work in Charlotte. There had been an electrical storm and something had happened to their landline phone. A serviceman promptly came out. Crawling into the crawlspace, he solved the problem quickly. After coming to the back door where Mary was working in the kitchen, he asked, "Pardon me, Mrs. Martz, do you have cable TV too?"

Now Tom, seeing the cable hookup in the living room after they moved in, said, "Let's see if this works" and attached the cable to the TV. "Yes! It works!" So for a couple of years they had cable. Until this visit by the repairman.

"Gosh, I don't know," she said, playing it cool. "You would have to check with my husband, Tom. He is at work now, though. Won't be home until about 6 pm."

At about 6:15 pm that evening, sure enough, the phone rang asking for him. Tom took the phone from Mary and heard, "Mr. Martz, this is the cable TV company calling. A phone repairman was out at your house today and, well

sir, it looks like the previous owner's cable is still hooked up. Mr. Martz, do you know whether you are still receiving our cable service there?
Now Tom, not always a fast thinker, had been told by Mary about the question asked by the phone repairman. When he left, she had called Tom. He was prepared.

"Actually, yes, I have been meaning to call your company about this. It seems you have been storing your cable programs in my house for the last two years without my permission. I thought about charging you rent. Just haven't gotten around to doing so yet."

"Mr. Martz, nice try. We will have a repairman out there tomorrow to disconnect our service. Should you want to have cable in the future, we will be happy to reconnect you for the appropriate fee. Goodbye." And so the phone call ended. And also the cable service.

CHAPTER 4
BOOK 3

That evening, books spread out on the dining room table with only a ham sandwich to satisfy his hunger, the search began in earnest. Mary had discovered something earlier in the day that she didn't want to reveal to Tom yet. She wanted to be more sure. It would take the daylight of tomorrow and the large lighted magnifying glass in their studio to be sure. If it really was what she thought, then this mystery was more than they had thought. And it proved that this painting may be telling a story.

Tom, who was leafing through a book called, "Colette a Passion for Life" by Genevieve Dormann and printed by Abbeville Press, said, "Hey, look at this. It is a photograph of Colette sketching a couple of cartoon drawings of her husband, a guy called Willy. It's not the same as an oil painting but at least it shows she did some art."

"Keep looking. Maybe there will be other drawings or paintings in the book. She certainly is an interesting woman."

"I'll say! I just read about the riot she caused at the Moulin Rouge. You were right. She was the first person who appeared nude. Usually the women wore flesh-colored leotards. She was in this play called Rêve d' Egypte. This play was written by this woman, Missy. An interesting character too, as she always dressed like a man. Anyway, this Missy was an archeologist kinda guy in the play who was intrigued by the occult. Missy, who is a man in the play, falls in love with this mummy...Colette...who rises up and unwinds her bandages in a striptease in order to seduce him, Missy. See there was this rather long kiss between these two women in addition to Colette's nudity. And, well this riot… Mary, shaking her head and laughing said, "I can see where your attention has gone this evening. Any other signs of artistry? Painting preferably!"

"How about you? Anything in what you have looked through that says anything about her taking art lessons or painting?"

"No, but I did find this cute quote in one of the books. Can't remember which one now. It was said by Colette's four-year-old niece who evidently had a German governess. It is from 1923. Colette wrote it in the sound of the German woman's accent as the child said it. Here it is."

> *"Here is the Summer, it iss wery varm*
> *Ant the Sun sheintz like*
> *a crate pig Star*
> *ant the Moon iss lightink*
> *us up there all through*
> *the Night.*

"Isn't that the sweetest thing you ever heard? Imagine this little girl saying that in 1923!"

"I suspect I will see this quote hanging out in the studio…right?"

"Yep. Hey, I've been thinking. We have six or eight books here. Right?"

"Yes. So?"

"Well, I think we have to come up with a systematic approach on how we solve this problem. Otherwise, we are just turning pages. Let's list what we need to find out from our sources in order of importance. How about we each list five."

"Sounds good to me. What are your thoughts?"

Mary said, "I think we each take a few minutes and write a list down. Then we compare the list in ranking of importance and focus on just two or three things. Sounds good?"

"Sure. Let's try it. I'll get the chalkboard from the kitchen, and we can use it to put the answers on when we share them." He went into the kitchen and brought the two foot by three foot rectangle chalkboard and stand into the dining room.

They both worked silently for several minutes, figuring out their answers on a separate piece of paper that they would then transfer to the chalkboard.

 Each one of them, looking distantly then writing on a piece of paper and then looking off distantly again. Mary finished first and waited for Tom. Finally, two or three minutes later, he too put his pen down.

"You go first," Mary said.

Tom took his paper over to the chalkboard and wrote:

1. Mention or example of Colette painting or drawing
2. Mention or picture of Colette in Honfleur itself
3. A Colette novel taking place in Honfleur
4. Colette novel with a young woman and a man with a red Fez
5. Mention of artist and writers who stayed with her outside of Paris

"Good list," Mary said. Here is mine in reverse order:

1. Artist friends
2. Writer friends
3. Living in Honfleur
4. Mention of her painting or drawing
5. Hidden coded message

"Wait, what do you mean reverse order. Does that mean number five is your number one pick?"

"Yes."

"So, coded message is your number one?"

"Yep-a-roonie!"

"What do you mean 'coded message' "?

"You will have to wait till tomorrow when you get home to find out. Let's just say I have to examine the painting again closely in daylight and use the large magnifying glass in the studio. But I may have seen something that tells me there is a coded message on the painting."

You're kidding! For real?"

"Yep-a-roonieo!"

"Cool.... The plot thickens!" Tom didn't know how true that statement was.

CHAPTER 5
BOOK 3

The next morning began slowly. The discussions regarding nudes following a few hours of reading led into personal, intimate fact findings about nudeness and its results. Sleep came easy for Mary and Tom later. Morning came with much more difficulty. A "cup of hot brown" was necessary...perhaps two.

Fortunately, the coffee pot was set on automatic, and the coffee maker prepared the evening before. Even though the house was a large now 2,500 square foot saltbox, the warm coffee smell carried up the stairs into their bedroom.

"Coffee is made, thank God!" Mary exclaimed. From her raised position with arms bracing her in a semi-sitting position, she looked over at her Tom. He laid there with a big smile of satisfaction on his face, looking back at her.

"I kinda like the way we end research. This could be a fun project. I suspect there will be more stimulating findings tonight, perhaps. Especially based on your number one ranked important fact to investigate. What was it? Something like 'coded message' "?

"Yep-a-roonie. But as I said last night, you will have to wait till you get home to find out what my research shows. Okay?"

"You will show me your research? If you show me yours, I'll show you mine!" Smile.

"Boys! We can discuss that later after the big reveal. Until then, focus!"
They had a slow breakfast after two cups of coffee. Tom would be late arriving at UNC Charlotte that day. Fortunately, the Chancellor was over in Raleigh at a system-wide meeting. No one but Scotty, his assistant, would notice his lateness. When she saw the smile on his face, she suspected she knew. She liked this couple. He was a good man to work with and he depended on Scotty and her historic knowledge of the University and its people. She also could make up for his misspellings and bad grammar. She knew about Tom's dyslexia but would never say a word. She and he were a good team.

Most of Tom's day was spent working with projects related to the campaign. The University was in its first really sizable fundraising efforts. The Chancellor and Tom worked hard to provide the funding necessary for the staffing that was needed. Their efforts were paying off. Even at this early time in the campaign, 2004, University of Alabama was trying to steal Tom away from UNC Charlotte. Alabama's eventual success played a future role IN THE SEARCH OF COLETTE.

For her part, Mary's day was somewhat the same as a typical day. She and Duke, the yellow lab, headed out for their usual 3 mile walk into the neighborhood adjacent to the small grouping of houses on Walnut Ridge. They always started early before eight to avoid the South Carolina heat and particularly the humidity. They had a slightly late start this morning. Mary wasn't disappointed in the reason for her lateness. She too had a big smile on her face thinking of her Tom and how silly he could be. Duke, unleashed, off they went.

You really couldn't call it a neighborhood as it only comprised about eight or nine houses along Walnut Ridge itself. No cul de sacs or streets running off it. Just eight houses in a row. Tom and Mary were close to the neighbors to their east, Kenny and Brad. They also had two labs, a chocolate and black. They taught Mary and Tom to let Duke roam the neighborhood on his own just as Cody (chocolate lab) and Star (black Lab) did.

Other than that, there was the nice old farmer. He had given off a stern impression when you first met him. Each summer, he made sure Tom and Mary had lots of free "Madders," his term for tomatoes.

There was Beth and her husband across the street. Mary loved children and Beth had a slew…just like Mary had had. Five stairstep kids in a row with only about twelve to eighteen months between one and the next. Beth, being a good Catholic, had a hard time giving Mary a copy of a new book out before one of Mary's trips to Paris with Tom. It was Dan Brown's "The Da Vinci Code". When giving it to Mary, Beth held it by thumb and first finger out away from her body and handed it to Mary. Mary became a surrogate grandmother to the five kids. Mary and the kids just flat out loved each other.

Coming back from the late walk, Mary was hot and sweating. Although she would take another bath that day, this day deserved two. Fortunately, the previous owners had added two rooms to the house, the office downstairs that had been a screened-in porch, and a huge master bathroom with Mary's wonderful soaking bathtub.

She and Tom, under the influence of a bottle of champagne (some of their best work together, painting and otherwise was done this way) had painted the most incredible copy of Monet's water lilies painting. Mary had a large poster of one in the collection of the Kansas City's Nelson Atkins Museum of Art. Her ability as an artist to deconstruct the process Monet used allowed her to teach and coach Tom as they stood in the bathtub's eight foot by four foot size and painted the scene on three wrap around walls. A bottle of champagne later and it was finished!

In the evening, the reflection off the small fountain, "Rebecca at the Well," made the three walls appear to be shimmering water around and over the waterlilies. This bath was much appreciated that day.

Following the bath, she dressed in appropriate garb for work in the studio. She would not be painting, wearing the clothing she normally wore to paint, however, put her in a good mood for the investigation. She and Duke marched out to the studio, Colette Honfleur painting in hand.

The late morning sun was perfect, just as she had planned. Streaming rays of sunlight through the east facing studio window fell on her art studio desk. She laid the painting on a cushion of an old quilt. Putting the painted surface downward, the stretcher faced upward, visible to her. Mary knew the painting stretched on the wood rectangle was not totally unusual for a painting of this age but it wasn't the typical way a painted stretching was done. Honfleur had an unusual amount of canvas beyond the attachment nails on the sides of the stretcher. Extra canvas covered almost all of the visible wood on the back side. That was what caught her attention yesterday when she saw the different artist brush strokes. Mary saw just a hint of the pencil writing on the wood under the canvas lip. Often the writing notes of an artist would have been made on the original frame. That frame was lost. Sold to an unknown other purchaser for cash at the Camden South Carolina antique store. No way to trace the buyer. At first, seeing the small letters on the stretcher she did not think much of it. Over the day an idea developed as she thought more about it last night. Now Mary was hoping what she suspected would be real.

Slowly, the screwdriver lifted the edge of each old, rusted nail one by one. Just enough to put the thin sharp point of the needle nose pliers under the head of the nails. Using a small block of wood as a fulcrum support, she applied a light pull on the neck of the nail. While pulling upward slowly, she also twisted it back and forth to loosen it from the wood. With typical calm and patience, the first eight nails out. Each spaced approximately four inches from the previous one. Finally, the whole flap of excess canvas was free and she could carefully fold it back.

As she had hoped, suspected there in front of her on the stretcher wood was notes from the artist, Colette. The writing in pencil. First pencils were used by artists as early as 1560 in England. The first pencils encased in wood began in Nuremberg, Germany, in 1662. The modern pencil lead was created in 1795 by Frenchman Nicholas Jacques Conte. To make the lead, he mixed powdered graphite and clay. These he formed into sticks and hardened them in a furnace much like a potter would his clay creations.

Colette's notes of course were in French as Mary knew they would be. She had a basic understanding of written French having taken two years in High School and one year in college. Latin helped too. Going to a catholic high school of course she had had four years of Latin. Still to translate these notes she would need help of a French/English dictionary. A second exciting possibility also was realized. She had uncovered writing in pencil of the artist.

Not writing on canvas in oil paint. Writing in a hard substance that left a message whose letters could be matched against other writing by the person scribing them. Perhaps these could help she and Tom verify that this painting was truly by the writer Colette.

Mary took out her Canon camera and took several photographs of the stretcher and the message she found. She then picked up a pen and wrote what she saw on a piece of paper, folded it up, and put it in her pocket. Following the procedure she used on the first lip that she did the same on the other three sides. Taking more photos and writing the stretcher's message was completely recorded. She would begin working on the translation that afternoon. Mary now began putting all of the nails back in place through the canvas and into the wood. Just as she had found them that morning. An unknown secret securely hidden. Once again.

CHAPTER 6
BOOK 3

Driving into the semi-circle drive in front of 4269, there he saw them. His sweet Mary and her ever faithful companion, almost to the point of annoyance, Duke, sat on the front porch. A big smile on both of their faces. Okay, to be honest, a yellow Lab dog almost always has a big smile on its face. It was once said of Labs, "The are such happy friendly spirits that if someone breaks into your home, the Lab will great them with a smile, invite them in, and show them where the money and silver are hidden." That was Duke.

But on this day, Tom could tell Mary was extremely happy too! He suspected she had found something. Her smile big she and Duke both bounded off the step to greet him.

"You found something?"

"More than something...somethings! Wait till you see them. There definitely is a story...a mystery for us to unravel. Do you want to eat first or dig right in?"

"Are you kidding! Dig right in! Where? Dining room? Or living room?"

"Dining room. It's all laid out there. Photos, notes, and translations."

"Writing?"

"Yep-a-roonie-O. Writing! Matchable writing! Matchable to Colette by an expert I believe. Still we have lots of investigative footwork to do. What would you think of a trip to Paris this winter? Perhaps January 2005?"

"I'm in. Should we make reservations soon?"

"Done! Did them this afternoon. We leave on January 11 next year. And are there until January 19! I booked the hotel too! A two-star hotel called, get this, Hotel Paris France!" She smiled. "We are set. Now, let me show you all I found!!"

They walked into the house through the front porch door and turned right into the dining room. The dining room table had all the books laid out. More importantly, it had photos developed of what Mary had taken earlier in the day. Jiffy printing came though. There were also her original notes and then the translations. Mary went through the process and how the extreme overlap of the canvas and a hint of pencil writing just barely visible on one side gave her the idea to look beneath the fold.

"Here is the original French."

M'a dit Jadin 1910
Assaminat 1914 ff
1918 nr
1924 vl
Premier paiement noir a js
Amis americains trois lettres +1 deux lettres +1

29-31 Marquet, Matisse, Picasso, Cocteau en St Tropez

"What does it mean?"

"In translation, this is what I found!"

Told me Jadin 1910
Assassination 1914 ff
1918 nr
1924 vl

Fist black payment to js
American friends three letters +1 two letters +1

29-31 Marquet, Matisse, Picasso, Cocteau in St Tropez

"Wow! Assassinations! Do the dates line up with anything of note?"

"Yep-a-roonie-o! 1914 the assassination of Arch Duke Ferdinand of Austria. It set off the First World War! Then in 1918 Nicolas the third, the last Tsar of Russia and family were assassinated. This ended the Romanov dynasty. Lastly, Vladimir Lenin died of a stroke in 1924. And, to top it off, he was replaced by a person with the initials J S!"

"Joseph Stalin!"

"Yep! And get this..." Mary opened a book on Colette, The Passion for Life, where Tom had found pictures the day before..."here is a picture of an actress who plays "Jadin" in a play based on the book that Colette wrote called Le Vagabond. Jadin is a singer and actress who goes missing in the book. The book tells of a woman like Colette who is performing in plays she has written to get away from a controlling husband. In the book, she adds the fact that Jadin went missing, though no explanation on why. The book was written in 1910!"

"This sounds like we have a lot of work ahead of us before this trip to Paris. I brought home two more books that arrived by courier from Chapel Hill today. That puts us at ten books to read about this writer's life. I suspect we should get a copy of Le Vagabond and other novels she wrote too." He paused for a moment then said,

"Hey, doll?"

Mary looked at Tom and the troubled look on his face. "What is it, Angel?"

"I don't think we should tell anyone about this...other than that we are trying to find whether it was really painted by Colette."

"Why?"

"Well, if it really is a scene from a story told to Colette by someone and it has three assassinations tied to it and two Americans funding the assassinations there could be some hidden danger we are not seeing. I don't remember anything in my history classes linking Americans to any of the three deaths. Quite the opposite. The funders may not be known to the authorities. And, if they are known but this was never revealed...well, the authorities may be hiding something from the world. I just think we should use caution and be careful what we tell people."

Mary studied him for a few moments before speaking, "You really are concerned, aren't you?"

"Yes. Something just tells me there could be trouble ahead unless we are cautious. And it is not from reading spy and murder mystery novels. This is from notes that an artist made on hidden areas under a canvas on the stretcher. I don't think she would have done so without some purpose. Let's look in our readings to see if we can find that purpose. And it still doesn't take away from the fun of finding out in other ways if Colette painted the painting. That will still be fun."

"I understand what you are saying. I think your thoughts may be right. Other than to brag about something, we really have no proof of at this point it really is not worth bothering others about. It will be an exciting side to the search for other proof of her painting it, though. Agreed! We keep it to ourselves at least for now."

Tom and Mary began reading the ten books they had acquired through the UNC Charlotte Library. Later that fall, they added four more books that they purchased through "Better World Books," a not for profit book supplier started by former Notre Dame graduates. One of the biggest fillers of landfills it turns out are unsold books from book dealers or old discarded library books and those of everyday discards of readers. The company was founded to generate funds for literacy, giving struggling people all over the world the basic skills to succeed.

Mary had discovered "Better World Books" by accident in the early 2000s as the company was just starting up. It became her first choice source for books, often not found in other places. The books came from libraries all over the country as they culled their shelves for new volumes.

Armed with fourteen books now you would think they would find some definitive written proof that Colette was indeed an accomplished artist. Other than the cartoon-like sketches in the earlier books they found nothing...

...that changed in January 2005!

CHAPTER 7
BOOK 3

Mary and Tom departed Charlotte Douglas Airport on a Northwest DC9 for a three-hour layover in Detroit. Mary had found cheap flights on line, which added to the travel time the couple would have. Still, it is the adventure that counts, not the time or money. Mary's long held philosophy.

The flight from Detroit was uneventful...but also flying coach class, without much, if any, sleep. The hotel shuttle driver that met their flight was over a half hour late...on time in France. A quick trip to Paris from Charles De Gaulle and they arrived safely at their new home for the six nights, Hotel Paris France, 72 rue Turbigo 75003.

Outside the hotel was a beautiful blue awning over the glassed-in entryway and breakfast lounge. That awning would be a "welcome home" sign every evening after a long day of exploration and search. Delphine greeted them as they entered the lobby. She was the same person who had interacted with them by email, first with Mary, when she made the arrangements, and then on subsequent emails to set up the airport pickup.

At first the couple was given room 21. Unfortunately, it had a non-flushing toilet. Delphine, who spoke perfect English, moved the couple to a higher room, 51. It not only had a street view of the rooftops but being above traffic level, it was quieter. It also was...a PINK room! Mary loved pink, calling it "panky". That girl could be silly.

The first couple of days were filled with searching for street markets they knew and those they didn't. One, which became their favorite they visited often on subsequent trips to Paris, they found on a meaningful day, January 15. The Market d'Algiers at metro Ledru-Rollin had everything, old paintings, silver lots of brocante stuff and fabrics. Mary loved fabrics! Today she purchased a very large and thick handmade linen sheet for only 10 Euros. Later they figured out it was a Catholic Church Altar cloth. That made making love on it some kind of special! They laughed each time thinking of it...after the fact, of course.

But this was not the reason alone that January 15 was special. What made it special was that Tom stumbled upon a hidden "underground" group of shops in the Jouffroy passage located in the 9th err. Along the way to finding that the couple did one of their other fun Paris things...dumpster diving! Well, they never really dove into a dumpster. Instead they had the knack of finding treasures thrown out and laid on the sidewalk for anyone to take. Except for the really big items like chest of drawers and dining room tables, they picked up almost anything. This particular day to go along with their "sacred" sheet they found a "Holy Water" bottle. The small silver spout at one end was attached but the handle of the spout was broken off. Sacred sheets and Holy water bottle. A sign!

At the d'Algiers market, Tom also purchased a remembrance of his childhood. Silver rests for knives, forks, and spoons between dinner courses. Shaped with silver Xs on each end a silver bar attaching both Xs kept the utensils from making a mess on the tablecloth. He purchased all ten for 10 Euros.

When the transaction was completed, the vendor asked, "Where are you from?" Tom replied, "The United States." To that, the vendor said, smilingly, "We cannot all be perfect, now can we?"

Tom answered with, "No, but we love the French anyway!" Touché!

Taking the metro back to the hotel, they asked Delphine where she suggested they eat dinner. She gave them the address of a really small restaurant within a few blocks of the hotel on rue de la Folie Méricourt. The owner and chef was a young Frenchman about Delphine's age… perhaps a boyfriend? Oui? The food was incredible in this really small French restaurant. He could easily remind one of the young restaurant owner and chef in a modern-day TV show, Emily in Paris.

Okay, all this is nice, but what really made January 15 special was what happened in the Jouffroy passage. It was there that the couple stumbled across an art gallery, Galerie Dominique Weitz. The gallery specialized in art of the nineteenth and twentieth century up to 1940! It was filled with original paintings, prints and photographs of those periods. It was overwhelming!

Monsieur Weitz seemed like a very nice man, so Mary decided to tell him about the Colette painting and ask if he had ever seen any works by her.

"Excusez-moi monsieur, parlez-vous anglais?"

"Bien sur, madame. Un grand nombre de mes clients sont Britanique et Americains. How may I help you?"

"Monsieur, we have a painting that we believe was created by the great French writer, Colette. Have you ever seen any oil paintings that were painted by her?"

Monsieur Weitz considered Mary and her question for a few moments and replied somewhat skeptically, "No, madame. I do not believe I have ever seen or heard of her painting. She was, of course, a very talented woman in many aspects. During her time many young women were taught in school the finer things of life…art, music. But, painting? I would be somewhat surprised. Tell me about the painting."

"It appears to be a scene of Honfleur, Normandy, France painted in 1929-31. It is signed on both the front and back. We have the painting at our home in the United States. We did bring photographs of the painting with us to Paris. However, we left them at our hotel room. Could we show them to you?"

"Madame and Monsieur, I have to tell you that I have my doubts. But of course I will be happy to look at the photographs. I am closing the store in

just a few minutes. Could you bring them to the gallery on Monday? Would 10:00 in the morning work for you both?"
"Merci, Monsieur Weitz. Monday at ten in the morning would be perfect for us. Merci beaucoup!"

"I must say again, I have my doubts. Let's look at them and see."

Both the couple and Monsieur Weitz bid each other a good evening and the couple left the gallery for the metro ride home to the hotel...and the nice dinner that evening at "Brin de folie"

CHAPTER 8
BOOK 3

Tom and Mary woke up Monday morning charged up to go to two places. The first a 10 am meeting with Monsieur Weitz at his gallery. The second, to wander the streets of the 16th, Tom's childhood neighborhood.

They had a quick breakfast at "Paul's", a chain patisserie, this one found in the Marais. By the time they arrived at the gallery, following a few stops in other passage ways, it was 10:45 am...right on time in France.

"Bonjour," Monsieur Weitz said as they walked into the gallery. Tom and Mary both replied the same.

"You have brought the pictures for me to look at, yes?"

"Oui."

Tom pulled the photos out of his "secret spy" passport pouch hung around his neck and under two sweaters on this cold morning. Mary herself had on new striped over-the-knee socks, matching striped leg warmers both of which Tom had purchased for the trip based on the last winter Paris trip's weather. It can get cold and damp in Paris in January. Mary also had on black anklet socks and black tights, a long gray knit woolen skirt over a black satin slip, two woolen sweaters, one orange, the other green, her new-old second hand woolen herringbone coat and her woolen headband. Voila!!! Warm!!!

The gallery owner took the photos and looked through each one three times.

He pulled out a magnifying glass and looked once again, shaking his head. Looking up from the photos his comments had changed...there was no longer skepticism.

"This painting has very good composition. I repeat again that I have never seen paintings by Colette. You may have something here! I have only seen one sketch of her first husband Willy on the back of a letter. It was a good sketch. She obviously could draw. Perhaps!"

Then he added, "The painting looks like it is telling a story, oui? Look at the characters the artist has included in the painting. A writer might do this with a painting she is painting. She would tell a story! Hmmm! I think you should go to the Place Colette and ask the Friends of Colette association there about this. You may have found a real mystery!"

He didn't even know how much of a mystery they had found.

"Thank you for bringing them for me to see. I hope you will come back one day with the answer to the mystery. I would look forward to finding out if in fact this treasure of France was also a painter."

With pleasant "au revoirs" Tom and Mary, spirits now high, left the gallery and headed back to the hotel for a quick bite of lunch before heading to the Palais Royal and the Place Colette.

A metro ride later, they exited at Place Colette and the Palais Royal and searched for "Friends of Colette". They couldn't find any markings for it, but they did find the "Minister of Culture" office there. They showed the photos to a woman in the Ministry and after looking at them she said, "You should go to the gallery at 155 in the Palais Royal and perhaps they could help you. It is in the Arcade d' Colette. But I am sorry to say, they are not open today. They are closed on Mondays."

Both Tom and Mary silently said in their minds "Dang!" or something to that effect anyway.

"Merci, Madame," and out into the cold they went.
"What do you want to do, doll?"

"Let's wander through the Arcade to find the 155 Arcade d' Colette so we know where it is tomorrow. Time is closing in on us. Tomorrow is the last full day we have in Paris. We leave on the 19th."

"Sounds good." And so they wandered through the Arcade. They missed it on the first pass but stumbled upon it the second time around by accident. Tom had seen some toy lead soldiers in a shop. They were the same ones he and his brother Wade had when they lived in Paris in 1956. Forty-five Euros for one soldier that cost them twenty-five francs in 1956...when a franc was a quarter of a cent! Talk about inflation!

As they left the little shop there in front of them only a few steps away were posters for an exhibit of Jean Cocteau and Picasso, both good friends of Colette's. The biggest surprise of all...it started the next day...in the Gallery in the Arcade d' Colette...the gallery they were looking for. This had to be another sign! Two of the people that Colette named on the stretcher of the canvas of the painting. Only two missing Matisse and Albert Marquet! That changed a few minutes later.

Continuing their walk, they headed east along rue de Rivoli towards one of their favorite antiquing places...Village St. Paul. It seemed interesting to both of them when they previously visited the area that it was a very Jewish neighborhood with the name of a Saint. Ecumenical people must have named it at one time perhaps. Of course they learned that there was a large Catholic Church in the district...named Saint Paul.

Now perhaps old Saint Paul had a hand in this. Perhaps it was a coincidence. Perhaps it was just fate. But for whatever reason Tom decided it was time to turn north just as Rivoli changed names to rue Saint Antoine. It was on a small street they called rue Sevigne where they turned left. That's when they saw the first poster announcing it. Straight ahead of them in Musée Carnavalet was a show of "the great forgotten Fauvist," Albert Marquet!

Mary and Tom looked at each other and both said, "You have to be kidding?! Really?!" They each wanted to yell "1,2,3,4, you owe me a Coke!" But of course being in their 50s, they would be embarrassed to do so.

Instead, they looked at each other in amazement realizing that three of the members of the stretcher painting party were revealed to them in loud support of their search. And, on the exact day they had strong support from a dealer with knowledge of artists of the period saying to them, "you may have something there," they had no choice. They paid a small fee and entered the show.

Now Mary Martz's maiden name was Markway. It sounded like a shopping center food store. However, it was the American naturalization official's bastardization of the French name Marquet. Mary's father's ancestors had immigrated from the Alsace area of France as had the German/French heritage Martz family. The Alsace Lorraine area of Europe had constantly been back and forth from France to Germany and back to France. Marquet was certainly French. Martz was certainly German. Still, the heritage of the families were from that part of Europe.

Mary and Tom, over a bottle of Champagne, painted a wonderful duplication of Albert Marquet's painting of the Samaritaine department store from across the Seine River at Pont Neuf on a rainy night. It was painted on the back of what had been an old musical organ, which some antique-brocante dealer had fashioned into a single drawer cabinet. Mary and Tom turned it into their kitchen island. She loved to tell everyone that the Samaritan was where "Tommy's mother, Mary Martz, used to buy his underwear when he was a small boy." Much to his exasperation. She would say, "just kidding!" Then they both would laugh at it. And, he knew it was actually true. His mom had done that. And also at the Army PX too!

That painting was there. Their painting looked just like his. The show was marvelous. Perhaps a hundred Marquet paintings. What they didn't know was they would have another opportunity to see the paintings when they were exhibited around the United States. Those exhibits were purposely shown by the curators at less famous art museums. The curators wanted a broader spectrum of viewers to see the paintings then what would often be the case in large metropolitan museums in the United States. The second viewing for Mary and Tom was in Columbia, South Carolina, two years later.
It was time to find a place for dinner and then head back to the hotel to

prepare for the next day's search. A quick ride across Paris found them in their new "favorite" restaurant, Scossas on the 16th at Place Victor Hugo. Not quite two city blocks from Tommy's 1950s home in the apartment at 55, rue des Belles Feuilles. Mary had saumon a' l'estragon and Tom had risotto au poulet! Tres magnifique! Both! On top of the fine dinner, as they left the restaurant they spied it on the side of a wall...a poster for a Matisse exhibit on display at Musée Pompadour! The fourth member of the stretcher painting team!

CHAPTER 9
BOOK 3

January 18, 2005, was the last full day of the trip. It started simply enough. Find a good boulangerie for breakfast croissants near the hotel. That finished, they were off for some other adventures until the Palais Royale Gallery when it opened at 14:30.

Taking the metro to the Châtelet station, a walk west to Pont Neuf bridge and headed south across the bridge to the 6th arrondissement. The Ecole Nationale Supèrieure des Beaux Arts located in this arrondissement might have someone who could assist them in the Colette mystery. One problem they found. The Ecole was closed for winter break between fall and spring semesters.

Heading back along Quai Malaquais they decided to grab a quick lunch at Cafe des Beaux Arts. On this cold day, French onion soup was in order. Once lunch was finished, it was time to catch a metro back to the Palais Royale. Before doing so, they found and went into three galleries they spotted on rue de Seine. Asking each of the galley owners if they had ever come across any paintings by Colette, Tom and Mary met with slight disappointment. No one said they had ever seen anything by her. Showing the photos to the owners, they each looked closely but shook their heads and repeated what they had heard at Galerie Weitz. "I have never seen anything. This painting looks very good. You may have something here!" Okay! Better than nothing. Off to 155 Galerie de Valois, in the Arcade Colette!

It was now slightly later than the opening time of 2:30 pm when they arrived at the gallery. A sign in the window announced that the opening would be delayed until 5:00 pm...two and a half hours later. What to do?

There was a very fashionable restaurant in the Palais Royale. The decision was made. Coffee for Monsieur Martz et la Pastis for Madame Martz. As one waiter in another restaurant once observed, "Well, we know who wears the pants in your house!" Not true. Tom liked strong coffee. Mary liked cloudy liquid that tasted like anise. Pastis was created in 1932 in France by Paul Ricard as a result of the government banning absinthe seventeen years earlier. Usually she had it on hot summer days in Paris. Today, though cold, it sounded refreshing to her. Besides, they intended to rent the table they were sitting at for an hour or so. Something to sip slowly made sense. The restaurant also provided them with a clean restroom for a potty break. On a cold day in January, that too was much needed.

A little over an hour later they, as Americans, felt the guilt of holding the table. A French person would never feel such guilt. You occupy it. It is yours! Guilt they had so they gave up their table and opted to cross the street and go into the classy shops in Le Louvre des Antiquaires. Once inside, they found several art galleries. On the second floor, they found one that specialized in Impressionist paintings. Impressionist paintings were a bit before the time Colette had presumably painted the painting but it was still worth a try. They entered the shop.

Two young, glamorously dressed women greeted them as they came into the store. One wearing long black touch-the-floor, clinging to the hips, flared pants. That is, they were pants, until she moved her long leg. Then the split up the side of her right leg revealed it was actually a long skirt. It was made to hang around the legs to look like pants until the flash of skin revealed the truth. Under a jacket cut to reveal her long neck and fastened with one button at mid breast the jacket flared wide to the hips, caressing them to the top of the spit of the skirt. Beneath the jacket, she wore a black and white diagonal striped satin or silk blouse. One piece of jewelry adorned her. Around her neck was a necklace made from round flat black-hinting-at-red stones that formed a tight ring around her throat at the top of her collar bone. This hint suggested someone's control of her, much like Manet's 1863 painting of Olympia displayed the perfect look for a gallery of Impressionist art. This look likely created the same titillation for the customers as Manet's groundbreaking work did at the Paris Salon. Is she a person of substance...or for hire?

Her partner was dressed similarly. However, her skirt revealed easily that it was part of her tight fitting short black dress. The only question is whether it is leather or some other 'biker look' tight fitting material. As she walked over to them it too caressed the top of her thighs. Mary knew her man was in heaven! Egad! What places will do to sell art!

"Excusez-moi, est-ce que l'une de vous, jeunes femmes, parle anglais? (Pardon me, do either of you young women speak any English?) Mary asked, trying to hide her obvious dislike of the store's displayed sexism.

Much to her surprise, the young woman in the split up the side skirt said, Yes, Madame, we both do. How can we be of help to you? I am the owner of the gallery and this is my assistant manager."

Now both Mary and Tom were dumbstruck! Imagine owning a galerie in the Louvre des Antiquaires and probably being under 30 years of age. Perhaps a family-owned business?

Mary asked if they would look at the photos after telling the Colette story. She knew her man's thoughts might be elsewhere with these two young "babes". She was wrong...partially...as he listened intently to every word the young women both said.

In the end, they also had never come across anything done by Colette. They too thought there might be something with the painting. Their parting suggestion was to take the photos to another gallery on the third floor of the building who specialized in paintings of this period, Dominique Bert Tableaux XX.

Mary asked one last question before they left. Have either of you ever heard of Colette, while living at her home in the South of France in Saint-Tropez, about 1929, having the painters Matisse, Marquet, Picasso, and Cocteau painting there?"

This brought a flash of something to the owner's mind. She wasn't completely sure how it would pertain. She simply replied, "Well, perhaps Madame, as many of the artist of that time painted throughout the Cote d'

Azur. This could be possible. Why? Do have some sense that perhaps this happened?"

"Oh, no, not really. Just a note I saw somewhere. Perhaps when we meet in a few minutes with the fellow who is having the Picasso and Cocteau exhibit, he can tell us for sure. Merci."

The owner of the gallery's mind was in gear as they left the gallery. Something about the painting sparked a lost memory.

Up the stairs they went to that gallery. Now, it was Mary's turn to be enchanted. Standing in front of them as they came through the door, a dapper looking youngish man, perhaps 35 or 40, greeted her. Occasionally, Mary was known to flirt with a handsome man...just for fun. This one certainly qualified.

Taking her hand in both of his and looking into her eyes, he said, "Bonjour Mademoiselle, comment puis-je vous être utile?" (Hello Miss, how can I help you?). This was said only to her. He did not even glance at Tom. Then he lowered his head as he raised her hand and kissed it! Ugh!

Out of the corner of her eye, Mary saw Tom's jaw muscles tighten.

Not even trying to say it in French, as Mary wrenched her hand from this guy, she said, "Do you speak English?"

"Why of course, Mademoiselle."

"Okay, look" ...not hiding her increasing disgust for this fellow,..."I am not a Mademoiselle...I am a Madame. This big, handsome fellow with me is my husband. Do you follow me?"

Glancing at Tom and pursing his lips as his eyes trailed up and down Tom, he replied, "Ah, so this old fellow is your husband. Forgive me for thinking he was your father." Tom's hands formed fists.

"We came to your shop to show you some pictures of a painting we think was painted by the French writer Colette and to ask you if you have ever seen anything like this that she may have painted?"

"Ah, yes, Mademoiselle" ...looking at Tom with a smirk..."I mean Madame. Let me take a look."

Tom reluctantly gave the pictures to Mary to show the man. He looked them over and then said.

"I am sorry Mademoi...Madame..." turning to Tom..."et monsieur, I have seen nothing like this. However, I am only temporarily standing in for my friend who is the owner of this gallery. You see I am a clerk at the clothing store down the hallway. The gallery owner will not be back until 6:00 pm. I am sorry."

Mary knew she needed to rush Tom out of the shop as quickly as possible. Although he had a reasonably long fuse, it was burned to the end. She herself wanted to kick this dude in the balls.

"Merci!" she said, grabbed Tom's hand, and pulled him from the store. "Ugh!" she said loudly enough for bystanders to turn. "Let's get out of this place. Between your little cute friends earlier and this guy, Paris is leaving a bad taste in my mouth!" Tom couldn't agree more, though the first shop had been somewhat fun. He would never confess that to her, though. Still, she knew him well enough to know it.

CHAPTER 10
BOOK 3

The young woman with the touch-the-floor slit skirt wheeled around the flare of her skirt rising high on her hip, revealing much of the slender female legs. She said to her assistant in French, "Marguerite, I have to leave. Something important has come up. You will have to close the gallery alone tonight."

Marguerite, with the pout on lips that drove Louise-Francis crazy, "Mais pourquoi, Chéri? Ça veut dire qu'on n'ira pas vampiriser ce soir? Ne vais-je pas t'embrasser la chatte en extase? Pas brouter ton cresson? (But why Cheri? Does this mean we will not go vamping tonight? Will I not kiss your pussy into ecstasy? Not graze your watercress?) The lower lip protruded more on the young woman's face. A look of sadness and seduction.

Louise-Francis, whose name came from her grandfather's stories about the two actresses that he had "seduced" in the early years of talking pictures, looked wantonly and tempted, but instead grabbed her coat and headed for the door. "Peut-être un peu plus tard! Je vais vous appeler! J'aimerais que! Merci! (Maybe a little later! I will call you! I would like to! Thanks!) Out the door she went almost at a run.

"Putain de chatte!" (Fuckin' cunt!) Marguerite said under her voice. "Elle devra d'abord me manger ce soir!" (She will have to eat me first tonight!) "Tant pis! D'ici là je trouverai un penis a chevaucher! Elle peut avoir les restes!" (Oh, well! Till then I'll find a penis to ride! She can have the leftovers!) With that she went over to the desk, pulled out the chair, sat down, hiked her short dress up well on her thighs, and placed her hand down below. "Merde, si quelqu'un entre dans cette satanée galerie, il peut juste me regarder descendre!" (Hell, if someone comes into the damn gallery they can just watch me get off!) Her fingers went to work.

As Marguerite was doing that with herself in the gallery, Louise-Francis hailed a cab. It took the young woman to the large apartment that he provided for her as he similarly did the money to ensure she had the gallery in the Le Louvre des Antiquaires. He, the great grandson of one of the two men that her grandfather had wanted to entertain at the castle when all hell broke out. She had heard the stories and how her grandfather was almost disinherited...and almost could never have children. Surgery saved that. Grandfather had not almost been disinherited for what he had attempted to do, they, all the family males and some of the women too, had enjoyed similar episodes at the castle. Over time, the young ones like Louise-Francis had heard stories of the castle "fun". That particular one had turned out so badly that great grandfather had been quite upset at what had happened to the castle. Her grandfather's and father's inheritance had gone to the repairs leaving future generations, herself, to do what she did now. Live off her lover's...kindness.

The man to whom she was placing the phone was about the same age as her own father. Perhaps five or ten years older. Hell, who can tell when they get to be that age. He, at least, could still rise to the occasion. And the occasional tryst was enough to keep him happy and her in the lifestyle she deserved. He wasn't a great love. She actually preferred the likes of Marguerite, or Marguerite and one of the young men they often shared. Still, she put up with him. What she was about to tell him might actually mean more gifts. A girl can always use more.

The call from the three bedroom apartment on the 4th floor of the elegant old building in the 16th arrondissement went to his private cell phone in New York City. She looked out the large floor to ceiling French doors of "her apartment" at the lights on the Arc de Triomphe. An apartment on the end of Avenue Victor Hugo as it merged into the traffic circle of the Etoile was a real find. Tres belle! He spared no expense for her. She was good at what she did and she knew it.

The call was instantly picked up, a welcomed surprise to him. He was bored and lonely...though his wife was in the bedroom reading or watching TV after her long hard day of...martinis. Thinking to himself that he should take a trip to Paris anyway to check in on the banking situation in Paris at Place Vendome, not far from her gallery. I'll make a reservation at the Paris Ritz as soon as we end this surprise phone call. He smiled at the thought of the pleasures.

Although married with four children, all of them older than her, he had no hesitation to "get it on" with this young thing. That activity he would continue to do until he tired of her, like he had the other young ones before her. At twenty five she still had a few more good years. Perhaps as many as five. He liked them young. It was a hereditary trait thing for sure. He was just like all the men in the family before him.

Into the phone, "Hello, my love! What a wonderful surprise. I was just thinking of you and that I needed a trip to Paris. Perhaps next week! Will you be available for me, my sweet?

In her French accented English, having been born in Paris by her French mother and fathered by an American Hadley, she spoke both languages. Still the French accent was pronounced. After all, she was raised in Paris, educated in Paris and Switzerland, and now lives in Paris. Of course that French accent was most pronounced! He loved it, found it sexy.

She said to him, "That would be wonderful love. I cannot wait. But, first, I must tell you of something that happened in the gallery today. I think you will find it interesting. I hope it is not troubling."

Now his interest was up...and his manhood slowly went down. "What do you mean, sweet one?"

Louise-Francis began telling him about the American couple who were inquiring about whether she had ever seen an oil painting done by the famous French writer Colette.

"The women handed me some photos of the painting. It was a monochrome painting, she told me. Anyway she showed me the signatures on both the front and back of the painting. It looked to me like it could be that of the writer. As I looked at those pictures, I saw something else, though."

"Yes, what was that?"

"I remember a story my grandfather told about the event at the castle that your great grandfather had attended with that actress LuLu. The event where she was the entertainment. But the problem with the Army caused that to fall apart. You know the one...she is one of the actresses my name came from."

"Anyway, looking at the photo, the painting seemed to tell a story. There were odd characters in the painting that reminded me of the story of a lost manuscript LuLu told the castle participants about. Everyone, including your great grandfather, wanted that manuscript. I'm really unsure why? Perhaps because they knew it was written by this great French writer. I really don't remember more of the story than what I've said. But I know my family, your family, and the other one in Chicago or Detroit, I think, all had talked about a missing manuscript related to this event. Anyway, everyone seemed to have an interest in that manuscript. Do they still?"

"Interesting. Go on."

"Do you think it could have been a novel written by Colette? And, then she did this painting of something about the story? The painting is dated 1929 - 31. It just seemed curious from what I remembered hearing as a child and then seeing a painting supposedly done by a famous French writer. Kind of a coincidence. I think I remember hearing the manuscript was in French. What do you think? Did they think it was by Colette? Did they ever find it? If not, could it be valuable? And what about the painting? Could it be worth a bit of money too?"

His interest was more than piqued. That was the time frame of the castle event. He actually, though his voice would not betray him, was a bit shaken by what she had said.

"I'm sure it is nothing." He wanted more information. He needed to share this with the family contact in Detroit. And the true bloodline of the Hadley family...not her side of the bloodline. The story may not have ended as the families had all thought. The future generations of all families having been alerted to be on the lookout.

"By any chance did the couple leave a way to contact them? If you ever come across another painting done by this...you say Colette?" He knew exactly who Colette was but didn't want to let on he knew.

"Yes, he gave me his business card. He works at a University in America. And she wrote a home address and phone number on the back of the card too. I have their contact information. Why?"

"No real reason. I have contacts who collect odd items like paintings done by out-of-the-ordinary people. I thought perhaps I might ask around. Seems like an interesting story. Take a photo of the card and send it to me via email."

"Now, my love, when shall I be in Paris next week and how long will we have? I have to say I am all pent up for you!" Looking down, he saw that was a true statement again. "Perhaps your young friend, the one who works in your gallery, might join us again for one or two nights of fun. What do you think?"

"Sure, why not. I'll ask her. You will have to work hard to satisfy us both. Are you in physical condition and in the mood to do that? It could be quite exhausting!"

"Nothing to fear. I am UP to it. Besides, watching you two have fun together is a great help to my performance!"

The dates were decided. The call ended. Her thinking had been correct. There is something there. Something very suspicious. Perhaps valuable! And, the time with him will be much more enjoyable since he suggested it should be with Marguerite there to enjoy.

Now," she thought, "a quick call to Marguerite to let her know that she could join Marguerite before she mounts someone without me. He or she will just have to share!"

As she was calling Marguerite so as to not be "left behind" ...The man in New York called a number in Detroit. A summit of the families would have to be arranged...sometime soon!While all that was happening with Louise-

CHAPTER 11
BOOK 3

A SMALL MUSTACHED MAURICE CHEVALIER DELIVERS AN ADDRESS

Francis and the man in New York, fortunately, it was now time to go to the Arcade Colette to visit with the, hopefully more gentlemanly, man who was having the Cocteau/Picasso show.

He was there alone. A small man of about 5 foot 5 and in a dark winter suit with a silk cravat of multi colors around his throat. He looked like an older, smaller version of a mustached Maurice Chevalier. The smile on his face, bright!

In French, he welcomed them into his gallery. It didn't take long for all three parties to understand, those that spoke English spoke little French. He, that spoke French...spoke no English. This was going to be a challenge. As best Mary and Tom could do, working as a team, they tried to cobble together enough French mixed with English to tell the gentleman about the mystery they were on. He kindly nodded, tried to understand...it was failing. Then it happened. Tom pulled the photos out of his "spy-passport pouch" and handed them to the man.

He studied them. Studied them some more. His eyes were bright with a glint of pure interest and intrigue. He particularly studied the oil painting signature on the front. He then said, "Je suis désolé de dire que je n'ai jamais vu ses signatures à la peinture. J'ai bien sûr vu sa signature à l'encre et au crayon. Les signatures en peinture sont très différentes." Mary and Tom pieced together what he was saying, "I am sorry to say I have never seen her signatures in oil paint. I have, of course, seen her signature in ink and pencil. Signatures in paint are much different."

Reluctantly, he handed the photos back to Tom with a purse of his lips and the familiar French shoulder shrug. This shrug with a simultaneous shaking slowly of his head and now a small frown intended to convey, "I am sorry I am of no help."

The three stood there for a few moments. Tom could tell Mary's mind was at work. She was trying to decide if she would and should share with him the one other hidden piece…one of the last photos Tom had in his pouch… a particular photo with all of the names of the people painting together in St-Tropez. She decided and whispered to Tom. He looked into her eyes and said, "You sure?" She replied, "Yes, but just the one."

Tom opened the pouch yet again. Searched among the other pictures and pulled out the one. He looked at Mary one more time. She nodded her head yes. He handed the photo to the gentleman.

The old Maurice Chevalier figure's eyes opened wide in amazement. His smile became larger. He stammered, "C'est incroyable! Incroyable!" "Je pense que tu as trouvé un vrai trésor, un trésor si d'une grande importance pour l'histoire de Colette! (I think you have found a true treasure! A treasure of great importance to the story of Colette.)

Mary and Tom smiled at each other as the old gentleman took each of their hands and shook them wildly with great pleasure. Pleasure for himself for being included in the discovery story. But also grand pleasure for the understanding of the full talent of a treasure of France…Colette!

Mary now tried her best attempt at French, filled with starts and stops but finally pieced together and asked, "Savez-vous connaître une personne experte avec qui nous pourrions parler de Colette? (Do you know an expert person with whom we could talk about Colette?)

Without answering, the old man pulled out a piece of small three by five card and wrote:

Madame Anne de Jouvenel

01 47XX XX XX

XX Rue SXXXX DXXXXXXXX

7500X Paris

Mary looked at Tom and he could tell she was thinking something...but what?

Just then, two couples entered the small gallery space. Mary turned to the old man, "Merci Monsieur. Tu as été très gentil et serviable. Merci. Bonsoir." (Thank you, Monsieur. You have been very kind and helpful. Thank you. Good evening.)

"Bonsoir Madame et Monsieur. Ça a été mon plaisir. Bonne chance et bon voyage." (Good evening, Madame and Monsieur. It has been my pleasure. Good luck and safe journey.)

Exiting the gallery Mary stopped them in the covered walkway. "What is it, doll? What are you thinking?"

"Angel, this is our last night in Paris. I know it is after 6 pm now. But, we have this address. I think we should head over there and try to see this person. For some reason the name rings a bell with me. What do you say? Are you up to continuing the adventure? We can grab a late dinner somewhere and pack later. Up for it?"

Tom looked out from under the portico. It was raining pretty steady, for rain in Paris. It was also quite windy and cold. He looked at her and the anxious face. "Are you sure you want to do this?"

"Hell yes!" and Mary hardly ever used profanity. "We are on an adventure of our lives. Let's see it through!"

CHAPTER 12
BOOK 3

Out of the Palais Royals they walked west on rue de Rivoli a short distance to the Galeries du Carrousel du Louvre. Although the wind was blowing hard out of the northeast, it felt as if the rain was coming down on them from the front no matter which way they turned. They turned left through the tunnel opening under the Louvre and headed south around the Place du Carrousel and across out the other side of the Louvre of the equivalent tunnel on the south side.

Once out on the Quai François Mitterrand, they had a choice to make. They could stay on the east side of the Seine, somewhat protected by the wall around the Louvre from the wind, and cross the Seine to the west at Pont Royal, or they could cross now at Pont du Carrousel and face more exposure to the wind. Choosing to stay in the protection of the wall, they opted for the Pont Royal bridge crossing.

Midway across the Pont Royal Bridge, it happened. A huge wind hit, this time from the west, and sailed Tom's original French beret hat off the bridge and into the cold Seine waters 27 meters below. A premonition of another "accidental" occurrence, which would happen in 2019 at exactly the same spot on the bridge. The hat had been purchased on their marriage-honeymoon trip in 2001. It was the first of the three French berets that Tom would own in the 2000s. Both looking over the stone rail at the disappearing beret in the cold waters below, they continued to just stare for a moment. Shoulder shrugs and "Oh, wells" and off they trudged some more. Tom's head, much more exposed to the cold winds. Mary had a warm wool headband and wool sock-cap on her head. She looked at him for a moment and thought, "should I"...thought some more and said, "He will be okay." Off they went.

Now, Paris winter rains are an interesting breed. You feel like you are being hit by tiny ice pellets, but they are actually just very cold little raindrops. The speed and intensity of the feeling of them hitting you is greatly increased in a high wind, as it was this night. Though the rain feels like it should be freezing on the sidewalk and street as it does in the United States, it hardly ever does this in Paris. In fact, even when it snows, it hardly ever stays down long enough for the need of it to be plowed or even salted.

Turning left once over the Seine, they turned right heading west on Quai Anatole France. Walking past the Musée d'Orsay, in their minds, a much more enjoyable and friendly museum than the Louvre...with Impressionist paintings much more to their liking. Just past the museum, the Quai Anatole France turns slightly left and becomes Quai d'Orsay. With heavier winds from the north at the Pont Alexandre III and the opening into the Esplanade des Invalides, they turned south and entered the large green space. After a couple of hundred yards in the exact center of the esplanade, they came upon the street they needed in order to find the address on the three by five card given a very cold and wet hour ago.

Heading west again, they began looking for the street building numbers. A little more than three streets further, they found it...but didn't. A new mystery began. There was no number XX!

As they looked and looked for a sign of the number, a gentleman on a ladder repairing a door saw them. The door he was repairing had been damaged in the storm. He watched them curiously!

Looking at how the big door was having been pulled from its hinges, no wonder, Mary thought, Tom's beret was a goner. The man continued to study the scraggly, completely soaked couple looking and looking for something. He stepped down from the ladder and in Spanish said, "Pardon me Madame and Monsieur. Do you need some help finding something?"
Latin and French were enough for Mary to figure out what he was asking. Without showing him the name on the three-by-five card, keeping that part of the card covered with her hand, she showed him the address.

Again in Spanish and pointing to the door to the building, he said, "It is here. This is the building. She lives on the third floor." Taking Mary by the hand with Tom following, he led them up the stairs and pointed to the door on the right. With that, he went back down to join a companion to finish the work on the damaged door.

Shoulder shrugs to each other and Tom's "Nothing ventured, nothing gained." Mary rang the doorbell.

A few moments later, the door slowly opened and Mary and Tom were greeted by a smiling, sweet, charming, lovely, and extremely petite elderly French woman. She may have been close to five feet tall if she had really high heels. The top of her head barely reached the center of Tom's chest on his six-foot frame. She spoke no English.

Mary did her best to try to explain what the two rat-soaked strange American couple were doing. She showed the lady the pictures. The French woman's eyes brightened, and she invited the soaking wet couple into her beautiful apartment filled with old antique furniture, Persian carpets, and oil paintings on every wall. It looked like Mary and Tom's home in Rockhill furnishings...only they were in this lovely sweet French woman's apartment instead!

The lovely woman went to a small antique leather-top note table and removed a piece of stationery, an envelope, and a pen. Through the still-open door, she pointed at the other door down the hallway and explained, "Elle y habite. Elle est Américaine. Elle est à l'église américaine ce soir pour la musique."

Mary turned to Tom. "I think she says the person we are after lives in the apartment down the hall. She is an American, and she is at an English church for music tonight."

Thanking the woman, Tom took the notepaper and pen and began to write :

1/18/2005

Dear Madame,

We were given your name by the gentleman in the Galerie Arcade Colette.
We have a painting we believe was painted by Colette.
We will try to call you or reach you by letter soon.

Sincerely,

Tom & Mary Martz

Unfortunately, we leave for the USA tomorrow. Thank you.

————————-

Then, Tom slipped the note and one of his UNC Charlotte business cards on which he had written their home phone number into the envelope.

A quick "bonsoir" to each and the Martzs left the nice woman's apartment.

Just as Tom bent down on one knee and was about to slip the note under the correct apartment door, as they stood between the two doors at the top of the stairs…

…Anne came up the stairs…60ish with a motorcycle helmet in hand!

"Bonjour, Madame et Monsieur. Puis-je vous être utile? C'est mon appartement.
(Hello Madame and Monsieur. May I be of assistance to you? This is my apartment.)

Tom rose as Mary responded in English. "You are an American, yes? I'm afraid neither of us speak much French. Could we speak in English?"

With a smile and bright glint in her eye, Anne replied, "But of course, my dears. Now what is it you would like to talk about?"

"We were given your name and address by the owner of Galerie Arcade Colette to talk with you. You see we have uncovered what we believe is a painting that was done by the French writer Colette."

Slightly interrupting, the woman replied, "The gallery owner gave you my address?"

"Yes, here it is on this card he gave us." Anne took the card. Read it and started to laugh.

"I'm sorry, my dears. You have stumbled upon the wrong Anne. You see I am Anne Kimball, from Bar Harbor, Maine. You are looking for a French woman by the name of Anne de Jouvenel. I'm so sorry!"

"Oh, rats!" was Tom's reply. "We wished to share the pictures we have of our painting with her to see if she could verify it is Colette's. We were told she is an expert on Colette."

Anne Kimball continued to chuckle and said, "I believe she lives in an apartment above the art shop across the alleyway on the main street. I think you must enter from the store front area. Let's go check it out." Handing the photos back to Tom, she added, "This is very un-French. But I am having great fun. Let's go on this adventure together."

Taking Mary by the hand, she headed down the stairs. Tom, close behind. Once outside, they passed the two men continuing to work on the door. Out to the main street and turning to the first store front, the art shop, they looked for another door. Nothing. Anne Kimball led them inside and proceeded to tell the store clerk that they were trying to find a person who lived in the apartment above the shop. It was explained to Anne the entrance to the apartments was off the same alleyway as was Anne's doorway...only across the alleyway.

Out they headed and sure enough there was a doorway and a callbox with the names of the people in each of the apartments. Anne tried to work it with no success.

The second work man came over to the three and in Spanish asked if he could help. In perfect Spanish, Anne Kemball told him what they were doing. Anne translated his reply for the Martz couple, "My wife is Anne de Jouvenel's housekeeper. I will call my wife and she will arrange for you to meet with Madame de Jouvenel. My wife is in our apartment at the moment. It will take her a few moments to get here." He pulled out his cell phone.

Sure enough, a not-too-happy Spanish woman appeared and said a few things to the gentleman. He replied. A couple more words of conversation between them as Anne Kimball who understood every word chuckled.

The Spanish women went to the call box, spoke quietly. Nodding, her head turned to the four others and said, "Madame de Jouvenel is on her way down to meet with you." She then said something to her husband and hastily left the scene just as the door opened.

Out came a woman as Mary explained to her friends later that just "dripped' in old French style!

"Pardonnez-moi d'avoir à vous rencontrer entre deux portes. J'ai peur de rentrer chez moi et de devoir."

Anne Kimball translated: Pardon me for having to meet you BETWEEN TWO DOORS. I am afraid I just returned home and must leave again. How can I help you?

Anne Kimball explained the painting and the mystery and asked Tom to show the pictures to Madame de Jouvenel. He pulled from his spy pouch all the pictures except for the ones of the back of the stretcher and gave them to Anne Kimball. American Anne then gave them to French Anne.

Anne de Jouvenel looked and looked at the photos. Eyebrows raised from time to time but then says, "No, I am certain she did not paint. I have never seen a painting by her. It must be some other Colette." Disappointment!

The four spent a little more time together thanking her for spending the time and looking at the photos. As they began to part, Tom reached into his wallet and took out his business card. He handed it to Anne Kimball and asked her to give it to Anne de Jouvenel just in case she thought of something. When that was done, Madame de Jouvenel departed the group and went back into the apartment.

Tom took Mary's hand and they started to say thank you to Anne Kimball but were stopped.

Anne Kimball said, "I'm not so sure there isn't something here. This is an area I'm interested in. You know the woman you just met is Colette's second husband, Henry de Jouvenel's, granddaughter by another wife. Colette and he were only married for a short time. He divorced Colette because she was having an affair with her 16-year-old stepson while she and Henry were married. This woman, Anne de Jouvenel, is his son's daughter. There is no love lost between the family and Colette. All of Colette's estate went to her third husband. She may not really know if this is done by Colette. Send me copies of the pictures. I run into these people all the time. This is a mystery I would like to be involved with!"

Then Anne Kimball added the final arrow to the target, "Ask yourselves, why would someone who could paint like this artist did, sign only 'Colette' at that time...unless she really was...Colette!. There was no other Colette, only she."

"Let's stay in touch!"

Now this could have been the end to their adventure, solving the mystery. They had some proof now, though circumstantial, that Colette had indeed painted the painting. There were the pencil notes on the stretcher. There was the fact that so many of the gallery owners, including the old man at Palais Royal that said, "you may have something," and even the slight hesitation of the step-granddaughter of Colette's, Anne de Jouvenel, before she said, "No, Colette never painted." Most importantly, there was Anne Kimball assisting that she thought there was something as she "came in contact with these people all the time." Now what did she mean by that?

Disappointment? Not really. Challenge? Yes, this experience now inspired them to continue to research. Surely somewhere there was real proof that Colette painted, whether she actually did this painting or not.

That night over dinner at the small restaurant near the hotel, just before packing for the trip home, they agreed. They would heighten the investigation. They had no idea of the turn of events that would soon happen.

Elsewhere, a summit was arranged that night. It took place later that year in New York. All three family senior representatives were there. Its outcome launched a series of multiple eyes watching Tom and Mary over the next several years... those efforts were coordinated just to make sure. Over time other calls were made. More meetings took place with reports and updates. Stealing the painting had been discussed but decided it may cause unnecessary alert. Seventeen years later after that first summit, action was needed...and it took place. The action necessary was triggered by the publication of a book... and the outline and writing of a second.

CHAPTER 13
BOOK 3

Upon the return home to Rock Hill, South Carolina, in 2005, the Colette search continued. Things happened very quickly.

Mary, investigating the interesting woman Anne Kimball, found out she lived half the year in Bar Harbor, Maine, as she had told them. She lived the winter weather in Paris, France, at her second home, the apartment where the Martzs met her. That was only the beginning of what Mary learned.

Anne Kimball had been the former Provost of Lenoir-Rhyne University in Hickory, North Carolina, a small private university in North Carolina. Another interesting coincidence to the chance meeting in Paris of three people with some connection to the same State, North Carolina. What was the biggest coincidence of that chance meeting turned out to be incredible. Anne's academic expertise and studies was...French and German writers of the late 1800's through the mid-1900s. She was an expert on Colette, Cocteau, and others. She had published several books on writers of that era.

Mary insisted that they write to Anne Kimball to thank her for her help. That first email they wrote to Anne simply said,

> Friday, January 21, 2005 10:58 AM
> Subject: Hello from Charlotte and thank you!

> Hi Anne,

> Mary and I arrived back in Charlotte at 12:30 am yesterday. I am at UNC Charlotte today.

We wanted to drop you a quick email to again thank you for your help on our mystery search of the "Colette" painting. We are having copies made of the photographs for you and will send them out in the next few days.

Welcome to the Mystery Search!

All the way home on the airplane we talked about the great adventure and how wonderful it was to run into your neighbor and you. Who knows where this will lead us. At worst, it has already led us to some new friends. For that we are very grateful.

Mary and I promise to keep you updated in letters and emails as we find out more from this side of the Atlantic. We hope your connections may help from that side.

Thank you again for what you did Tuesday night for two additional crazy Americans.

Next, a first class letter to Anne Kimball followed at the end of January with an enclosed letter to Anne de Jouvenel. The note to Anne Kimball asked if she would personally deliver the note to Anne de Jouvenel. The letter to Anne de Jouvenel was translated from English to French by their friend and Tom's colleague Joel Gallegos, head of International Programs at UNC Charlotte. Their note simply said:

Chère Madame de Jouvenel,

Merci de nous recevoir à la soirée du 18 Janvier 2005.
Nous sommes des Américains avec les photographies de la peinture de Colette.
Nous apprécions sincèrement le temps que vous avez passé avec nous.
Merci beaucoup,

Thomas et Mary Martz
4269 Walnut Ridge drive
Rock Hill, South Carolina, USA

Tom's business card was also enclosed.

Dear Madame de Jouvenel,

Thank you for meeting with us the evening of 18 January 2005.
We are the Americans with the photographs of the "Colette" painting.
We sincerely appreciate the time you spent talking with us.
Thank you very much,

Thomas and Mary Martz

————————————

Then one day Tom on his computer at UNC Charlotte had a surprise. They received an email from Madame Anne de Jouvenel. The email said,

> Cher Monsieur et chère Madame Martz,
>
> Je vous remercie de votre petit mot que je ne méritais pas car je vous ai reçus vraiment entre deux portes!
> C'est quand même une chance de vous avoir rencontrés car je venais de rentrer et devais repartir très vite!
> Je voudrais savoir où vous avez trouvé cette peinture car la mention "by Colette" est bien curieuse.
> Cependant je confirme que ce n'est pas du tout sa signature et que le mélange "by" et Colette peut indiquer n'importe quelle Colette qui est un prénom répandu.
>
> Bien a vous,
>
> Anne de Jouvenel

————————————

Dear Mr and dear Mrs Martz,

I thank you for your small word which I did not deserve because I really received you BETWEEN TWO DOORS!
It was nevertheless a chance to have met to you because I had just returned and was to set out again quickly!

I would like to know where you found this painting because the mention "by Colette" is quite curious.

However, I confirm that it is not at all its signature and that the mixture "by" and Colette can indicate any Colette who is a widespread first name.

But, where did you find this painting?

Yours sincerely,
Anne de Jouvenel

——————————

CHAPTER 14
BOOK 3

The greeting party for Tom was waiting on the front porch steps as the small red SUV pulled into the drive. Both the smiling yellow lab and the beautiful, smiling woman, known as Mary Beth to some and Marie, MB, Mary, and Biz to him, walked over to him too. With the usual deep kiss, hug, and hand around her waist, they strolled towards the house porch steps.

"Wait 'til I tell you what I found today!" she said. "More proof that Colette painted. Wait 'til you see the email and the two volume book that arrived today from Better World Books!" He could tell she was excited. Her big smile always told him so.

"Yeah, well I'll see your books and email and raise you one email!"

Mary looked at Tom, shook her head when he said such crazy things of which she had no clue, and said, "What does that mean?"

"Just, I received an email from France today...that well...is kind of interesting to say the least."

"And I got an email from France today too. And it is also interesting. But the books I have downright state what we want to hear. Dinner first or should we dig into our reveals to each other?"

"Reveals. You first." They entered the house and sat down together on the living room couch. A hand-me-down from Mary's parents that she and babysitter Rita had covered with a handmade cream-colored linen covering. Duke, the Lab, joined them at Mary's feet.

"Okay, remember I sent a letter to La Société des Amis de Colette? Telling them about the painting and asking them if they knew if Colette painted. Well, I received an email from Gerard Bonal today. He is the President de la société des Amis de Colette."

"Really? What does he think? What did the email say?"

"Thank God for computer translating programs. I had to copy everything from his email to the translation program. Here is what his note says." She began reading it to Tom.

> From: Gerard Bonal
> Sent: Thursday, February 10, 2005 12:28 PM
> To: Mary and Tom Martz
>
> Madam, Sir,
> We cannot inform you without to have seen the table in question. But we doubt much that it was painted by Colette.
> Indeed, one knows of it only pastels carried out during the First World War. In addition its house (which it sold in 1924) was not close to Honfleur but in Brittany, close to Saint-Malo.
> In 1929 - 31 date that you indicate to us, Colette had a house with Saint-Tropez, in Provence, i.e., very far from Honfleur.
> What could perhaps light your research would be to see whether the signature of the table and the inscription with the back are well of the hand of Colette.
> Afflicted not to be able to say some to you more.
> Well sincerely,
>
> Gerard Bonal President of the Company of Friends of Colette

"Well, I'm not sure why this excites you? It is sorta a downer if you ask me. He states that he doubts that it is painted by Colette. He says she did not live near Honfleur. And, he tells us that she could not have painted it in Honfleur as the dates the painting says because she lives in Saint-Tropez, Provence."

"Buddy boy, you are not listening correctly."

"Uh?"

"What he says is, First, that he cannot verify the painting without seeing it in person and looking at the signatures to compare them with others. Second, that the home that she lived in was in Saint- Malo, Brittany, and she was not living in Honfleur. But we knew that. And I did a map search. Saint-Malo is only 142 miles from Honfleur. Hardly a 'long way' from each other. Lastly, and this is the best part because the stretcher already told us this fact, she painted this painting in 1929-31 in Saint-Tropez with Marquet, Picasso, Matisse, and Cocteau. He didn't see those pictures!"

"Hmm, you're right. This is not a downer at all. It kinda adds credibility. He tells us she did pastels during World War One. We both know if you can do pastels with any ability that oil painting is a sure thing. Wow, you're right. This is good news!"

Tom added, "Do you think we should go back to Paris to meet with this fellow and take the painting with us this time?"

"Possibly. Let me share the other good news. I received this two-volume set of books from Better World Books today. It is written by two co-authors, Fernande Gontier and Claude Francis."

"And?"

"And, in the book Fernarnde Gontier wrote that Colette was an amateur painter in addition to being a writer, actress, and dancer! She also says that Colette gave some of her paintings away to friends. Others she stored in a home in Verdun, France, which was destroyed by bombs in World War Two! And get this! One of the friends she gave paintings to was a close, and I mean 'intimately' close friend of Colette's. That person, Princess Edmond de Polignac, also known as Winnaretta Singer! The Singer Sewing heiress! And, she had an estate.... da,da,da ta da! New York State!"

"You're kidding?! Really? You found this for sure in print in these books?"

"Yep-a-roonie-o! Right here!" she said, tapping the two books.

"So that's my presentation buddy-boy, buddy-boy! Whatcha got that can top that? Huh?"

"Well, that is a challenge. Perhaps, not topping that. But, certainly adding to it. Look at what I received from Anne de Jouvenel today."

Mary read the email that Tom had printed off and especially reread the last sentence, "But, where did you find this painting?!"

"Right," Tom replied. "She knows it is real! She won't say it for sure. She probably thinks we are trying to cheat or scam her in some way. Perhaps ask her for big money to return it to her or something."

"Okay, let's not be hasty, but I think the proper thing to do is to get it back into the hands of the family...and I mean probably her step-granddaughter's family. Colette only had one child. And, this is hard to believe with Colette's bisexuality but the daughter was a lesbian and not appreciated by Colette and the de Jouvenels!"

"Kind of a tough call what to do with it. At least we need to get it back to the Friends of Colette's or to the French Government. Don't you think so?" Mary asked.

"I think so. Probably the French Government for them to decide what to do with it. I bet what happened is either an American soldier discovered the painting in the bombed-out house in Verdun or the painting was from the Estate of the Princess de Polignac's in New York. Either way, the French Government should decide, in my mind."

"Right. I agree. Let's have dinner and we can keep up the search and make a final decision in the next few weeks or months." She paused looking at her Tom. "Something else is on your mind. I can tell."

"Yeah. I still wonder about the notes on the stretcher referring to assassination dates and code initials. It has to mean something. I worry that it not only is 'a can of worms' but it also spells danger!" Mary felt a cold chill up her spine but said nothing. They ate dinner, both thinking about Tom's last thought.

CHAPTER 15
BOOK 3

As the search heated up, so did life! First, a successful fundraising campaign finished that year in 2005. It led to another major University seeking to hire Tom from UNC Charlotte. He and the Chancellor, James Woodward, had been a good team. He really didn't want to work with anyone else.

The other University had approached the Chancellor three years before asking for permission to talk with Tom. In the south, the code of ethics at Universities is you ask the current university where a person is employed for permission to approach that candidate. Tom had no idea of this earlier attempt. Now, following the campaign, the other University approached him directly. He probably would not have taken the position with them except for two reasons.

The first reason is his good friend, mentor, and campaign partner Chancellor Woodward had announced his retirement. Tom would have to work with a new chancellor. Perhaps this would be the right time to leave. The rumor was that it is tradition in the south for members of an administrative team of one leader to give their resignation to the new leader. In that way the new leader could hire his or her own team. You might be hired again or not. Whether that was true was unclear but it made the offer from the next University inviting to at least investigate.

The second reason, go where the money is! After this next move he and Mary agreed they would never again do.

"They," in Chancellor Woodward's words, "will throw money at you! It will be hard for you to turn it down. But do you really want to go to the 'Deep South'?"

"Are you kidding, Jim? I already work in the south at UNC Charlotte and live in Rock Hill, South Carolina."

"Not the same, Tom," Jim warned. He had been right on both accounts. The University approached Tom, throwing money his way. The President of the University actually flew to Charlotte on a private plane to meet with Tom after Tom at first turned that University down.

He and Mary moved to the next location and though the Colette painting hung on the wall in the walnut office of their new home, it was a bit removed. Over time, the mystery was set aside and if not forgotten, put on long-term hold.

Two years later, Tom's dream job was offered at his alma mater. Unfortunately, he was hired by one president, a really good man. An African American President in a state not used to an African American leader for one of its two major public universities. Under undue pressure, that President retired and a politically driven person took office as the new President. He had worked hard to undermine the previous President and lobby for the job. Not quite three years following that move, another move was forced on Tom and Mary.

The new move was to Husson University in Bangor, Maine, in 2010, a great "right size" private University. Life was back on track. They fell in love with the new University. The President, Bob Clark, was a good man whose dedication to the institution and its students you could believe in. The city of Bangor, though a bit "gritty," was filled with good hard working Mainers. The house they found was right up there in their hearts with the one in Rock Hill on Walnut Ridge Drive. Best of all, Ken and Deb, their neighbors next door, were like a brother and sister to Tom and Mary.

Tom and Mary began thinking about the mystery once again. And, coincidentally, they were now living in the same state where Anne Kimball lived half the year. It was time to reconnect with her. Just as they were ready to do so, more life happened.

Two of their daughters, Sara and Catherine, became pregnant at the same time. One living in Kansas City and the other in the White River Junction area of Vermont. Not a problem. Mom has a bag, can travel. And so when the girls were due for delivery, about a month or two apart in 2012, Mary headed out first to assist Sara and follow up with helping Catherine.

Then another big complication hit, and it hit Tom hard! He went on what was termed, "Tom and Paul's Big Adventure." A trip to Korea, Thailand, and Japan to recruit students for the University and meet with Husson University's Asian Alumni.

Everything went well. The Alumni saw Paul Husson, the University's founder's son, as having been their surrogate father while they were in college so far from home. He stayed in contact with all of them. The student recruiting side was equally as successful and a significant partnership was formed with a sister University in Seoul, Korea.

In a taxi cab in Chiang Mai, Thailand, trouble hit in the form of a lone mosquito's bite of Tom just below the left shoulder. He remembered it well. Sixteen days later to the day, dengue fever hit full on. The first doctor thought he had strep throat. He prescribed alternating aspirin and Ibuprofen. Exactly the wrong things to prescribe to someone with dengue!

There were two fortunate connected actions that helped Tom. First, he described to his son-in-law Jason, a pathologist at Dartmouth Hitchcock Medical Center, how he was feeling. Jason was suspicious right away. He asked Tom about what test the doctor had prescribed. "Did you tell them you had just been to Korea, Thailand, and Japan?" When Jason received Tom's answers that he had told them about the trip but no tests other than strep was performed, Jason said, "Dad, I think you have dengue fever. Stay away from aspirin and Ibuprofen. Both thin the blood. I'm going to make a call and you will hear back from me or someone else shortly."

Jason called a doctor friend in Bangor. Jason's quick call to him resulted in the Infectious Disease Center at Eastern Maine Medical Center calling Tom and telling him they wanted to see him right away. The result was not confirmed for several days but the doctor was concerned. She said he should be hospitalized. Finally, after a long discussion, not happy with the outcome, the physician relented to Tom's request to let him go home. In hindsight, he feels he made the decision while not thinking clearly...truly under the cloud of dengue.

Armed with the doctor's pager number, cell phone, and home phone number, he was allowed to leave the hospital but not before she spoke with Mary by phone. She ordered Mary to stay away from the house. Stay where she was. They were not sure this was not an airborne disease.

Tom was ordered into home quarantine. He stayed that way for nearly two months. His colleagues from the University dropped off food for him on the front porch almost daily, though he had very little appetite and much of it was eventually tossed.

Full recovery did not happen until mid-fall 2012.

The next big punch to Mary and Tom was landed in December of 2013. This one hit them with a thud!

Mary was diagnosed with breast cancer, and her type was non-curable. Their lives were shaken. Any thoughts of any searches other than the best treatments possible went out the window. They ended up buying a home in West Lebanon, New Hampshire, to be close to Catherine, Jason, and two grandchildren, Alice and Jude. Tom began working towards full retirement.

Things were okay for a few years, nearly six in all. Tom and Mary, not thinking about the mystery search, did go to Paris twice during that time. Once in August 2015 to meet up with Mary's baby sister (early 60s in age) and her partner/boyfriend, Henry. The four had great fun.

Then in 2019, following an outstanding Pet Scan, Tom surprised Mary with a suggestion of a trip to Paris. Mary said "Yes!" In September 2019, Mary and

Tom headed back to Paris for an adventure that became the first of the several novels they would pen, "The White Light Within," based on their true travel adventure.

2020 brought hard times in so many ways, not just for Mary and Tom, but for the United States and the World...Covid 19 hit! Long, slow, back road drives through New Hampshire and Vermont became their entertainment.

On October 20, 2020, Mary, now in hospice care by Tom at their home, made three requests of him.

They were sitting in their bedroom, Mary sitting up in the bed with Tom at her side in a wicker chair. It was a wonderful evening. He had made what she considered, "the best scrambled eggs ever!" They laughed about someday him finishing a cartoon book on his life that he had found in an old drawing pad in the basement. He had started it in his mid-thirties. He was now approaching 71. Nowadays, it would be called a "graphic novel". To him, it was a "classic comic".

Then his sweetheart hit him with two further requests. Write the first book, "The White Light Within" based on the recent trip. It was about the Russian spy experience based on a Russian gallery owner, her Russian father, an astrophysicist, and several other good characters, mostly female. Mary helped make up the rest of the characters they did not know. The gallery, called 'iSpy Gallery,' was real, like most of the characters and story. Then looking deeply into his eyes she said, "And finish the investigation into the story told in the Colette painting! We need to know the answer. It will be fun. In our hearts, we will be doing this together. Do this with me!" When she said it, he had no idea how deep that statement was.

October 21, 2020, his Mary transitioned...leaving with him the challenges of the last evening. The last challenges they shared together in this world...physically. Mentally, a whole different story!

Paves de rue. Pont Neuf, March 2001
Photo by Mary Martz

CHAPTER 1
BOOK 4

Tom began writing the book "The White Light Within" on January 14, 2021, as Mary had requested. The first draft was finished by October of that year. Four additional drafts later by his two gifted editors, Kali and Amelia, it made its way to a publisher and was now in bookstores.

Mary's second request is currently written and being edited. And so, as he writes, we move into the contemporary time period, and what is happening with Mary and Tom's mystery, "Between Two Doors: In search of Colette".

Throughout his life, several key women have played important roles with Tom. His mother, also Mary E. Martz. His Aunt Jo, acting as a second mother to him as a boy and young man. Tom's good friend and "surrogate mother" Milie Freitas, who 'adopted' him when he worked at UC Berkeley and rented a house from her. And, of course, his own woman, Mary Elizabeth, MB, Mary Beth, Bizz, and to him just plain Mary, doll, babe, and sweetheart!

Two other young women play important roles in his life. They become major characters of the next two books, this one, and the third one he intends to write this year. One of the young women, his former colleague at Husson University and administrative assistant, a volunteer editor of his books, Kali "Roundkick" Anderson McNutt.

The second important lady, Tom's massage therapist, Tammy "Green Hornet" Lynn.

Now to tell Tammy's involvement in the story you need to understand that Tom had long suffered from herniated disks. To try to avoid surgery, he received help from deep tissue massage therapy while living in North Carolina. The massage therapy worked. No surgery.

Tammy started giving Tom massages in 2013. The cause of this treatment began with Tom being prescribed a new magical drug in 1999. The drug was the new cure for everything.... the next aspirin!

Although its primary purpose was to lower cholesterol, medical science didn't know all the wonderful things it could do. Everyone should be on it, they said, even young children! Tom's cholesterol was 160 total at the time,130 HDL and 30 LDL, still a low dose was prescribed. Insurance picked up the cost. Hey, you could save more if you purchased twice the dosage pills and used a pill cutter to cut them. Everything was wonderful! Cheap and safe!

The drug did everything it should do doctors thought until fourteen years out. At the beginning of the fourteenth year, some strange muscle cramping began. The first one was a "Charlie Horse" in the back of his left upper leg. This eventually led to strange muscle cramping everywhere. Transient cramps, never in the same place. It also produced muscle weakness, loosened joints, and other strange physical issues. While the heart and vascular muscles supposedly got stronger, it appeared the connective tissues, tendons, ligaments, and skeletal muscles suffered. Something to do with the mitochondria, he learned.

Fortunately, his Bangor doctor realized what was causing the problems and took him off of the drug. Studies were beginning to be released that told of similar problems in other people. So Tom decided to do what had helped him in the past, find a massage therapist who knew deep tissue massage. The alternative appeared to be a future in a wheelchair. He tried several massage therapists. Some were okay. None were truly successful.

Then one day by chance, he happened to go into a spa on the northside of Bangor. They had a massage therapist, and he made an appointment. That appointment destined him to have someone who saved his life from that wheelchair. He met a young, talented, expert in deep tissue and athletic massage therapy, Tammy "Green Hornet" Lynn.

Kali "Roundkick" Anderson McNutt, Kali Anderson when he met her, came to Husson University as a work study employee. Although Tom had not hired her, he soon saw that this young woman was smart and could do just about anything. What Tom needed was a partner in the office who could cover his shortcomings, specifically spelling and grammar. Having lived in France as a young boy during his formative years, his grammar was all over the place with both languages. No one could tell if he was using French spelling rules or American spelling rules either. He sure didn't know. There was the other big issue too...he was dyslexic!. Kali, a talented writer, researcher, and editor fit his needs. A perfect partner.

During the nearly ten years they worked together, Kali was subjected to the interesting and often humorous stories Tom told. Were they true? They sounded so! As Kali was hearing these stories, so too was Tammy in the massage therapy sessions. Tom talked through them all. Stories of travel. Stories of other Universities and cities. Mystery stories, love stories, spy stories, they heard them all.

Both young women eventually heard the story of a trip to Paris in 2019 that was an intriguing spy-mystery. They both heard about a strange painting and a search that Tom and Mary were on, trying to find if it was painted by a writer named Colette.

In 2021, they both learned Tom was going to write a series of novels in retirement. He shared rough drafts of the first one with both of them. Tammy became a sounding board for all of the stories he would write. Kali volunteered to be his draft editor. He needed both women's talents for sure... and more. He had no clue how much!

CHAPTER 2
BOOK 4

October 2021 found Tom planning a "trial trip" to Paris. Could he make this trip again? Would he even enjoy Paris again without his Mary? Should a 72-year-old man even attempt the trip by himself?

Again, coincidence, synchronicity, or just plain good luck came through. Family friends of his and Mary's, the Munroes, volunteered to accompany him on a trip. James, Kristen, and their three daughters, Gwyn (17), Grace (15), and Tillie (13) upon hearing about his desire to go to Paris again, gladly accepted the challenge to escort Tom. The date was set for June after school ended for the semester. On June 15, 2022, at 5:25 pm, Air France flight 333 departed from Boston Logan International airport for Paris, France. Onboard the flight were Tom, James, Kristin, Gwyn, Grace, and Tillie. Their adventure began...more than the Munroes would realize until a few days after the return flight on Air France Flight 334 on June 26th.

Tom booked the six travers into a wonderful apartment through Airbnb near the Republic. It was a fifth floor walkup with no elevator. The apartment itself was two floors of a small Paris building. The owner of the apartment had renovated it so that there was a glassed-in atrium at the center court of the building. The apartment was just an incredible space with five bedrooms and two baths. It was perfect for a family of five and Tom.

Access to anywhere in Paris was either a good fun walk or a quick metro ride or both. The only downside...temperatures in June were in the mid to upper 90s F and no air conditioner. Fortunately, there were plenty of fans, plenty of breezes at the top floor, and dry air with little humidity, which was odd in Paris. Best of all for Tom, the young women all wanted to help with his bags and kept a careful eye on the old guy. The perfect family to travel with to regain his confidence.

What he did not share with them was his ultimate mission to revisit with an old man about a painting and its artist and her friends. That would happen on the next-to-last day for Tom. The family would also not know until much later what the visit provided for Tom and the turn of fate it delivered to him.

CHAPTER 3
BOOK 4

Kristen had made reservations for the Louvre earlier in the week but had changed them to the last day thinking that a final bit of culture was a good experience for teenage daughters. What could be a better cultural experience than a trip through art history dating back to the beginning of man through to the mid-1800s. Reservations were set for 1:30 pm.

The day began with a slow morning. Tom and James went out to purchase various pastries...more than they could eat. They were men. See something they like...buy it. Tom continued to settle for the pain croissants, but the rest of the troop had a continued choice of pain au chocolat, brioche, religieuse, and more. If you are in Paris...well eat all the pastries you can!

Breakfast finished, they headed off walking to the metro station close by, at the Place de la Bastille. A short ride later, they arrived at the metro station Louvre-Rivoli, found a small cafe nearby, and had lunch. Seems all one does in Paris is walk, eat, and admire the city's beauty. Exactly what Tom and Mary had loved to do. This was what Tom had hoped for. Well, teenage daughters had a few other ideas. So while the men had shared some "Man Time," Kristen and the daughters had shared some "Woman Time"...shopping!

Now it was time for their Louvre reservations. When one has a reservation, one assumes that means you move to the front of the line. And, in fact, you do. You move to the other line at the back. You see, the Louvre is a place that draws huge crowds, even crowds of people buying advanced reservations. Bag checks and several inspections later, you finally make it into the crowds of other art viewers...thousands and thousands of them. Long lines to many of the most viewed pieces of art displays. If you are patient, you can actually move close enough to the painting or sculpture to actually see the artist's brush stroke on the canvas or tool mark in the stone. Not really Tom's experience. He and Mary much preferred the d"Orsay with their style of painting, Impressionist. De l"orangerie for the same but with the incredible works of Monet. The Musée Marmottan was the Martz's favorite. It's an old home owned by Claude Monet's son that had been given to the people of France. It had Claude's own collection of art as well as many of his "Water Lily" pieces...most looking perhaps unfinished but magical just the same.

The youngest daughter, Tillie, and her oldest sister, Gwyn, teamed up and went off on a tour of the Louvre on their own. They had both gained a great deal of independence on the trip and continued to use trips on the metros or walks back to the apartment by themselves to prove it. Tillie only lost one time. It was a bit frightening for her as one would expect for a 13 year old. Her older sister quickly found her. Life was good again.

Grace, a truly gifted young actress, hung around in the museum with her parents. It was nice for Tom to see this. The whole family showed such love and care for each other. There were really never any arguments and compromise was quickly found when different ideas of what was to be done for the day were expressed by the three teenage women.

For Tom, it was the care and concern that they all shared for him that really stood out. However, in the Louvre, it was the perfect time for him to separate himself from the family and see if the old guy could still be independent...and also to follow up on the search he and Mary started some years ago.

Arrangements were made of a location in the Louvre where they would meet in two hours. That arrangement changed later out of a combination of desire and necessity. At that moment, however, the separate grouping set out to explore the musée on their own.

An hour into the separation, it was at the sculpture of Venus de Milo that Tom noticed him. The sculpture created by Alexandros of Antioch in the years between 150 and 125 BC depicts Aphrodite. Should the name actually be "Aphrodite de Milos" instead of Venus de Milo is up for debate. After all, a Greek statue named after a Roman deity is a bit odd. Is she Greek like the sculpture or Roman like the name?

Tom didn't notice him at first. The arm grabbed Tom's arm and what appeared to be a syringe in the man's other arm started moving quickly in the direction of Tom's bicep.

The crowd was dense around the statue and in that moment a woman tripped and fell into the man with the syringe causing him to miss Tom. The needle hit a woman, a rather heavy-set person, in the loose skin of her tricep. She screamed. Tom pulled his arm away and looked the man in the eyes. The face was a rather un-frightening one. However, there was shock and disappointment obviously showing. A face with glasses and straw hat sitting atop a head about 5 feet 8 inches off the ground. Finished pulling his arm from the man's grip, Tom moved as quickly as possible through the crowd away from the arm grabber.

As Tom moved away, he did not see the woman who had been stuck slump to the ground. Patrons of the museum screamed for help. While shocked art viewers tried to aid her, the woman who had bumped the needle stabber apologized to him. As he started to move after Tom, her leg shot out between his legs, tripping him. Quite by coincidence, the woman's husband turned just in time to see what had happened. Then a second accident happened as the husband's right elbow swung hard during his turn and landed directly into the now falling head of the tripped man. The elbow landed squarely to the jaw. The blow rendered the man unconscious with a broken jaw. At the prison infirmary later that day, his jaw was wired shut to repair the broken jaw. For the next several weeks, the man would be eating chicken soup through a straw fitted between the two lost front teeth. Those were lost from the blow. Good news, Interpol knows who he is.

The needle that hit the woman's arm passed through one layer of skin and out another layer of the fatty wrinkled skin. When a small amount of liquid inside the syringe was pushed out through the needle, it sprayed not into the woman's arm but into the surrounding air. None of the liquid entered the woman's body. The syringe was later pulled back out of her arm by the responding EMTs and was sent to the police lab. The substance in the syringe was identified as Gelemium, "Heartbreak Grass". A poison known to be used by Russian contract killers.

After the accident, the husband and wife were able to follow Tom as he raced out of the Louvre. He needed a quiet place to think. The couple found him a few minutes later, sitting by himself on a park bench in the Jardin du Palais Royal. He appeared curiously watching workers install a new type of porta potty "Happee seivies" or "MadamePee," an open air urinal for women and a similar new device for men called "MisterPee". The second one was not nearly as interesting as the first one to Tom. The installation, in preparation for a month of July celebration of the French birthday, Bastille Day, and the ending of the French President's six month stint as President of the Council of the European Union.

 While he watched the workers install the new red utilities for women and plain gray ones for men, the Paris Choir practiced an acapella version of Ravel's "Bolero." The curiosity of the new utilities and the intoxicating sound of the music eased his tension, allowing him to consider what had happened and what to do next.

Not looking to his left, he felt the presence of a woman sit down beside him. Then a man sat to his right. She spoke.

"Beautiful, isn't it? The music, that is. The interesting utilities in front of us are amusing, aren't they?"

Chuckling, he replied, "Doesn't leave much to the imagination, does it?"

"We women had to put up with that with our men for some time. Only fair that it finally happens for women. Don't you think so?"

Tom turned toward her. He knew her from somewhere. She was obviously American. "Do I know you? You look vaguely familiar." Then the man spoke. "Great day for the Louvre, wasn't it? Too bad about the 'accident'. The fellow nearly shot his 'insulin injection' into your arm and not his own. Hope he is not suffering a diabetic reaction for his mistake."

Tom turned to the man, "Fred? Fred Smith?" Turning back to the woman. "Of course...you are Mrs. Smith! Now I remember you! Wait! You have to be kidding? You all are following me again?"

"Yes, Tom, and for good reason," Fred replied. "You would have been assassinated back there at the Louvre. We intercepted the assailant. Let's just say he is out of commission for a rather extended period. He has to have some extensive facial surgery. It will be done in a prison hospital. Those hospitals in France are not known for the best reconstructive surgery. No reason to do anything except utilitarian work. He will be able to eat some solid foods again someday; however, it will have to be cut up in rather small pieces I suspect. You see, he had an unfortunate meeting with my right elbow."

Mrs. Smith chimed in, "But that will not stop the attempts on you, Tom. Your first book uncovered some unpleasant truths about the President of Russia and our former President. Sadly, the book will not be in the bookstores anytime soon, as you were promised by the publishers this year. It will be held off until after the election in 2024."

"What! Why?!"

Mr. Smith took over, "Because it reveals some national security issues that cannot be revealed at this time. Sorry. The US Government, specifically the CIA, FBI, and NSA have purchased all of the first printing....and the second one too. Your book has done well by those purchases, especially the second one. The funds to yours and Mary's scholarships will do very well. Unfortunately, it just cannot be released yet."

"Tom, we were very sad to hear of Mrs. Martz, Mary's, transition."

They knew she wanted that term and not "passing" or "death". How did they know this, Tom wondered. They obviously were still keeping close tabs on them, and now just him.

"Thank you. I appreciate it. But can I ask you both a question?

"Of course."

"Fred, when we met with you at the Embassy and had lunch with you at the restaurant, you told us that we were no longer on a list. We were who you thought we were. Just two nice US citizens. What changed? Why were we...and now I, being watched again. Why?"

"As I said, your first book upset two very powerful world political leaders. That was enough to warrant some retaliation on you when the book was going to be released. Like us, they have ways to find out what will happen. Somehow, they knew your book had been written and what it was about."

Mrs. Smith, "As much as the internet companies would like for everyone to believe the "cloud" is secure...to agencies that know how to hack them...they are not. The Russians and former supporters of the ex-President have this knowledge and used it."

Fred took over again, "But that's not all. In much the same way they learned of that book, they have picked up on the fact that another is being written by you now. And it not only is upsetting to them, it is upsetting to four very wealthy and powerful US families. One a major media conglomerate owner who is allied with the former President. You have been right to not use the "cloud" to write the book and to use hard drives and flash drives for writing and back up. We have been monitoring your home for the last several months to ensure that no break ins occur. Still, they know of your search for the answer of who these families are."

Mrs. Smith again took over, "Be very careful, Tom. We will try to watch your back as we did today...but you must do so too. You understand? You may have opened a Pandora's Box with this second book. We just wanted to warn you. We will leave you now to listen to this beautiful music...and to think about these new utilities in front of you."

They both stood up and shook his hand. And as they were about to walk off arm in arm leaving a bewildered Tom alone, Fred turned. "Tom, the French Department of External Security will have picked up all the security tapes at the Louvre while we have been talking. They are secured for the moment. Eventually, forces will see them and realize that you were the intended target. Perhaps not before four or five days. Then I suspect French police will insist on seeing the video and wish to talk with you about what happened. They will want to know why. It is important for national security reasons for you not to divulge anything about either of your books to them. Do you understand? Do we have your agreement?"

"Yes!"

CHAPTER 4
BOOK 4

Was he scared? Hell, yes! Was he bewildered? Not really. He and Mary had realized they were wandering into a potentially dangerous area. However, reality now hit and hit hard! An attempt on his life had taken place. Not a fictional one. A real one! By whom? Was it the Russian President? His US crony? By one or more of the two original partners' families in the assassination plots from long ago? And what was this about a media mogul? Who was that and why was he involved?

He decided he needed more information. And he was very close to the first real lead to answer the question "Did Colette paint the painting?" 155 Gallery Arcade d' Colette. He was only steps away.

Tom quickly found the gallery. From the outside, it looked much the same as it did seventeen years before. It still had posters, newer ones, that revealed the gallery still dealt with writers of the early twentieth century, including Jean Cocteau and Colette. It was open and he entered the door, ringing the same small bell hanging above the doorway. At first he didn't see anyone. Then a young man in his thirties appeared from the back room.

"Bonjour," the young man said. "Puis-je vous aider? May I help you."

Tom asked if the young man spoke English and learned he did...excellently.

Tom began the story.

"Many years ago, in 2005, my wife and I visited this gallery. It was owned by a very nice older gentleman. A rather small fellow."

"Yes, he was my grandfather. The gallery was started by his father, my great grandfather, who was a good friend of Jean Cocteau, Colette, and others. My father inherited the gallery from my grandfather after he inherited it from my great grandfather. I'm the fourth in the chain. My father would still have it except he died unexpectedly about a year ago from a heart attack. Quite unexpectedly. He was in good shape. We ran together and played tennis twice a week. It was quite a shock, especially since grandfather had died by a hit and run driver as he crossed rue Rivoli in January 2005. Didn't you say you visited with him in 2005? You must have visited with him sometime just before his death.

Tom was now shaking and trying hard not to show his nervous concern, but this was, as Mary would say, "A weird turn of events!"

"Yes, gosh I am truly sorry to hear about both of your losses. I too lost my sweetheart, Mary, to breast cancer fairly recently. One never gets over the loss of someone special. Even though I had only met your grandfather for about an hour one evening, he seemed like a wonderful person. I am sure your father was just like him."

"Thank you. Yes, both were wonderful." He paused for a moment, appearing to be lost in thought. "What did you say your name was?"

"I don't think I told you my name. It is Tom Martz. My wife was Mary."

Suddenly the young man started from the room, "Wait right here. I think I have something for you!" and he ran to the back room. A couple of minutes later, he returned with a small old strong box and a key. He opened it and pulled out an envelope. On the envelope was written a note: pour Monsieur et Madame Martz devraient-ils jamais revenir. (For Mr. and Mrs. Martz should they ever return.) He handed the envelope to Tom.

Tom opened it carefully. Inside were three things. Tom's business card from UNC Charlotte and a note from the young man's grandfather instructing the father what to do with the envelope. The note from the grandfather translated to:

"I have met with this nice American couple recently. I had forgotten this letter my father received from Jean in 1932. It talks about the painting the couple told me about and of which they had photographs. This note verifies their finding. They may one day return. If they do, I wish this letter would be given to them."

Carefully, Tom pulled out an old envelope, the one which was addressed to the young man's great grandfather from Jean Cocteau. Inside was a handwritten note to the young man's great grandfather. It was written in French. Handing it to the young man, Tom asked, "Can you translate this for me?" The letter read:

"My Dear Renaud;
Today is the 15th of January 1932. Although warmer here than in Paris, St-Tropez is in the heart of this year's Mistel. The winds are heavy with rain and the cold and damp makes this note a fitting writing for such a day. You see, dear friend, I am writing about a sad mystery that my friend Colette has shared with me, Albert Marquet, Henry Matisse, and Pablo Picasso. They do not yet know that I have solved the code contained on the stretcher of a painting done by Colette. It is one she had done from memory. It is a scene of the story of a young woman named Jadin...and much, much more.

The story began in 1910 when Colette was performing with a troop of actors in the town of Honfleur. It is a frightening story as it is about the assassination of three people and perhaps this young woman, Jadin, as well. The payment for the assassinations was a black enameled, jewel-encrusted gold sculpture fist. It was provided by two Americans with coded initials hiding their identities. As promised to my fellow painters, who are gathered once again with me at Colette's home here in the Cote d' Azur, I have unlocked the puzzle of the coded initials. What it reveals is too frightening for me to share with them. That is why I am writing to you, my great friend, Renaud. I want you to know of the journal I have written and hidden here in Colette's home.

The journal has been placed in a clay crock sealed with beeswax. I placed the journal first inside a small bag made of sailcloth treated to make it waterproof. Following that, I placed it inside the crock. Hopefully, this will protect it for I know not how long. Over time, I may change my mind. At this moment, I have decided the information is too harmful to share. I will admit to my friends that I have failed in solving the mystery. Perhaps this will be the end of the story. However, I needed to share the fact that I solved the mystery with someone. That someone is you, Renaud.

Should you have any reason to search for this journal, I have placed it beneath the floorboards of the attic. It is located two feet by two feet from the northwest corner of the attic's sloping ceiling. I think it should stay there lost for some time...perhaps forever.

With sorrow for bringing you this burden, my good friend and confidant. Your eternal friend,

Jean"

"May I keep these envelopes and letters?"

"Oui, Monsieur, they were meant for you. Perhaps one day if you find this journal and you do not wish to keep it, you will use my gallery to sell it for you. That would be my pleasure."

"Merci, I will consider that. Au revoir."
Tom headed for the door.

"Oh, Monsieur Martz! This letter and story sound ominous. Be careful."

Tom nodded his thanks, opened the door, and was gone. Inside a quick flash of concern ran through the young man's head. Could this explain the hit and run death of his grandfather and the unexpected heart attack of his father. He shook the thought from his mind. Still?

CHAPTER 5
BOOK 4

Fear still gripping him, he made several quick decisions. He went to two separate bank machines close by and withdrew the full amount of cash available for the day using two cards, his card and Mary's. In total, that gave him nearly 700 euros. That along with the 500 euros already in his wallet from earlier bank machine withdrawals that week and the 1000 euros in his, as Mary called it, "spy case" for his passport, was just short of 2200 euros. This would have to carry him over for the next four or five days. He couldn't use any credit cards after this evening, he told himself.

Next, he went by metro to the 5th err and the Hotel Cluny Sorbonne. Tom and Mary had stayed at this hotel with their daughter Sara in 2001 on their first trip to Paris. He secured for four days the same room he and Mary had on that trip, number 11.

In the hotel lobby, he sent a text message to all of the Munroe family's phones. "I left the Louvre a while ago and am going to visit my old neighborhood in Paris. I made reservations at the restaurant Scossa at 8, Place Victor Hugo, 75016 for 7:00 this evening. I'll meet you there. We will be seated outside. Sorry, but the Louvre was just overwhelming to me! :)"

Leaving the hotel, Tom took the metro from Cluny la Sorbonne to Gare d'Austerlitz. There he purchased a phone card he might need to use later.

On his own iPhone, he called the Gallery and was able to reach the young owner to tell him about the attempt on his life earlier in the day, just as the man had feared. Tom told the young man he was headed to St-Tropez. He needed a place to stay that was undetectable. He must only use cash. Could the young man help him?

Fear now crossed quickly through the young gallery owner's own mind. Should he involve himself more? He decided he would.

"Yes, I have a friend Bridget. She has a place in St-Tropez that has a guest house in her backyard. It has a wonderful view of the St-Tropez harbor. Here is her number and address. Can you write it down?"

Tom did so. The gallery owner asked, "What time should she expect you? I will call her myself now and tell her you will be coming. She will tell me I owe her big time, I'm sure. But she is my friend, and she will do this for me."

"My train arrives tomorrow in Saint Raphael Valescure at 9:00 pm. It appears to be around an hour drive by cab. She should expect me at about 10:30 tomorrow night. Tell her I will have a good bottle of rosé to share with her. And thank you for doing this for me."

"Be very careful, my friend. Be very careful." The phone call ended.

Tom crossed the Seine River on the bridge, Pont Charles de Gaulle, and walked the short distance to Gare De Lyon. He purposely had used his phone to make a call from the other station just in case anyone would ever check where his phone calls originated. The last time he would use his phone would be to text the Munroes the next day at the airport. After that, he would turn it off. He would operate without a phone for the duration of his stay. Except for the one and only time it was turned back on...in St-Tropez...by someone else.

At the train station, he purchased a one-way ticket with cash. The train left the next day. The day that he and the Munroes were to return to the US. His ticket for the 3:37 pm train, with one transfer, was set to arrive at his stop at 8:37 pm. It was scheduled to leave Paris two hours and ten minutes after he would miss his flight home with the Munroes.

CHAPTER 6
BOOK 4

The morning of the trip was a comfortable and similar pattern to the other mornings in the grand apartment. Up early for he and James and off to the bakery for the morning pastries. Kristen was up early too, ensuring that she and James were packed. The girls? Well, they are teenagers after all...they, as usual, slept in until the pastry hunters returned.

At 10:30 am, the SUV cab arrived on the street in front of the building. Everyone was downstairs, outside waiting. The luggage was loaded and off they headed to Charles De Gaulle. Kristen noticed that Tom only had one bag, his roller bag. His small tan duffel bag must be packed inside it.

"You didn't forget your duffel bag, did you? We still have time for you to run...well walk...upstairs and retrieve it. Or can one of the girls run up?"

"I packed it in my roller bag. I was going to bring the load of pink toilet paper back for Sara and Cath. It was a tradition that Mary and I started twenty years ago. You can't find the stuff in the US. I decided this morning it was foolish so I left them for the next renters." This was not totally a lie. He did leave them for the next renters. And the duffel bag was packed inside the roller. He wanted to be encumbered with just one bag today.

Two hours before the flight, they were checked in and Kristen noticed another change to Tom's routine. "You aren't checking your bag this time?"

"Nope, we always did so going over to Paris because bags always arrived quickly here. In Boston and other US airports, not the same. It takes forever. I thought it would be easier to catch the Dartmouth Coach after customs. We will see if that works. Still, I may need one of the girls to help me put it above in the luggage rack."

Quickly, all three girls said they would do it. Tom could see the pride on both Kristen's and James's faces. Yep, these parents had raised three special, caring young women. They had all taken care of him on this test trip.

They each found something to eat for lunch, knowing that they would be served another meal about an hour into the flight. The choices were small ones. Salads, wraps, water, and lots of chocolates and other sweets. The family was on vacation and treats were in order.

The meal completed, it was now time to peruse the duty free stores. The sweets area was one that was paid special attention. Choices were made of the many candy treats not found in the US stores. There were also multiple potato chip offerings: Tyrrells slow-cooked crisps of black truffle and sea salt, sun-dried tomato and mozzarella cheese, cheddar and chive, and everyone's favorite sea salt and cider vinegar.

Tom hadn't made any purchases when they met up by the boarding gate.

"Just couldn't decide on anything to take back as gifts. I saw a few things but...oh, well, the kids won't expect anything anyway...I hope!"

"Besides, you guys cleaned the stores out!"

Boarding began and they, in coach class, were nearly the last group to board. Just as they started to hand their passports and boarding pass to the agents, Tom said, "I've changed my mind. I did see something in the duty free store that will work. You guys go ahead. I'll be there shortly!" Without waiting for a response, he hurried toward the stores.

Kristen looked at James and the girls and now did one of Tom's famous "Hoosier shoulder shrugs". They handed their boarding passes and passports to the agents, were checked on board, and proceeded to their seats. Grace at the window, Kristen next to her, James in the aisle seat. Across the aisle was Gwyn, then Tillie and Tom's open seat.

The five settled into their pre-flight routine, earphones on, video monitors watching the mechanics and loaders do the pre-flight work. Flight attendants checked with passengers on their seat belts. The announcement made that the cabin doors be secured.

Tillie nudged Gwyn and nodded to Tom's empty seat. Gwyn reached across the aisle and got her dad's attention and pointed to Tom's seat and said, "Tom's not on board!"

James turned to Kristen and whispered loudly the same. Panic was on all five faces. Just then, a text came through on all still turned-on cell phones...

"Hey Munroes, something has come up. I have decided to stay in Paris and do some research on my second book. I'll catch a fight later in the week. Don't worry. You guys proved to me I can do this. Thanks. I'll contact you later once I am back home. Love and White Light. T."

The plane began being shoved back from the gate by the tractor, the five looked at each other and gave the "Hoosier shoulder shrug". All this happened as Tom was departing the airport, pulling his roller bag up to the assigned cab. Kristen, not realizing her "Find My Phone" app on her cell phone was still tracking Tom, turned her cell phone off.

Four other people on board the Airbus flight A334 were now confused and worried. Two were friends of the "Smiths". Two were Russian assassins. Four last minute cell phone calls were made. Two in English and two in Russian. The calls were too late.

CHAPTER 7
BOOK 4

At exactly 8:09 pm on his watch, the train pulled into the station. Tom found a taxi and paid in cash for the ride from St Raphael Valescure to St-Tropez. In his hand he carried the peace offering bottle of rosé wine.

At the same time back in Paris, a young gallery owner prepared to close his gallery. A distinguished man with a dark hat, dark suit, and mustache entered the gallery, ringing the small bell.

"Bonjour, monsieur. Can I help you?" He took a chance that the man was American and spoke in English. A lot of his customers were American. Those who had visited the Louvre.

He was wrong. In perfect French with a slight eastern region accent perhaps, the man replied. "Well, yes, as a matter of fact you can. I am seeking some information. But I also see you are closing up. I really don't want to be a bother. My visit will only be a short one. Why don't you close the gallery so that we will not be disturbed. We can talk in the back room."

With that, the man pulled from under his jacket a gun with a silencer attached to the barrel: a Makarov 9mm.

"Hurry now. This won't take long."

"Monsieur, I have a wife and small daughter. Please do not hurt me. I will help you however I can. But please, leave me to join my family once you have learned whatever it is you want."

"Lock up and let's chat!"

The young man did as he was told. They both went into the back room, turning off the gallery lights as they did.

There was one chair under an old desk. The desk was piled with papers. The room was not big, but big enough for the young man's needs. A door on the right opened to another room about the same size. It was the work room. The place where paintings, drawings, books, and other materials could be packaged and sent off to the buyers. Both rooms together were about half the size of the small gallery. On the desk sat the picture of the young man, his wife, and his daughter. The daughter looked about 6 years of age.

"Sit down. I want you to tell me all you know about an American man who called you yesterday. He is the man I am looking for. His name does not need to be spoken. We know he called your place using his cell phone yesterday. We were able to trace the call from his phone records. What did he want of you?"

"He talked about the artist and writer Jean Cocteau. About a missing diary of his. And about the writer Colette."

"Why was he interested in them?"

"He owns a painting he believes is painted by her...the writer...Colette. He wanted proof that she painted it. He said something about wanting it to go back to its rightful owners. Either the family of Colette or the French government."

"And this missing diary. Why is that important?"

"He believes that she was painting this picture with Jean in the south of France." Not wanting to reveal the fact that Tom now had a letter from Jean that verified that fact. He added, "Someone had told him of the existence of a journal that Jean had written that mentioned the painting. He wanted to know if this was true. I told him I knew of nothing like that." Taking a chance at lying.

"Do you believe he will be headed to the south of France? To find this diary?"

"Monsieur, I really do not know. I just know he wondered if I had ever heard of it. I said, perhaps one day long ago, from an old American woman. An expert in Cocteau and others. I told him it was vaguely something I remembered. I have never heard anything else from anyone about it."

The man in the hat and dark suit stood to leave. At the office door, he turned.

"Oh, monsieur. Just one more thing." His hand raised the gun directly at the young man's forehead. An easy shot. The young man's jaw dropped. Fear filled his eyes as tears started to fall.

"Please, monsieur. No!"

Sitting on the desk behind the young man was the picture of him and his family. The daughter was looking at the man with the gun with a smile on her face. It must have been a happy day.

To this day, the man in the hat doesn't know why. Perhaps it was because of his own daughter. But for some reason, that day...he was very unprofessional.

"Stand up. Put your hands over your head with your fingers laced together and walk into the work room."

The young man complied. His legs were shaking. Tears were still falling.

"Get on the floor and put your hands behind your back. Put your feet together one ankle over the other."

The gunman found what he needed. Strong twine, used to tie the packages, and rolls of packing tape.

"Now close your eyes!"

Fearing that this meant he was about to die, the young man again pleaded, "Monsieur, please don't shoot me! Please!"

"Shut up and lay still or I will do so!"

The man with the gun took the twine and twisted it around the young man's wrist several times, so tight that it cut into his wrists. He did the same with the man's ankles. Next, he tore up a black work apron he found on the workbench.

"Raise your head off the floor!" He ordered. The young man did so. The strip of heavy back cloth was held over the young man's eyes as the man wrapped and secured it firmly to his head with packing tape. When the tape would eventually be removed, so would a lot of his hair. It would hurt, but not nearly as much as he might have.

The gunman stood up. Looking at the young man lying immobile on the ground, he had second thoughts. They passed quickly as he remembered the eyes on the young girl's face. Satisfied with his work, he walked to the door. The man would be there for some time.

"Once you free yourself, you are not to talk to anyone about what has happened here this evening. No one. Not even your wife. You hear me? If you talk to anyone, including the police, I will find you and the next time so will my bullets. Do you understand me?"

As best he could, the young man signaled that he understood.

"Good! That is good! Monsieur, you have a wonderful family. Your daughter has a LUCKY father this evening. You owe her a lot! Good night, monsieur."

He turned off the light to the workroom and then the office. Exiting the Hall of Colette, he headed for the Seine River. He removed his hat and replaced it with an American baseball cap, the letters "KC" squarely on the forehead of the royal blue cap. He also removed the cheap suit coat and threw it in the trash, along with the first hat. The mustache had been pulled off as soon as he was out of sight of the building.

He walked to the Pont Neuf bridge and crossed to the Ile de Cite. Off Quai des Orfèvres, the power boat waited for him. After he got on board, it powered east past Ile Saint Louis and eventually past the headquarters of the Brigade Fluviala.

Captain Etienne Michel was just relieving his second in command, Lieutenant Guy Guenard at the start of Etienne's 12-hour tour. Neither they, nor the man and his crew racing past the headquarters on the speedboat, had any idea that their lives would cross one day in the not-too-distant future.

At the same time in St Tropez:

Emotionally drained, Tom sat on the bed in the guest house. He and Bridget had shared the whole bottle of rosé. She was a young woman, about the young gallery owner's age. She was the college roommate of the young man's wife. Explaining to Tom that she had been a bit put out by the request for him to stay with her, she had finally agreed. Now after several hours of talking she not only felt more comfortable, but she also rather enjoyed the company of this older man.

"I will be leaving on a two-week trip tomorrow with my boyfriend. But you are welcome to stay in the guest house as long as you want." They agreed on 500 euros a week. He paid her the first 500 in cash that night. The next morning, she was gone before he got up. He didn't see her again, as he would not be there when she returned, but neither one knew that.

As he sat on the bed looking out the window onto the bay down the hill, Tom decided a shower was needed. "A quick rinse," Mary would say. His hostess that evening had been kind enough to prepare a small Provincial dinner. They had enjoyed the late evening on the outside terrace of the main villa looking at the lights in the harbor. For at least one night, he was comfortable.

Tonight, a good rest was needed. Another long day was ahead of him tomorrow. He really did not know exactly how or where to begin the search. He would figure that out later. For now, shower first and then sleep.

CHAPTER 8
BOOK 4

The couple strolled arm in arm, weaving back and forth a bit under the alcohol's influence. The French beret sitting proudly on top of his six foot one body. Part of his green striped sport shirt hung loosely out from under his dark blue linen sport coat. The remaining third of the shirt was partially tucked unkempt in his natural colored linen slacks. He was the right age for the target...over 60 years. The woman, perhaps in her late 40s, was heavily made up. Her tight black and white clingy dress barely covered her. Its strapless bodice pulled revealingly across what part of her breasts were not exposed. The couple staggered in through the front hotel door. He obviously found her on the street somewhere, probably in the Pigalle area of the 18th. Now here they were for a night of it in the hotel of the 5th err. Their last night!

The man across the street at the outside cafe table had witnessed it all. He knew it had to be the one. No Frenchman would wear that foolish chapeau. He decided he would give them an hour and then end it. Time for another Pastis on this warm night. He looked at his watch, 11:30 pm. It would all be over shortly.

At 12:30 am, the man stood up, put euros on the table, and walked across the street. His crepe-soled shoes made no noise. Dark tight euro slacks and a black shirt made him less visible as the streetlights on this rue were not bright. He stood by the door smoking a cigarette, acting nonchalantly as though he expected someone to be coming to pick him up.

The front desk clerk left the counter and went to the back room to retrieve something. It was time. Quickly, the man opened the door and headed for the stairs. He learned from his team who had hacked into the hotel reservations system that the man and this woman would be found in number 11! It was at the top of the first flight of stairs toward the back of the hotel away from the front door. Perfect.

Climbing the stairs quietly, two steps at a time, he simultaneously screwed his AAC Illusion 9mm suppressor onto the Beretta. Silently, he put his ear to the door and listened. No sound.

Taking out the tools, he quickly picked the cheap lock. The door opened slowly, revealing the small room. Only a bed, a chest of drawers, one old wooden chair beside a small writing table, and on one side of the bed a round nightstand closest to the door. On it was the sole lamp in the room. Barely room for a person to walk around the bed. The door must have opened inward toward the bathroom, he thought.

He closed the room door and now stood between it and the bathroom door. Between two doors. He stepped forward into the room, the doors now slightly behind him.

The couple were locked in each other's arms in the post-coitus position. Him spooning her. His light silver hair shone with the faint light coming through the ill-closed window shade. Arms wrapped around her under the sheets. Her leg hung out of the sheet, revealing itself up to her hip. Used clothing strewn hastily around the floor of the room. Both were facing the door sound asleep. Both naked.

This would be easy! He paused to consider his options. Kill the man first and silence her with his hand quickly? Then he could take his time enjoying her before killing her too. He could do that by covering his hand over her mouth. Women always scream, though she might bite him. He would have to work quickly. This could be difficult. He could quickly knock her unconscious with the gun or a fist. That would silence her. It would make his future work with her easier but not nearly as much fun.

The other option, he could kill her first. The man would perhaps stay asleep. If he didn't, a man's usual reaction would be different than that of a woman.

His reaction would be to try to defend himself. A scream would be a sign of weakness. Men seldom screamed.

Looking at her uncovered shapely leg, he decided on the first option! The time making the decision had caused him to pause a moment too long.

As he eased the gun up to take care of the silver-headed man and then enjoy her, the gun flew from his hand. The rubber encased, two foot long, five pound rod, striking quickly upward, had broken his wrist. His hand dangled worthlessly as he swung his head toward the direction where the strike had come from. Now the downward moving rod smashed hard into the top of his head. His knees buckled and he crashed to the ground unconscious. At that moment, four armed GIGN police tactical unit officers streamed into the room.

The unconscious man was turned roughly on to his stomach and the zip ties pulled tight and securely around his wrists and ankles.

Fire alarms in the hotel screamed as guests streamed out of their rooms in to the hallways. What appeared to be hotel employees on all floors were guiding them down the stairs when the first Pompiers arrived at the scene. No one would question how they arrived so quickly. If they had, they might have learned that two squads had been stationed less than two blocks away in the courtyard of the Sorbonne.

Mr. Smith and Mrs. Smith rose from the bed. He grabbed his shirt from the chair and slipped it on his torso. She smoothed out the clingy tight dress. The clothes on the floor were just decoys. Both had been wide awake waiting. They put their drawn guns away. His, in the holster on his ankle. Hers, in her purse. Both guns under the covers had been aimed at the man coming through the doorway.

"Glad you guys made it in time!" he said in French. "We thought that Inspector Vanasse would have to deal with him all alone."

"Ah, then you did not see the red dot on the man's forehead from the sniper across the street? He was one second from the shot. That man was dropped to the floor from the inspector's blow just in time. Good thing for him...this fellow. His brains would have been blown all over the room. A bit messy, for sure. In the end it all turned out well. Did you get some...nice private time.... in preparation for the event?" A sly smile on the GIGN leader's face.

"Memorable for sure!"

"How will this be reported? Will it make the newspapers and TV?"

"Ah, monsieur, this is France. If we don't want a story to leak out, it remains not so. This will be kept under wraps for a few days. I am sure that the director-general for external security will be in touch with you at the Embassy tomorrow. He and you should coordinate and handle this."

The GIGN officer said, "May I ask you, however, the man who is registered for this room, Mr. Martz, who is he? Where is he?"

Mr. Smith replied, "Let's just say he is an old and good friend of Mrs. Smith and mine. As to where he is...well, at this moment...we are unsure. That will be part of the discussion that will take place tomorrow with the director-general. In the meantime, merci for your assistance in this operation. Mrs. Smith and I are very grateful to you for ensuring our safety."

"It was our pleasure. We will now get this fellow out of here unseen through a back way. We will inform the US Embassy where he will be located. Your colleagues will want to join us in our interrogation of the fellow when his head stops ringing."

"Will you and Mrs. Smith enjoy the rest of your night here? I suspect it will be as safe as anywhere. We will have two of our officers in the room next door to ensure no other intruders. And of course the desk clerks will be our men too."

"No," Mrs. Smith replied. "My husband and I will return to our home. He wants to get me off the street and out of these clothes...but not in the way you are thinking... I hope. Right, Fred?"

Fred smiled.

The GIGN officers left. Fred turned to inspector Vanasse. "Thank you, Nicolas. That was expertly done."

"If I had been unsuccessful with the baton, then I would have shot the fellow. Either way, he would have been unsuccessful with Madame...perhaps he would have been able to fire one shot" ...eyebrow raised..."but only one shot. Too bad, Fred!" They both chuckled...though Fred's laugh was just a bit more tentative.

"What do you two think? Is he Russian? Why?"

"Don't know," Mrs. Smith replied. "If he were Russian...former KGB...the gun would have been a Makarov and not a Beretta. What do you think, Fred?"

"Sweetheart, you are the gun expert. I'm not about to question what a gold medalist in the Olympics pistol competition thinks about a gun. It certainly raises lots of questions. Appears more than one person may have interest in making sure Tom is no longer with us. Troubling for sure. Wish we knew where he is and what he is up to."

"No credit card usage since the dinner at the restaurant the night he booked this room?"

"Nope. And he did use his bank card and his deceased wife's card to withdraw funds from bank machines that day. I suspect he is on a cash-only basis now. What do you think, Nicolas? Think he is still in Paris?"

"My friend, I think he has departed Paris. I think we should check with the airlines. However, he would have used his passport to do so. We can check that easily enough. Otherwise he would have to take a train. If he paid for a ticket in cash we would have to check all of the train station videos for these last couple of days. A bit time consuming. The facial recognition software will probably help. Unless he changed his looks significantly from his passport."

"We talked with him two days ago. At the time, he had a beard that was becoming scraggly. Hair was longish and untrimmed too."

"Ah, that might explain what I found in the bathroom. For a two-star hotel, I am afraid the cleaning is not quite as it should be. I found a few clumps of gray hair behind the toilet. We can have that checked but I think he may have shaved his beard and cut his hair."

"The only thing in the brown duffle bag was a package of pink toilet paper. He must have another bag with his shaving equipment and scissors."

"Pink toilet paper?" both Mr. and Mrs. Smith asked simultaneously.

"Yes, pink. Strange!"

CHAPTER 9
BOOK 4

The last two July 4th celebrations in Bar Harbor, Maine, had been hot. This one was the same as those last two...temperatures over 100 degrees Fahrenheit. Although hot, fortunately it was not too humid. There was also a soft breeze off the ocean. It would be bearable.

Kali and Josh found their favorite spot on Main Street, Peekytoe Provisions. It was less than a quarter mile from where the parade formed up at the YMCA baseball fields and park. Unfortunately, last year Peekytoe had installed a low wooden fence around the seating area of the picnic table. It still offered the perfect site for the family of three, Kali, husband Josh, and Kali's stepdaughter, Lily, to watch the parade.

"It's still about a half hour before the parade starts so how about I get us some lunch and cold drinks while my two girls guard our spot?"

"Sounds good, Josh. How about lobster rolls all around. I bet Lily would love an Old Soaker Root Beer to go along with hers. Unless she would rather have a Peanut Butter and Jelly Time sandwich with it. I'll try a "No New Friends Sour" blueberry cheesecake sour. That sounds interesting. And water all around. What are you going to have?"

"Normally, I would go for an IPA but this one sounds interesting from the Fogtown Brewing Company in Ellsworth...I think I'll try a "Night Nurse". She sounds exciting!" Said with a smile and a wink. He knew the only "night nurse" he really needed was his beautiful woman sitting with their daughter.

Kali smiled back and said, "She does sound interesting. I'll let you get to know her and tell me what she's like!"

As Josh got up to head in for the orders, a small woman who looked to be near 90 approached the table.

"Would you mind if an old soul would join you, dears?"

"Of course not." Kali got up to help the old lady but realized the woman was quite spry as she was already starting to sit on the same side of the table with Lily, facing the street.

"My name is Anne. What are your names, dear?" she said to Lily.

"Mine is Lily. This is my stepmom, Kali. And my dad just went in to the store to buy our lunch. His name is Josh. We are the McNutts."

"Well, that was quite a proper introduction, young lady. How old are you?"

"I'm 8 years old. I know I shouldn't ask your age. So, I won't."

Anne laughed and smiled at Kali. "A very smart young lady."

Turning back to Lily, Anne said, "Since you did such a proper and mature introduction, I suppose I should do the same. My full name is Anne Kimball. I live here in Bar Harbor during the summers. During the winters I live in my apartment in Paris, France. Have you ever been there?"

Kali's mouth dropped in shock!

Lily replied to the woman, "No, I have never been there yet. There is some talk about the family maybe going to Paris at Christmas, though. Isn't that right, Kali?"

Kali didn't respond for a moment, still in shock. Then she said, "Yes, Lily. That is true. We may go there this Christmas with a friend of ours."

Then turning to Anne, Kali asked the question, "Anne, by any chance do you remember ever meeting a couple by the names of Mary and Tom Martz?"

Now it was Anne Kimball's turn to look shocked.

"Why yes, dear. I did meet them. We were on an adventure together. I unfortunately lost touch with them. How do you know them?"

"I worked with Tom at Husson University in Bangor."

"Yes, I know of the university."

"Tom is retired now. Anne, I am sorry to tell you, Mary died of breast cancer just two years ago."

"Oh, my. I did not know them well at all. Just a chance meeting one cold, wet, and stormy night in Paris. Between two doors as I recall the evening went. We stayed in communication for a couple of years then I am unsure what happened to them. I think they moved. I sent a couple of emails to them at UNC Charlotte...I think that was the university. But never received a reply."

"This is so sad. Just from the short visit we had that evening you could tell she was a beautiful soul and quite a charismatic person. Such a loss. I was helping them discover if a painting was done by the French writer Colette. Do you know, did they ever find the absolute answer?"

"Anne, this is so remarkable that this coincidence is happening. The short answer is yes. Tom, in retirement, has become a writer himself. I was his administrative assistant at Husson University. I am now acting as a volunteer editor for his books. The first one is at the publishers now. It is called, The White Light Within."

"But, more importantly, he has finished a second book. Anne, it is called, Between Two Doors; In Search of Colette. He was in Paris just recently to find absolute proof that the painting was done by Colette!"

"My goodness, this is exciting! You must tell him when he gets back..."

Just then, two things happened. Josh arrived with the food and drinks and the music from the parade started a quarter mile away. Josh was introduced to Anne Kimball. He then asked if he could get her something to eat and drink.

"Well, that is quite nice of you young man. I can see why Lily here is such a fine young lady. She has two very kind and thoughtful parents. I will have what you both are having. But instead of a heavy beer...a woman of my age has to watch her girly figure you know...I'll have a glass of rose wine. But, dear, I insist that I pay for mine. It is just kind of you to offer to get it for me."

Josh would not hear of it and off he went into the store again for her lobster roll and rose wine. Just then, the Scottish bagpipe and drummers could be seen right behind the lead Parade Marshal's car.

Anne turned to both Lily and Kali and said with a wink, "What do you suppose they really wear under those skirts...I mean kilts?"

Lily giggled. Kali smiled and laughed. They watched as the high kicking drum major led the kilted bagpipe and drum core past their spot. Kali watched him especially with a smile on her face. He was a large man with a bit of a girth. A friendly smile on his face and the most expressive full mustache and heavy eyebrows. Those he used often when one talked with him to express his thoughts. He and the others marched on just as Josh returned.

Following lunch, Kali said, "Tomorrow I and another person will be meeting with Tom in Bangor. I cannot wait to tell him that I ran into you. He will be overjoyed!"

"Dear, that reminds me of what I wanted to tell you just as the skirted men paraded by." She smiled and winked at Lily. "I was about to say, I think there may be absolute proof of the painting being done by her. Tell him he is to go back to the gallery in the Hall of Colette. A friend of mine, you see I used to be an expert in this area..."

"Yes, Tom mentioned that in the book."

"Really, I will have to buy a copy of the book when it comes out. Anyway, this friend of mine had a letter from a writer by the name of Jean Cocteau. Are you familiar with the name? You are, that's good," she said as Kali nodded her head yes.

"The letter was to this man's father who was Jean's good friend. My friend told me of the visit with Tom and Mary long ago on the same night as my visit with them. He said that he put the letter somewhere special for Mary and Tom. Unfortunately, the old man...he would have been even older than me today...was killed by a hit and run driver. I don't know if the letter is still at the store. If it is, my friend told me it provides absolute verification of the painting having been done by Colette. It was done by her with the guidance of three good friends of hers, Albert Marquet, Pablo Picasso, and Henry Matisse. You must tell Tom this."

"Let me give you my home phone number and address too. Tell him I would love to see him and talk more about our adventure. Tell him also of my sorrow for him of losing his sweet wife, Mary. Such a dear!"

"I will tomorrow, Anne. I promise."

With that, Anne got up as did they all. Anne gave Kali and Lily a hug. She shook Josh's hand and thanked him for his kindness. Then she turned to Lily.

"I still wonder what they wear under those skirts. Don't you?" she said with a wink and a smile. Then she strolled off through the crowd.

CHAPTER 10
BOOK 4

They both thought it independently. Is it strange that Tom hasn't contacted me to remind me of lunch? He always emails or texts reminders. Oh, well. Tammy waited at her Bangor Athletic Massage and Bodywork studio until 11:40 am, a full 10 minutes past time. Tom was usually 15 minutes early. Perhaps he just went straight to Bagel Central today. She locked the door and headed south on Franklin Street. At Hammond Street, she turned east to Central Street. There, she crossed the street and turned north half a block and entered Bagel Central. Kali McNutt was already there. No Tom!

"Hey, Kali. Where is Tom?"

"I don't know. I thought he would be coming with you as usual. Did you get a text or email from him?"

"No. You didn't either?"

"Nope. That's unusual. I hope nothing is wrong. Perhaps he's tied up in traffic if he's driving over today."

"Yeah, that must be it. Hey, how was your July 4th? Did you do anything fun?"

"Yes, actually. Something fun and unusual and it's tied to our old buddy Tom."

Looking at her watch, she added, "It is quarter of 12 now and I will have to be back at the office by 1 at the latest. Think we should order and sit down? Tom can join us as soon as he gets here."

"Sounds like a good idea. I have a one o'clock appointment ahead of Tom's massage. Let's do it and grab our regular table before the crowd gets here."

They considered the menu, and both decided on the one they each always ordered, the "BLTC" bacon, lettuce, tomato, and cheese for Tammy and the "Brady Gang" vegetarian for Kali. Each grabbed a bottle of water. After paying, they walked over to the table at the far end of the restaurant to watch and wait.

While waiting, Kali began to answer the earlier question about her family's July 4th and the Story. First, she said, "Yesterday we were at Bar Harbor for the parade. Did you go?"

"No, I took my new Kawasaki KX250 to the track to try it out. I know this doesn't mean much to You, but it is a powerful 38 horsepower bike. And guess what?! I did a really high jump. I mean, I had to be 25 feet in the air coming off this hill. The first time ever! I don't want to gloat or anything but it was incredible!" A huge smile painted on her proud face.

"But it kind of ended a little rough cause there was this guy who had harassed me all day on his bike. I accidentally put him in the dirt following the hill jump. I mean, it was accidental! I would never do anything like that on purpose. But here is the really interesting thing. He is one of the top motocross racers in the world. I mean, he is one of the leading contenders to win the championship this year.

Last night, my girlfriends Sara and Julie and I went to the riverfront performance of the band MotoMavs. Do you know the song, "Rev It up, Baby?" That is one of the band's hits. I hadn't really wanted to go because with the three-day weekend I had too much work at the studio to set up for today. But since my friends insisted, I went. Well, this jerks' friend is a motocross racer too and plays in the band. He is the keyboard player. Guess what happened?"

"What?"

"I ran into the guy at the concert…the jerk. And he is not a jerk at all! He is a nice guy. He apologized to me! Said he didn't know what came over him. Perhaps the nerves of getting ready for an upcoming big race. He has invited me to the Pro Motocross race in Southwick, Massachusetts, on Saturday. I will be in his pits with his team! He is tied with another guy for the lead in the World Motocross Championship Series."
"Wow!" Kali responded.

"I still feel a bit funny about it though."

"Why?"

"Well, it was nice to have found out that I put him down in the dirt, even though it was an accident. I mean he is a motocross champion. One of the best there is. And I put him in the dirt! I did it!" she said with a smile."

"That's great! Believe it or not, I know exactly how you feel. Something similar happened to me with my cousin Joel. He is a mixed martial arts fighter. Not a champion, but he is very good. He and I were sparing on Sunday. He is teaching me some stuff. Anyway, I floored him with a special kick I designed…from watching a kids cartoon show!"

"Seriously?"

"Yep! It's kind of fun to top a guy occasionally. I mean I would never want to do that all the time. I don't really have the need. But" …trying to hold back the giggle…"it was great!"

"I agree. But, let's not let them in on it. I mean, no sense in showing our dominance and hurting their male egos." Laughter. "Right?!"

"Right!"

"So, finish the story about what happened on July 4th at the parade."

"Oh, yeah, well has Tom ever mentioned to you a woman named Anne Kimball?"

"Boy, the name is vaguely familiar, but I can't remember why. What about her?"

"She lives half the year here in Maine. Bar Harbor. And she lives half the year in Paris. Tom and Mary ran into her when they were trying to find out if a painting they own was painted by Colette, a famous French woman writer of the late 1800s."

"Oh, sure. I remember now. Isn't he writing another book about the writer? Are you editing that book too?"

"Yes, well, here is a strange coincidence. Josh, and I, and Lily were sitting down at our favorite place to watch the parade. This sweet old lady came over and asked if she could join us at our table. We said of course she could. Josh had already gone off to get the food for Lily and me and himself. Anne, the lady, introduced herself to us. The name was so familiar, but when she said she lived half the year in Bar Harbor and the other half the year in Paris, France, I knew it had to be the same Anne Kimball."

"Are you kidding?! What a coincidence!"

Ten minutes later, Kali was close to finishing the story. Their orders were up, they continued waiting, but still no Tom.

Unexpectedly, a couple sat down at their table with them. There were plenty of other tables and chairs in the place but this couple chose to sit, him on one side where Kali sat, and her on the other side with Tammy. Odd, both young women thought, but said nothing. Perhaps they saw that the girls were talking softly. The restaurant is large but gets crowded. Perhaps sitting here with the young women, they would be removed from the lunch hour noisy crowd. The young ladies continued their Anne Kimball discussion. They were soon distracted by the low conversation of the couple at the table with them.

Scientific studies show that there are significant differences in the human auditory system between men and women. Bottom line, most women can pick up on other people's conversations in crowded, loud places easier than their male counterparts. At this moment, both women heard the other couple's conversation.

"Yes, his book is being printed. I read the first printing. It divulges sensitive national secret information. The government is going to buy up all of the first two printings to delay its public release."

"Wow, and you say this author is in New Hampshire?"

"Yes."

Both young women stopped their conversation, acting as though they were eating. Both stared at each other. Eyes big!

"I understand that there is a second book that is in progress now too. The writer has an editor here in Maine he is working with."

"Really? Close to here?"

"Yes. The problem is that not only does this book also contain very top-secret information but it also perhaps puts the fellow's life in jeopardy!"

The women stopped eating and stared at each other. Suddenly, both the man and the woman turned to Kali and Tammy. She said, "Do you know Tom Martz? He has gone MISSING!"

Les Toits de Paris. Le Printemps, dernier étage. 2012
Photo by Mary Martz

EPILOGUE

Fall 2022.

As you have just read in this book, I have gone missing. I hope that I am found. There will be a great team working to do so. There is my former administrative assistant and volunteer book editor, Kali "Roundkick" McNutt and my massage therapist, Tammy "Greenhornet" Lynn who are on the case. They will eventually team up with other friends from the first book, The White Light Within. The Smiths, along with Etienne, Nina, Ninette and Guy, will help Kali, Tammy and their families in the search to find the missing author...me, Tom Martz. Good luck guys! I'm pulling for you!

Mary and I started developing the story for this book after finding a painting in a South Carolina antique store in 2004. Thinking it could have been painted by the French writer Colette, we decided to find out for sure. After reading 16 books on her and several trips to Paris, we were convinced we were right. Colette, we concluded, had done the painting with the help of another artist. In the book you just read, you found out Mary suspected that based on the difference of brushstrokes on the painting.

Our idea was to prove this painting was done by Colette so we could either return it to her family, to the Friends of Colette, or to the French Government. We wanted no money for it. We want it to be in the proper hands of the people of France. We still do.

Any profits from the book are to go to the two travel abroad scholarships that Mary and I established at UNC Charlotte and Husson University. We do not want to profit from these adventures other than to have had them. That was reward enough. Which leads me to the purpose of this epilogue.

We wanted our stories to be fun adventures. When we told people about the Colette adventure in 2005 through 2012 everyone said, "the only thing this story needs is a good murder". Well, they got their wish. Several times over with this one.

That leads me to the point: Sometimes it is not good to get what you wish for.

You see, we wanted our stories to be light, fun, and entertaining. Filled with the white light of hope, truth, and love. We think we were reasonably successful with the first book, The White Light Within.

As I finish this book, alone without my sweetheart, I am not so sure I was as successful with the fun and light that we wanted it to share. Perhaps this book deals with a more difficult subject: greed and abuse of power.

After reading just part of our first book, a published author said of it, "I think you have a compelling story here. But honestly, I cannot tell if this is a love story, a travel log, a biographical writing, or spy story! I only read 100 pages and I am lost!"

Downer, I thought!

Then two thoughts hit me.

First, he is not the demographic the story is written for. You see, both Mary and I are "romantics". We believe in love above all else. So, to him, the answer from me is...it is a love story. Several in fact.

It is also a travel log. It shares with the readers our love for the city of Paris and its people. It is also a compelling spy/political mystery. It was all three. And it spoke clearly of those messages.

An interesting side note. Almost every woman who read the first book in my test group loved it. They especially loved the strong female characters. Mary and I were successful.

The second thought also hit me. He is right! It needed to clearly state what it was. It needed to be clearly understood it was not the type of book he wrote, legal, murder mystery. It was a different genre. Perhaps best termed: a romantic spy/political mystery.

The romance was important!

So, it is now in its fifth draft and edit as I am writing this epilogue for the second book, "Between Two Doors: In Search of Colette". Hopefully edit number five will find a publisher. If not, book one will have its sixth draft and so on and so on. Because you see, it does have a "Compelling Story" it tells.

And so does this one. This is less of a fun, light, mystery book than I/we had hoped. The times since 2020, when we started conceiving the first book, have turned somewhat dark and ominous. Even though there are light parts of the book and the attempt to make the whole book a bit fun, when you are dealing with the issues of abuse of power and greed it is almost impossible to do so lightly.

I struggled with the scene of the young gallery owner father of 155 Gallery Hall of Colette and the killer. I am glad the character softened and spared the young man's life.

I'm not sure that would have happened in another writer's book.

This story, unlike book one, has many characters to dislike. Even LuLu, who is a fascinating blend of two real live actresses of the 1920s through 40s (one, a friend of my parents), was at times very likable and at times distasteful.

Book two that you just finished, Between Two Doors: In Search of Colette, has one central theme and it comes through over and over again. Greed and Abuse of Power are evil and bad. Pure and simple.

If that theme did not come through to you clearly with the first read...you need to reread the book.

Fortunately, there are good people in this world...hundreds of millions of them.

People like Kali, Tammy, Anne Kimbell, and people like the characters of the Smiths, Nina, Etienne, Ninette and Guy.

And of course, the marvelous woman, Colette, who made this adventure possible.

They are all wonderful people. Some made up and many real live people. And of course, there is me, Tom, and an angel named Mary. Good people all.

Thank you for reading this book. Now, let's go find the author! He has gone missing!

ACKNOWLEDGEMENTS

The writing of acknowledgements for this book is easy. I have three wonderful people who have helped Mary's and my book get successfully completed and into your hands.

First, as always, I need to thank Mary's and my principal editor, Amelia Gilliland. What an incredible find as an editor she is. Amelia, takes reasonable story tellers and through careful evaluation of soggy and wrinkled writings, wrings them out in to what becomes a fascinating novel. Mary and I both thank her immensely for her skill and talent and friendship.

Speaking of Talent. Another member of the team is Nohemy Adrian. Talented, funny, and like Amelia a very kind person. Through her careful process she takes vague ideas for the book's look and then as if with magic suddenly the external cover and internal book design appear. And not just for hardcover, paperback books but for eBooks too.

The final person of the team I wish to thank is Stuart (Stu) Grant. If you have seen the website design that Stu created you understand what a talented and creative person he is too. Again, we were so fortunate to find Stu.

This brings me to the conclusion of this page of acknowledgements. It was quite serendipitous that the team which came together for Mary's and my books is an international one. Amelia is Canadian. As we joke with Amelia, our "northern cousin".

Nohemy is French. She lives near the house where Colette once owned. And lastly, Stu is British. Quite a marvelous group of people who came together to create for you this fascinating book.

It was Mary's and my distinct pleasure to write this acknowledgement for the creative talents they gave to this effort. Thank you Amelia, Nohemy and Stu.

Best regards and gratitude from Tom and his angel, Mary

TABLE OF CONTENT

Book One

Book Two

www.ingramcontent.com/pod-product-compliance
Lightning Source LLC
Chambersburg PA
CBHW070459300726
48975CB00007B/2243